Georgia On My Mind

Contents

Dedication

To all the careless men's careful daughters.

Playlist

Georgie

Mean (Taylor's Version) – Taylor Swift

You're On Your Own, Kid – Taylor Swift

James

Anti-Hero – Taylor Swift

Enchanted (Taylor's Version – Taylor Swift)

Georgie & James

Bad Liar – Selena Gomez

Everything Has Changed (Taylor's Version) – Taylor Swift

I Can See You (Taylor's Version) – Taylor Swift

Finally // beautiful stranger – Halsey

Butterflies – Kacey Musgraves

Man! I Feel Like a Woman! – Shania Twain

Dancing Queen – ABBA

Dress – Taylor Swift

Hands To Myself – Selena Gomez

You Are In Love – Taylor Swift

King of My Heart – Taylor Swift

Lover – Taylor Swift

Paper Rings – Taylor Swift

2

GEORGIA ON MY MIND

Prologue

One Year Ago

I really fucking hate these things. Why do we have to have seventeen thousand conferences a year where the same people talk about the same shit, circle jerking each other over out successes and patting each other on the back for a job well done?

This particular conference- The Future of AI- had potential, considering the intense changes artificial intelligence is having and the it they will continue to impact our sector in the coming years, but nope. Nothing interesting to report.

At least the Moscone Center is nice. It's a few city blocks worth of interconnected buildings surrounded by glass walls and beautiful art pieces. I'm grabbing a level-above-shitty cup of coffee from the lobby cart when I see John Morello walk out of the nearest auditorium.

Fuck, I can't stand that guy. He thinks because he went to Stanford (like 90% of us in the Bay Area) and made a few good investments with his trust fund that he's God's gift to Silicon Valley. I try to duck out of his line of sight (not an easy feat when you're six inches north of six feet tall) so I can avoid an inane conversation about his newest project, but thankfully he turns his attention to the iPad being held in front of him.

I let out a sigh, ready to call the rest of the day a wash and head home when my eyes land on the woman walking next to the douche lord. She's angled slightly towards me, so I can see her side profile and part of her face. Golden brown waves of hair cascade over her shoulder, an arch of freckles crosses her nose, a navy blue dress clings to her skin, from her full breasts to her wide hips, and I can see a hint of red on her lips as she speaks, never taking her eyes off of the iPad in her hands.

I feel pulled to her. I follow a few steps behind in their direction, not a total creep move since technically my next scheduled meeting is down the same hallway. Another auditorium lets out, and I lose them in the crowd.

Shit. Looks like I'm staying at this snoozefest until I can find the mystery girl again.

Thankfully, it doesn't take too long. After an inane two-hour seminar on the morality of AI in the arts (spoiler alert, AI in the arts is not good), I'm desperate for another jolt of caffeine. When I find the coffee cart, I'm blessed with the sight of navy-colored cotton clinging to the sweetest ass I've ever seen.

"I thought all the beverages were free during the convention?" Her voice is light and semi-frantic. The bored-looking employee just shakes his head.

5

"Only if the company sponsors it. These guys didn't."

"Frick, frick, frick." Mystery girl bounces on her toes and shakes out her hands. "I don't have my purse. I'm gonna be late. Can I come back in an hour to pay? I swear I'm good for it. I'll leave something for collateral. My shoes or my bra or something!" The kid looks at her like she has three heads, or maybe like he really wants her bra.

Meanwhile, I pull my card out of my wallet and tap it to the payment terminal over her shoulder. I know, smooth as hell.

"John Morello is not a man you want to keep waiting. I got this." She turns and beams up at me, embarrassment and gratitude playing together across her pretty little face. She doesn't even bother asking how I know who she's fetching coffee for; she just presses her body against me in a tight but quick hug.

"Thank you, thank you, thank you!" she squeals, grabbing the to-go cups and heading off in the other direction. I watch her run off, the hem of her dress floating up with each hurried step. She turns and yells over her shoulder.

"You're my lifesaver. I hope both sides of your pillow are always cold, and your shoelaces never come untied and trip you!" I laugh at the pint-sized little weirdo, positively wonderstruck. I think I'm obsessed with her. I fight the urge to run after her and get her name and phone number, but she's clearly in a hurry.

If I had known that would be the last time I ever saw her, I would have.

1

Georgie

You know what feeling really sucks? First day of work jitters. You never know exactly what to expect, who you're gonna meet, what the vibe is gonna be...it's nerve wracking. Most people only have to experience the indignity of the first day of work every few years or so if they're lucky.

You know what's worse than first day of work jitters? First day of work jitters when you've accidentally made yourself horny as all get out because you write smutty romance in your spare time.

Today is my 7th first day in two years, and the 4th in a row where my panties are all in a twist because I was up to the wee hours writing fun scenes for my characters who have WAY more active sex lives than I do. Yay, me.

The morning sun is shining through my tiny window into my tiny bedroom, and even though it's a cool summer morning and the fog is rolling in, I can still feel my skin warm from the rays. I've lived here long enough, but it still surprises me how different the sunshine feels here than it did in New York. Even on the coldest days, the California sun can heat a person from within.

I'm standing in front of the over the door mirror I got on sale at Target, looking at myself in the black slacks and white blouse that I also got on sale at Target, sipping from the mug of shitty coffee that I got - well, I'm sure you can guess where I got the shitty coffee from. The blouse is just slightly too tight on my lower belly. It's definitely going to ride up when I sit, but it's the nicest one I own.

My golden brown hair is curled, already frizzing a bit around my face, but whatever. It doesn't stand a chance against the foggy morning air anyway. That's why I keep an arsenal of hair ties and bobby pins in my purse. I kept my makeup simple. A bit of light brown eyeshadow, a swipe of (admittedly uneven) black eyeliner across each lid, no blush. And of course, I'm wearing my emotional support red lipstick. Some people say red is too much for daytime, but since I was 21, my MAC Ruby Woo has been a confidence booster and the one kind of makeup that I'm willing to spend more than $8 on.

"Well," I say into the mirror, doing my best 'Anne Hathaway in The Princess Diaries' impression "this is as good as it's gonna get."

I don't know why I'm nervous. I should be used to it by now, but I never am. I've been working with Sustained Staffing ever since I moved to San Francisco from White Plains, New York two years ago. I've had my fair share of temporary positions in that time. Temp work is not ideal, but neither is the creative writing degree that I never got a job with. I got seriously sick of bartending after a while. This is pretty much the only kind of office work I can get, and long nights and weekends in the restaurant business are not conducive to my peak creative writing hours.

Today I'm starting a four-month position as a temporary personal assistant to a guy at some tech company that created an app that...honestly I have no idea what it does. It might not even be an app. But it's definitely a tech company.

I think.

I was supposed to have two weeks of training with the person I'm filling in for, but according to the email I got on Friday night, she went into labor early. Now I get to dive into this position blind. I just hope I don't screw it up. The only thing worse than being a 26 year old failed writer with no other career prospects is being a 26 year old failed writer with no other career prospects that gets dropped by her temp agency for sucking.

I grab my tote bag and my keys, slip my feet into my one and only pair of black heels (these ones are from TJ Maxx, not Target, thank you very much), and head towards the door. Both of my roommates are in the kitchen, headphones in their ears, neither bothering to look up as I pass by. That's the beautiful thing about San Francisco. It's full of socially awkward tech geniuses who need roommates and won't talk to you about anything but the rent. I've lived with these two girls for a year, and to be honest, I barely remember either of their names. I know from the mail that one is Ryan and the other is Ashley, but gun to my head, I couldn't tell you who's who.

That's fine by me. I've never needed to be friends with my room-mates. Or my coworkers. Or my classmates. The truth is, I've been on my own since I was 16, which left me with a bit of a stunted adolescence and an extra shy personality. I've had acquaintances, classmates in college that I was friendly with or coworkers that I've commiserated with over lunch, but it's been a long time since I've had someone I really considered a friend. I thrive on my own. Or at least, that's what I tell myself.

If I'm being completely honest, I crave...something. I don't know. I used to get jealous when I'd see happy families at the park or mothers shopping with their daughters at the mall. When I'd work late shifts at the bar and a group of girls would start getting giddy and huggy after a few tequila shots, I'd secretly wish that I was part of their gang. I learned to suppress those feelings a long time ago, but sometimes I think it might be nice to have someone who cares enough about me to tell me to text them when I'm home safe or ask my opinion on their first date outfit.

But I don't have that, so what's the point of dwelling on it?

I step out into the chilly morning air, popping in my headphones and pressing play on my ultimate pump-myself-up playlist. Pop music fills my ears and I make my way towards the bus stop.

The office is pretty much the exact opposite of what you'd expect. Most offices I've been to in this city are annoyingly modern, open floor plans, a stray foosball table, those weird egg shaped chairs that look comfortable but really aren't. This is not that. Sure, it's got the typical floor to ceiling windows and row after row of Mac computers, but it's stodgy. It feels more like some hedge fund in New York. There aren't many tall buildings in San Francisco, including this one, but since it's at the top of a hill, there is a perfect view of the Bay Bridge, Treasure Island, and even over towards the Transamerica Building and Coit Tower. It's stunning, even on a foggy morning like today.

Every person in this office is impeccably dressed. I'm surrounded by people in suit jackets and shiny loafers, wrinkle free dresses and silk blouses, and I've spotted a fair number of red bottom heels already (thank god I didn't go with flats). I was expecting tech bros in gray t-shirts and flip flops. I honestly thought I was going to be overdressed. I wasn't expecting to feel like my stomach was going to drop out of my ass from nerves as the woman named Catherine who's giving me the tour talks a mile a minute about the company.

"So Streamline is the most popular CRM tool on the market. We service most of the big names here in the city, Silicon Valley and across the country. Currently, our teams are working on creating a better in company messaging system. The goal is to push Slack off the stage."

I nod, but I have no idea what she's talking about. She's thrown about a hundred different acronyms at me in the last five minutes. At one point I wondered if she was even speaking English. In all of my temp jobs, I've learned that unless you're writing code, the ins and outs of a tech company aren't that important.

"Of course, you won't have to worry about any of that."

Thank god.

"Your role here is to be the right hand man to James Adler. He's the CEO, as you know, and he's also the co-creator of the original software."

Honestly, I didn't know that. The temp agency didn't provide me with much information besides an address and a time to show up.

"You'll handle his schedule and his calendar. You'll attend all meetings and take comprehensive notes and provide them to him in an organized and concise manner. You'll handle his email inbox, his mailbox, and any other correspondence he receives during the day, and you'll also be in charge of running any errands pertaining to his professional or personal life at his discretion. There is a conference in Los Angeles that you will be attending with him. Oh, and we have coffee brought in every morning from Espresso Yourself across the street, so you'll be in charge of grabbing that. I took care of it today, but tomorrow, just ask for Rachel and she'll get you squared away. Any questions?"

"Umm..."

"Don't worry. Amy left a comprehensive list of all your duties and any other pertinent information in your inbox before she left. She knows better than anyone that James is..."

"James is what?" a male voice sounds behind us. Catherine winces, and I breathe in the scent of warm, woody cologne and mint. I turn, and holy crap. I really wish I had googled this place, because I am not prepared for the man in front of me.

He's tall, definitely over six feet. He towers over the two of us, even in our heels. He's dressed in a black suit that was no doubt tailored to him perfectly, and he casually runs a small lint roller over one of his sleeves, though I don't spot a speck of dust on him. He's wearing a stark white button up shirt, no tie. Even through the jacket, I can see that his chest is broad and his arms are...not small. Dude definitely works out. His hair is cut short on the sides and longer on top, not long enough to tie back, but enough to run your fingers through. Small creases form around his bright blue eyes, lines that tell me he's older than me. Maybe late thirties. He's so gorgeous, looking at him feels like a punch to the gut. Like I don't deserve to breathe the same air as him. He tucks the lint roller into his pocket and gives me a quick once over. I feel a slight air of dissatisfaction settling over me. I don't know why, but I can tell right away that he doesn't like me. I lift my chin and try to look formidable, but I feel like a squeaking mouse in front of a hungry python.

"Quirky, James. You're quirky," Catherine answers his question with a roll of her eyes, and James makes a sound in the back of his throat that might be a laugh. No sign of amusement reaches his face.

"This is Georgia Hansley. She's filling in for Amy for the next few months," she continues. I reach out my hand to shake his, give him my best "I'm a good employee, I swear" smile and introduce myself.

"It's a pleasure to meet you, Mr. Adler. And you can call me Georgie."

He looks at my hand for just a moment before he turns on his heel and walks away.

"We have a meeting in twenty minutes, Georgia. Bring a pen."

Well. This is gonna suck.

2

James

Fucking Amy. I'm going to kill her. As soon as she's out of the hospital with my new baby niece, I'm going to kill her with my bare hands...

Okay. No, I can't kill her. But I can hate her. She's so selfish. Who the hell does she think she is? Starting a family, going into labor two weeks early, reaching out to the temp agency to find her own replacement and having the nerve to choose the resume of the mystery woman I saw at a convention at the Moscone Center last year, the one with the bright red lips who barters underwear for coffee. The one that I couldn't take my mind off of for the entire fucking day, who has crept into my thoughts many times since, even though I know absolutely nothing about her.

Fuck it. Amy's going down.

Through the glass window of my office, I can see Catherine show-ing Georgia Hansley (at least I can put a name to the face now) to her desk and helping her login to our internal system. Her desk is perpendicular to my office, so I have a full view of her side profile. I need to pull down my damn blinds. It didn't matter when Amy sat there - I never made it a habit to stare at my sister's wife all day - but now, I can't pull my eyes away from the little brown fly away hairs sticking out from Georgia's otherwise perfect curls, the curve of her mouth as she smiles at something Catherine shows her on her company laptop, the way that the white blouse she's wearing tightened ever so slightly when she sat down, outlining the swell of her round breast...

My office door swings open and I'm pulled from my trance.

"Is it gone?" Streamline CTO and my best friend, Amir Salman, asks from the doorway, referring to the latte I chug down every morn-ing. He's holding his t-shirt over his nose for dramatic effect. The dress code at Streamline is stricter than most other companies in this city, I prefer to be well-dressed and I expect the same from my employees, but Amir has always had an aversion to the feel of suit jackets, so I let his daily uniform of a cardigan, T-shirt, and black slacks slide.

"I just tossed the cup."

"Good. The smell is disgusting." He crosses the doorway and closes the door behind him. Amir and I have been buddies since college. We were both in the computer science program at Stanford, and even though he's a few years younger than me (dude was a boy genius and graduated high school at 14) we bonded over a shared appreciation of the show Freaks and Geeks and became fast friends. We roomed together for years while we ate ramen, wrote code and tried to make our mark in Silicon Valley. Streamline was our breakthrough development, our baby, and I'm proud to have created something so big with my best friend.

"I'm well aware of your aversion to my coffee, dude."

"Then stop drinking it." Back when we lived together, I had to drink my morning coffee outside so he couldn't smell it. When it rained, I drank it on the toilet. Some people find Amir off putting. He's blunt, and frankly, a little socially awkward, but I love him.

"Over my dead body." I don't bother looking up from the overwhelming inbox on my screen. Part of Amy's job is to filter through the hundreds of emails I get a day and make sure only the shit I actually need to see ends up on my desk. Well, I guess it's Georgia's job now. Fucking gorgeous Georgia.

"Get whatever it is off your chest now, before the morning meeting. I'm not dealing with moody James today," Amir says. He's sitting in one of the chairs on the other side of my desk, looking right at me. For someone who doesn't always pick up on social cues, the man can read me like a book.

"I'm just frustrated. It's gonna be rough around here without Amy." Not a total lie.

"I don't know why you even need a PA. I do fine without one and I have a heavier workload than you."

"Not everyone is a computer, dude! Some of us need assistance." I immediately regret the bite in my tone, but Amir doesn't seem rattled.

"Catherine is training the temp. It'll take a day or two but she'll be doing your entire job for you by the end of the week, just like Amy."

He grabs a pen off my desk and stands. He's always taking my damn pens. I don't get it.

"Let's go. We have that financial presentation this morning. I want to get a seat in the back so I can nap with my eyes open." He's not kidding. It can look like he's deeply invested in what a speaker is saying, but really, he's off in dreamland. It's impressive, and a little freaky.

I sigh and stand, motioning towards the door, and follow him out. I can't bring myself to look in her direction as I say, maybe a bit loud, "Georgia. First meeting is happening now. Follow us."

"You got it Mr. Adler!" I can hear the nervous smile in her voice, and fuck it if the crotch of my pants doesn't tighten.

Well. This is gonna suck.

I couldn't get out of that conference room fast enough. Finance meetings are so fucking boring. Usually I can count on Amy to pay attention so I can zone out during these things, but with it being Georgia's first day, I decided I should stay alert. Good thing, too, because apparently, Amir and Georgia hit it off right away. No eyes-opened napping for him today. Nope, those two were trying to suppress their giggles while they drew each other little cartoons or some shit- with my fucking pens. I want to be mad at her for goofing off on her first day, but honestly, people don't take to Amir very easily, and I'm happy that they seemed to form a bond.

Back in my office, I unlock my phone and send a quick text to the receptionist at my therapist's office, asking if Dr. Patel had time for a video call today. I started therapy about ten years ago. Seems like a long time, but I spent twenty years suppressing the trauma of my mother leaving my sister and I with a distant aunt and disappearing from our lives when I was six and Jenn was nine. I've barely cracked the surface of my issues.

It's not even something I realized I was dealing with until my twenties, when the women I was seeing started to expect something more serious than a few romps in the hay with me, and I didn't have it in me to make a commitment. Without meaning to, I developed a real "leave before you get left" philosophy to my romantic encounters.

These days, I can get by with a session once or twice a month, but the tightness in my chest is telling me I need my head shrunk, fast.

Dr. Patel likes to call my infliction "fear of abandonment", but let's be real, I have mommy issues. I refuse to get close to any woman besides Catherine, my sister Jenn, and Amy, of course. It's because deep down, I'm afraid that they're going to leave me. Honestly, it might sound sad, but I don't really care. I'm thirty-seven years old, I have a great job, great friends, more money than I know what to do with. I don't think I'm missing out by not having a relationship.

Don't get me wrong - I fuck, it just never goes further. I always make sure my partners know that it's nothing more than sex, nothing more than a release. I always make sure they come - multiple times if I have my way- but I never spend the night, never call the next day, never think about them again, and I'm fine with that.

Now that I think about it, I haven't taken a woman to bed in months, haven't even thought about sex with anyone but my own hand. I mean, that's normal right? Guys lose their sex drives as they get older, don't they? Yeah, that's totally my problem. I have no sex drive, I'm old, I'm too tired to go out and pick up a woman. Move over, this guy's pulling right into erectile dysfunction station. Actually, you know what? No. I can't even joke about that. I'm not putting that out into the universe.

So why the fuck can't I get the curvy woman currently chewing on her bottom lip as she types outside of my office window out of my fucking head when I'm practically celibate? I'll tell you why. Since I saw her a year ago, she's been the accidental object of all of my fantasies. Who needs porn when I could think of my mystery girl's creamy thighs and how good it would feel to slip between them?

God, I'm being such a fucking creep. At this rate, Dateline is gonna be knocking on my door any day now.

I tried to find her again at the convention. All day I kept my eyes peeled, waiting for her to emerge. I waited long past five o'clock, skulking around the lobby and scanning the crowds as they filed out. I even tried afterwards. I swallowed my fucking pride and called Morello's office. I was going to makeup some bullshit story- a dropped change purse or something- as an excuse to get in touch with the woman by his side. It seems he realized I'd been avoiding his prick ass and didn't take kindly to that, but I conveniently never heard back from him. I resigned myself to the fact that the mystery woman was merely a mirage, a product of my overactive imagination, doomed to live forever only in my mind.

Not that I'm dramatic or anything.

My mind keeps replaying the moment during the meeting break where she stretched her arms above her head next to me, lightly cracking her neck side to side. Her tits pushed forward against that tight blouse and I was overcome by the scent of warm vanilla as she lowered her arms and shook her hair off her shoulders and down her back. I had to fake a cough to cover up a groan.

I can tell when a woman is hot, I've spent time with many attractive women, but none have ever gotten under my skin like this. I only officially met her two hours ago, and I'm infatuated. I can't stop myself from not so subtly watching her through the window. I figure, if she catches me, I can disguise it as keeping an eye on her on her first day, making myself available if she has questions. She pushes back in her chair just a bit, and her legs are visible under the desk. She crosses the right one over the left, the material of her black slacks shifting with her. She leans forward to start typing again, and the smallest sliver of the skin of her hip peeks out as her shirt moves up just an inch. I can't help thinking about what it would taste like if I licked that bit of flesh, nipped at it with my teeth...

My phone buzzes in my hand and breaks the trance.

Dr. P's Office: Hey James, he has time at 3 today for a session, I'll put you on his schedule

Thank god.

3

Georgie

My first two weeks at Streamline have been painful. Don't get me wrong, the people in the office are nice enough, although I don't really interact with them much. I've really bonded with Amir. We walked together to that first meeting Monday morning, and he talked the whole way to the conference room. He told me he has trouble picking up on social cues so if I don't want to talk to him, I have to tell him to his face, and his honesty made me love him immediately.

He is a self-proclaimed romance novel addict like me, and we've been eating lunch together, gushing over Ruby Dixon's *Ice Planet Barbarians* series and how much we hate closed door books- I mean it's romance, people, we're here for the sex! I've also started to get friendly with Rachel, the owner of the coffee shop who helps prepare and package the office's coffee order for me every morning. We've spent the last few days chatting about Love Is Blind and our favorite places to get cioppino in the city. Yesterday, she mentioned a spin class she goes to on Saturdays and invited me to come sometime, which was nice. I might actually go.

So why do I say my first weeks have been painful? Simple. James freaking Adler. It's like he's hellbent on being the world's biggest dick, but just to me. That's right, he's Mr. Sunshine around the office. He's kind, he smiles, he uses nicknames and asks about people's home life. He fosters a healthy and happy work environment for everyone but me. With me, it's formal. I'm not Georgie, I'm *Georgia*. His smile drops every day when he walks past my desk into his office. His office, where I can feel him glaring at me through his window. I'm supposed to be his personal assistant, I thought I'd be working more closely with him, but he pretty much ignores me. The only words he speaks to me are orders to follow him to a meeting, asking where his coffee is (on his desk, *like it's supposed to be,* every single day, by the way), and grunts of acknowledgement when I have to hand him something or ask a question. When he does deign to speak to me, he refuses to make eye contact, always rolling that stupid little lint roller over himself.

Oh, and I can't forget my new favorite phrase that I've heard about a million times in the last few days- "*That's not how Amy does it.*"

On Monday, I starred his morning emails in his inbox in order of urgency instead of the time they came in.

That's not how Amy does it.

On Tuesday, I wrote a short summary of a particularly long meeting at the top of the notes I provided him, thinking I was doing him a favor with the refresher.

That's not how Amy does it.

On Wednesday, Amir bought breakfast sandwiches for the whole office. He was sitting on the edge of my desk, typing my order into his phone (an everything bagel with cream cheese and bacon, thank you) when James walked out of his office, rolling that stupid tiny lint roller over his sleeve.

That's not what Amy orders.

Seriously. Even my breakfast order wasn't good enough for this man, and then he had the nerve to ignore me for the rest of the day. Not a word in any meeting, no thank you when I brought him his afternoon cup of tea, nothing. I'd quit, but I've gotten really used to a roof over my head and at least one square meal a day.

Now it's Thursday, and I have two more days chained to this asshole before the weekend. The thing is, I'm usually okay with people not liking me, I don't let it get under my skin, but I've had a particularly rough morning. I don't know if I have it in me to play games with James today. First, I woke up to pee at 4 am and could not fall back asleep, then when I gave up trying and went to the kitchen, I found that not only had one of my roommates finished off the last of my hazelnut oat milk creamer, my landlord left us a note that he's raising the rent - *again.* DAMMIT!

Breathe, Georgie.

Screw it. It's only 7:30 am, but I need to get out of here. I finish getting dressed and grab my stuff. I can grab the coffee early and then

25

have some alone time in the office before everyone else comes in. It beats staring at the four, severely overpriced walls of my bedroom.

The bus is mostly empty at this time of morning, since it's still before the morning rush. I climb on, and when I realize the only other two riders are two large men, I tuck my headphones into their case and put them away. Not that these men look like they want to hurt me, but I still feel the need to have all of my senses in tune just in case. Being a woman is so fun.

I stare out the window during the mostly quiet ride, the two men grumbling to each other across the aisle. It's so seemingly normal, like maybe they're friends or strangers that struck up a conversation that it takes a minute for my brain to catch up when one man lunges and hits the other square in the jaw.

Something you should know about me - I can't handle violence, particularly male violence. When I was younger, my father wasn't the most pleasant or patient man, and it only got worse after my mom died. I was always tiptoeing around him, trying not to trigger him or make him angry, but I was a teenager, so the occasional fight was inevitable.

I really don't like to talk about it, but one day it hit a tipping point, and I haven't been the same since.

I watch as the other man throws a punch, and another, fists flying in every direction, and my vision blurs. The bus feels like it's moving forward and backward at the same time. I try to stand, but I can't get steady on my feet. Thankfully, the driver notices the brawl happening in his rearview mirror and screeches to a stop, the doors of the bus opening. It must have been my fight or flight instincts kicking in, because even though my entire body feels like jello, I manage to get myself off the bus and around the corner. I lean against the brick wall of the building I stumble against and try to regulate my breathing.

You're okay. No one is going to hurt you. You're safe.

I repeat the mantra in my head until I can properly fill my lungs again, and then I do my grounding technique.

What do I see? A trash can, an electric scooter, and a rack of bikes.

What can I smell? Salty morning air, the faint scent of coffee.

What can I hear? The rattle of street cars.

You're safe. I keep my headphones in my purse and my head on a swivel as I walk the rest of the way to the coffee shop.

The office has a nice vibe to it when it's empty. I can't describe it, but I'm feeling main-character energy. I was still shaken up when I got to Espresso Yourself, and when I told Rachel about my crappy morning, sparing her the details of my mini panic attack, she tucked a chocolate croissant into my bag for me. I honestly think I'm in love with her.

I'm in the kitchen, warming up my pastry in the toaster oven and setting up the coffee station- a few boxes of black coffee and a couple specialty orders for the pickier employees- when I decide to do a little meditation. Now, traditional meditation has never worked for me, so over time, my old therapist and I came up with a different way for me to quiet my thoughts and reduce my stress levels. I turn the volume of my phone all the way up and press play, the sound of Taylor Swift's voice filling the air. Since I'm alone, I don't even think before I grab a plastic fork from the counter and start singing into it like a microphone.

I start really getting into it, performing some choreography that I may or may not have practiced for hours in my room, singing and waving at my imaginary fans in my imaginary audience when I hear a throat clear behind me. I gasp and turn, and guess what? My morning manages to get worse.

"Hey," I say, a little out of breath from my performance. "Mr. Adler, you're, uh, you're here early."

James is leaning against the doorway to the kitchen, arms crossed over his chest and his right foot tucked behind his left, looking incredibly sexy. It's a casual stance, so different from the straight spine, stick-up-his ass look he's had around me all week, and it packs a punch. He's really got that "smoldering romance hero lean" thing down. I think I might write a poem about the sliver of ankle I can see poking out below his perfectly tailored pants...

My god, Georgie, get it together. I can feel my face burning up. My boss- the guy who hates me- just caught me treating his office like my own personal Madison Square Garden and now I'm, what? Checking him out? Having a staring contest? Humiliating myself further?

"Uh, James. You can call me James. Everyone does," he says after a moment of awkward eye contact.

"Oh, okay. Well, uh, James. I was just sort of, getting the coffee set up and, uhm, preparing for the day and..." I'm stuttering.

I don't think I've ever been so embarrassed in my life. He's quiet for a moment, and I swear I see the right side of his mouth start to curl up into a smile. I'm staring back at him, and even though it's wrong, I can't help but take in how incredibly handsome he is. He's so tall and broad-chested, his presence is commanding. His eyes are bright blue, not like the ocean, but more like a burning, raging fire. His lips, which are usually pressed in a tight line when I'm around, look soft and plump. His jaw is sharp, angular, and covered in a light scruff that I bet would feel amazing brushing against the soft skin of my inner-

He speaks, thank god, cutting off my increasingly inappropriate thoughts and gesturing his chin towards the coffee on the counter.

"Amy never-"

Two words. It takes two words for my morning- my entire week- to catch up with me, and I snap.

"Oh please, Mr. Adler, tell me something else that your precious Amy never did. Seriously, what is your deal with her? Is she your lover or something? Because I haven't been able to blow my nose around this place without you telling me that I'm doing it wrong and Amy would've done it better. Guess what, my dude? Amy isn't here right now, I am, so you can either get on board with the way I'm doing this job or you can call the agency and have them reassign me because I can't take your prickly attitude or your stupid lint roller for one more freaking day." I storm past him, leaving my coffee and croissant behind. I'm not hungry anymore.

"Georgia!" he calls after me as I huff off to the bathroom.

"What?" I spin, biting the inside of my cheek. I will *not* let this douche see me cry.

"Amy never brought in the flavored creamers, that's a nice touch. Thank you."

He turns to walk to his office, and thank god because I can feel the first tear dripping down my cheek, no doubt leaving a trail of cheap mascara in its wake.

4

James

I had a plan, and the plan was working. All I had to do was keep my thoughts on the work. If I just focused on my job, only spoke to Georgia about things pertaining to that job, run a couple miles in the gym after work and then went straight home to Lucifer, my beloved cat, I would have very little time alone with my thoughts. I could get through this. It's just a random little crush on a woman. Sure, I've never gotten a real crush before, not since I was a teenager anyway, but Georgia is only getting to me because I unknowingly held her in such high regard for over a year and now we're in such close proximity all day. At least that's what Dr. Patel said. I'm a grown man. I can sweat a crush out of my system in no time.

The problem with the plan, of course, is Georgia. She's beautiful, that much is obvious. It's nearly impossible not to stare, not to take in the sway of her hips as she glides around the office like a goddess. It's bad enough that my mystery girl is here in my office and that she's a walking wet dream. No, she's also really fucking good at this job. She's incredibly organized, she takes impeccable notes and gives me highlights of all the shit I need to not forget, not to mention my inbox has never felt so underwhelming. She's taken on every single task I've given her and perfected it, and she gets along well with everyone in the office. Amy makes a good executive assistant to me because we get each other. Georgia makes a good assistant because she's smart and talented. She's perfect. It's maddening.

I made it through the rest of last Monday and most of last Tuesday suppressing any of the inappropriate thoughts about her threatening to creep into my mind, and I was feeling pretty proud of myself. That is, until Wednesday, when she showed up to work wearing *that* navy blue curve-hugging dress and tortoise shell rimmed glasses that made her look so fucking delectable. I've never been so happy to have a private bathroom attached to my office in my life- not even the time I got food poisoning from my lunch and was too sick to drive myself home. I had to lock myself in there and relieve the tension thinking about how badly I wanted to pull up that tight dress and *properly* thank her for all her good work.

Besides that one (ok fine it was twice... in a row) slip up, I felt like the days were going well. Until this morning, at least. I don't know what she was doing here so early, but there she was in the kitchen, singing some song about karma and...cats? I don't know. I thought it would be a good time to tell her that Amy never put in as much effort as she has this week and that I'm thankful that she's here, but that obviously backfired when she snapped at me for comparing her to her predecessor. I didn't even realize I'd been doing it, but now I'm back in my office, watching Georgie crack her neck at her desk and wondering how I'm going to un-piss her off.

I didn't realize just how blatantly I was tuning out Amir's complaints about some code deployment that I don't give a shit about until he was snapping in my face.

"Are you even listening to me?"

"No," I answer honestly, wiping a hand over my face.

"Is it because you're staring at Georgie like you want to go out there and mount her like an animal?"

"Dude." Always so blunt, that Amir.

"I'm not wrong. You look at her every chance you get." He shrugs, grabbing one of my pens and flipping it around his fingers. Catherine walks in, tapping a light knock on the doorframe, holding a laptop in one hand and a green smoothie in the other. She's our Senior Vice President and another friend from our Stanford days.

"What are you two doing? We've got a call in five minutes," she says, nodding at us to get up and follow her. This woman has kept us in line for almost two decades. We've offered her better positions, but she swears she's happy as SVP, that it gives her the perfect work-life balance, and if she had any extra responsibility, she wouldn't be able to keep us in line. (Her words, not mine). Honestly, what the fuck would we do without her?

"James was fantasizing about fucking Georgie on her desk."

"AM," I bite out "Why the hell would you say that?"

33

"Why would you do it in front of me? I'm not a coat rack." He smirks.

"You can't just quote random tv shows and expect to get out of being an asshole."

"You're right, it's my innate adorableness that gets me out of that."

"Amir," Catherine sighs, obviously exasperated with us, "please try to remember to think before you speak. James, keep your hands off the temp. Let's go." She turns on her heel and leaves the room, and I give my friend a not-so-playful shove on his shoulder as I follow her out.

The rest of the day was insanely busy, and despite his big fucking mouth, I decide to grab some dinner and a drink with Amir to unwind after work. I can't take another night of trying to run off my feelings on the treadmill. We're sitting at our usual place down on the water, sipping beers and eating mussels. In the warmer months, we like to sit outside, but since summer in San Francisco is cold as shit, we're at a bar indoors by the window, watching the fog roll over the bay.

"Are you going to talk about it?" Amir asks, dipping a slice of sourdough into the broth in front of us.

"No," I answer, finishing down the last of my beer and gesturing to the server for another. Since we were in and out of meetings all day, I've been able to avoid both him and Georgia.

"Fine. I'll talk about it." I roll my eyes. I should've known he wasn't going to let this go. "You have a crush on Georgie, and you're purposefully acting like an asshole so you can push her away and not have to deal with the fact that you like her."

"I'm not acting like an asshole, and I do not have a crush on her. I don't get crushes, you know that." I nod a thanks to our server as he sets another IPA down in front of me. Two is enough since I have to drive home.

"I do know that, because I know you. I also know your preferences in women," he says, scooping up the last mussel and popping it into his mouth. He slurps at it loudly, and I have to fight the urge to leave him here and drink at home with Lucifer. Unfortunately I have a feeling that I'm not getting out of this conversation either way.

"Georgie has brown hair," he continues "she's at least a foot shorter than you, she dresses modestly, but since she's curvy in all the ways you like, everything she wears makes her look sexy to you. She takes it easy on the makeup which gives her the innocent look you're attracted to, but I'm sure you've had indecent thoughts about her red lipstick. She's soft spoken and sweet but she's funny, so if you actually tried to flirt with her you could probably achieve a level of banter that would keep you on your toes-"

"Dude, it sounds like you're the one who has a crush on her," I spit out, growing frustrated with my friend's incessant nagging.

"She's not my type. She's your type. Are you even listening?" He has the nerve to sound like *he* is annoyed with *me*.

"Okay, she's hot. I mean that's obvious. But that doesn't mean I have a crush on her. I don't even know her." I sip my beer, hoping that acknowledging that I find Georgia attractive will be enough to shut him up.

"She's twenty-six years old. She moved to the city from some small town in New York. She's a writer but she's too shy to actually publish anything, so she's working with the temp agency for now while she figures her life out. She loves Taylor Swift and cats, her favorite movie is The Devil Wears Prada, she has a tattoo under her right boob of-"

"Am," I cut him off before he goes into further detail about her tits. "Why are you going all Encyclopedia Georgie on me?"

"Because you said you didn't know her, but I do. We've had lunch together every day this week. She's my friend. I call her peaches. Oh shit, that's cute. James and the tiny peach." I don't know how I missed that piece of information. Am likes to dole out nicknames like they're going out of style, but I didn't realize she's who I'd lost my lunch buddy to.

"Now you know stuff about her, and you find her attractive. You can accept that you have a crush on her."

"Amir-shit. It's her" I concede, tired of keeping this to myself. My friend just gives me a blank stare. "Her. The mystery girl. Remember?"

"The girl you've been mentally stalking all year?" God this guy keeps pissing me off. Why am I friends with him again?

"I have not been mentally stalking anyone. I just thought she was a beautiful stranger. Now she's here and working with us and she's a real person. It's fucking with my head. I'm crushing, are you happy?"

"Yes, but you were definitely mentally stalking her. Didn't you even physically stalk her too? I have a distinct image in my mind of you pacing outside of Morello's office that one time. And if my memory is correct, you've been jerking it to her for twelve months." I roll my eyes. Why do I tell this guy anything? "If that's the case, though, there is one thing you should know. She hates you," he says, popping a fry into his mouth. I feel my stomach drop out of my ass. I know she was mad at me this morning, but I thought it was just a one-off thing.

"She hates me?"

"Of course she does. I told you, you've been acting like an asshole all week. Unless you're comparing her to Amy, she barely gets a grunt of acknowledgement out of you. You treat her differently than everyone else in the office. You're cold towards her. You lint roll yourself over her desk constantly. She sees it, we can all see it, and it's embarrassing for her."

Shit. I've been trying so hard to keep myself guarded (and get Lucifer's damn fur off my Brioni suits) that I didn't even think about how I was affecting Georgia. I honestly didn't realize she thought about me at all until this morning. I run my hand over my jaw, the scruff of my beard scratching at my palm.

"Did she, uh. Did she tell you she hates me? In those words?" Maybe he's exaggerating, although knowing Amir, that's highly unlikely.

"Yup. Today, after she yelled at you in the kitchen. She burst into my office crying and said 'I freaking hate James Adler.' And then she stole my muffin. It was blueberry. I was livid."

He drops the bomb so casually, like he's telling me the weather and not ripping my lungs from chest. I feel like I swallowed a handful of sand.

"Fuck. I don't even- FUCK!" I yell, slamming my hand down on the wood and gaining the unwanted attention of some of the other diners. I drop my face into my hands.

"How do I fix this? How do I make her not hate me?" I ask, my voice muffled through my palms.

"Well, you could try not being a dick to her." He shrugs. This guy is infuriating.

"No shit. HOW do I do that when I didn't even realize I was being a dick to her in the first place?"

"How did you not realize it?"

"Because, as you so kindly forced me to admit, I've been crushing on her. I thought I was just giving myself space so that I didn't blurt out 'I LOVE YOU, PLEASE SIRE MY CHILDREN' in the middle of a fucking staff meeting."

"Okay, calm down. I get it. Get her alone and apologize to her. Really apologize. Acknowledge your behavior and how it made her feel and promise to not let it happen again. And then talk to her about something other than work. Ask her questions about herself, get to know her. She's pretty fantastic."

It sounds so simple and yet, I don't know.

"Are you sure that will work?" I ask, handing my card over to the server to pay.

"No. I've read thousands of romance novels since I was 16 and learned absolutely nothing." He forgets to inflect, but I know he's being sarcastic. "Thanks for dinner man."

I sign the check and follow him out the door, hopping into my blacked-out Jeep Wrangler. I have a few different cars, but my Rubicon is my go-to. I drive back to my penthouse in Pac Heights, ready to cuddle my cat and formulate a plan to change Georgia's mind about me.

5

Georgie

"I'm telling you, Rach, he's going to fire me." I sit at the table closest to the counter at Espresso Yourself, my hands tugging at my hair while my new friend (yes, I'm claiming it!) puts together the arrangement of boxed hot coffees, flavored creamers, various milks and sugar packets that I bring to the office everyday. I'm gonna miss free coffee when I'm shitcanned.

"Jesus, Georgie, if he was going to fire you, he would've done it yesterday when you called him a dickwad." She rolls her eyes, loading up the insulated bag with the goods. Amir told me all about his aversion to coffee when I made the mistake of offering him a cup earlier this week, and apparently, having coffee brought in from Rachel's place everyday is less assaulting to his nose than a coffee machine living in the office, so he has a running tab here to keep Streamline employees caffeinated and his nose happy.

"Besides," she continues, completely ignoring my anguish, "Can he even fire you? I mean you technically work for the temp agency, right?"

"First of all, I didn't call him a *dickwad,* and second of all - no, he can't technically fire me, but he can call the temp agency and have me reassigned." She gives me a look of understanding, and heads to the baked goods.

"In that case, take a Danish," she says, pulling something that looks like it's stuffed with cherries out of the glass case and placing it in a paper bag.

"Rachel, if you keep giving me pastries every time I'm depressed, you're gonna go bankrupt," I say, taking the Danish anyway. I'm not one to turn down free food, especially if it's glazed.

She laughs and hits me with a wink. I have to admit, I'm pretty jealous of Rachel. She's the kind of effortlessly gorgeous woman that you see on Pinterest when looking at outfits you'll never be able to pull off. Today, her strawberry blonde hair is tied in a loose knot on top of her head, really nailing that messy-perfect look. She's wearing thick, black rimmed glasses that, along with her impossibly precise winged eyeliner, make the green flecks in her eyes pop, and her outfit is a simple white shirt with dark blue linen overalls. She's like the living embodiment of "I woke up like this". Thank god she's nice, or I'd be spending a lot of time shoving down my internalized misogyny and trying not to hate her.

"G, it's Friday. Just try to ignore the butthole boss for eight hours and then tomorrow morning you can sweat out your frustration at spin with me."

"I'm not getting up at the ass crack of dawn to exercise with you after the week I've had, Rach." I'm down for a cardio session, but I'll be damned if I have to get up early on a Saturday.

"Nope! My friend Kira teaches at 11 on Saturdays, we can do brunch after!" She beams, handing my order over to me.

"THAT I can get on board with. Text me the address," I say over my shoulder as I make my way out the door and over to the office.

Catherine told me during my initial briefing that Fridays are kind of relaxed here at Streamline. They call them "Work for Yourself" days. It's a dress down day. Most people are sporting jeans. There are no mandatory meetings and employees can use the time to catch up, work on their own projects, even stay home without sacrificing any PTO or sick days. There are less people around than usual, and the ones who are here seem to all be working individually, so it's quiet.

I set up the coffee bar and head to my desk, hoping to avoid my inevitable dismissal a little longer. Maybe if I avoid James long enough, he'll forget that he wants to fire me. I notice he isn't in his office and breathe a sigh of relief.

"Hey!" Catherine chirps, popping her butt to the corner of my desk and pushing her Rapunzel-long locks over her shoulder. The sunlight from the window behind me illuminates her rich brown skin and I can't help but wonder if being hot is a requirement to run this place.

"Morning," I say, biting into the glazed cherry Danish

"James and Amir got called into an offsite meeting early this morning, so they'll both be out until the afternoon. I told James I'd just give you the day off, but he said he has something to discuss with you later."

Of course he does. He needs to discuss how fast I can pack up my shit and get out of here.

"So," she continues, "you're with me today. James was raving about your color coded digital filing system and I could really use some help getting organized if you're up for it?"

"Of course!" I try to sound cheerful, but to be honest, I'm totally fucking confused. James was...raving? About something I did? That makes no sense. He was probably being sarcastic, or maybe he's pulling a prank on Catherine cause he thinks my methods are shit. There is no way that that man has a kind word to say about me, especially when he is most definitely giving me the boot in a few hours.

"Yay! Ooh, and Amir left his AmEx here last night, we can order lunch later!"

Again, I'm not going to say no to free food.

The morning absolutely flew by. Helping Catherine get organized was pretty easy. She was already in much better shape than James was last Monday. We talked while I worked, and she told me about meeting James and Amir at Stanford, how formidable baby Am was, dealing with ass hole frat guys when he was still too young to vote, how James once kicked the ass of a guy who shoved Amir on the quad and almost got expelled (I cringed at that story, but thankfully, nothing in my body said "pass out now" like it usually does). It was nice, hearing about how these three friends have stayed together through the years.

"Catherine, can I ask you a question?" I lean over, grabbing a slice of bread to dip into my broccoli cheddar soup. She used Amir's card to order soups and salads from Boudin, spewing something about a brunch bill he stuck her with a few weeks ago.

"Sure." She nods, scooping up a bite of Caesar salad.

"Am I uh... am I getting fired today?" I feel silly asking, but I mean, I have a right to know, don't I?

She coughs, grabbing a napkin to spit out the romaine she's choking on.

"Why the hell would you be getting fired?" she asks, sipping from her water bottle.

"For yelling at James in the kitchen yesterday..."

"You yelled at James yesterday?" She looks at me inquisitively.

"Yes," I answer sheepishly.

"Did he deserve it?"

I think for a moment. "Yeah, he did."

She purses her lips, peruses me where I sit on the other side of the desk, then surprisingly, leans forward for a high five that I happily return.

"I love James, but he can be a prick, and we could use another body putting him in his damn place around here. And no, Georgie, you're not getting fired. He's been singing your praises to me all week. He said something about convincing Amy to stay at home with the baby for good."

I'm...shocked to say the least. "Then do you know why he wants to meet with me today? I assumed he was kicking me to the curb."

"I don't know. Probably something to do with the LA trip. Or maybe it's something non-business related. Amy did some personal errands for him every so often."

I nod, still not fully convinced that I'm not going to be unemployed in a few hours when there's a knock on the door.

"C'min," Catherine calls around a mouth full of bread. I turn and watch as James and Amir enter the room.

"Did you really steal my black card to buy fucking bread bowls?" Amir points to the spread in front of us.

"Fuck you, you know you still owed me for that brunch."

"Jesus Catherine, it was your turn to pay, and I REALLY had to pee, let it go!" The two bicker, but it's playful. I imagine they're used to this sort of power struggle dynamic. Honestly, I'm distracted by the scent of leather, warm and heady. A large hand presses to my shoulder. It feels hot and strong and powerful, and I nearly yelp at the sensation.

"Georgia," James's voice comes from behind me, but I'm too nervous to turn around and look at him. "Can I speak with you in my office?" His voice is low and, god help me, he sounds so freaking sexy. I nod my head yes, knees wobbling as I push back from Catherine's desk and follow him, watching my feet as I walk in step behind him, the sound of Catherine and Amir's arguing fading as we move.

I've been in this office plenty of times in the last two weeks, but this is the first time I've really taken it in. It's incredibly monotone. Black leather chair, black wood desk, black coat rack holding a black jacket in the corner. I would say it feels like the place where whimsy goes to die, if I didn't spot the three stuffed cat plushies sitting on the windowsill behind James' chair. I guess I never noticed them before since James is usually *in* his chair when I've been in his office, but there they are.

James Asshole - I mean Adler- is a cat lady!

I want to ask him about the toys, maybe tease him a little, but I remember I'm in here presumably to talk about my job performance, not to mention he hates me, so I don't think a little jab at his collection is the best idea.

"Have a seat, Georgia," he says, gesturing to the black, high back chairs that sit in front of his desk. I sit, folding my hands in my lap and staring at them. My nerves are firing on all cylinders. I mean, Catherine said I wasn't getting canned, but what does she know? My breath is shaky, and I try a calming technique I learned from an old therapist. Breathe in, second breath in on top, hold, and exhale. I'm at the "holding" part of the exercise when James says my name. I exhale quietly and look up, but he's not at his desk chair across from me.

No, he's sitting in the chair next to me, turned so his entire body is facing me, leaning forward with his hands clasped and elbows on his knees. He cracks his knuckles, one by one. I exhale audibly and try to ramp down the embarrassment searing through my veins. This position feels a little too intimate for a firing...

DO NOT think the word "intimate" around him, Georgie!

Friendly, I mean. The position seems friendly.

"You there, Georgia?" he asks, snapping me out of my surprised haze.

"Yeah, sorry. Sourdough hangover. What can I help you with?"

"I'm not here to ask for your help, Georgia. I'm here to ask for your forgiveness."

Uh. What?

He must sense my confusion because he goes on. "It's been brought to my attention that I haven't been particularly kind to you during these first weeks. I got the sense I had pissed you off after you let me have it in the kitchen yesterday, but Amir mentioned something about you telling him you hate me."

My cheeks flush. "I didn't say I hate you." I try to cover my tracks, but he snorts.

"Yes you did. Amir doesn't lie, sweet girl."

I'm mortified. Not only because he knows I said I hated him, he knows I've been talking shit about him behind his back, and he just called me *sweet girl* like an adult talking down to an angry toddler.

And yet, for some odd reason, my stomach flutters at the nickname.

"Okay, yes, I did say I hate you, but it was an 'in the heat of the moment' thing. I don't actually hate you. I was just flustered and annoyed that you kept comparing me to Amy. Please don't fire me. I swear I didn't mean anything by it."

He laughs and pats a hand on my forearm in an intima-*FRIEND-LY-* gesture. "I'm not firing you, Georgia. You were right, I've been acting like an ass. I didn't mean to, but my intentions don't matter. I hurt you, and I'm sorry." He runs the hand that was just searing a mark into my skin through his thick brown hair and sighs.

"Amy is my sister's wife. They've been together for forever, so she's family. She was one of Amir's and my initial investors when we started Streamline. She only works as my assistant because she says if she had to sit alone all day waiting for my sister to get home like a lesbian Donna Reed, she'd drown herself in the Pacific. I'm sorry I made you feel inferior to her because it's not true. We've just worked together for so long, it's an adjustment being here without her. I was trying to tell you that you do things differently than Amy and that's a *good* thing. I just didn't go about it the right way. And to be completely honest, I have real issues with change, no thanks to my mother. I know it's ridiculous, but Amy going on maternity leave felt like an abandonment in a way. I took out my hurt feelings on you, and that's not okay. I'm really, really sorry."

He sounds so incredibly sincere, I can't help but believe that he truly is sorry for the way he's been treating me. This day has already felt like an emotional roller coaster, and now here I am, ready to accept the fact that the asshole who has been making my life hell might not be that bad of a guy.

"Honestly Georgia, I've been telling anyone who will listen around here how great of a job you've been doing. The digital planner you set up on my iPad? Life changing."

I smirk down at my hands. "Catherine may have mentioned something about that."

"Yeah, she was pumped to have the morning with you today. And Amir hasn't stopped talking about you or your mutual appreciation of uh..." He pauses, a hint of smugness washing over his face. "Blue alien erotica, is it?" I groan and cover my face with my hands in a dramatic gesture, but really I don't care. Give me alien porn or give me death. James laughs and continues, "I know I made a shitty first impression, but I swear, I'm an OK guy, and I really am sorry. Can you forgive me, Georgia?"

I meet his gaze, and I can feel how genuine his apology is. I mean honestly, why was I getting so butthurt anyway? It's not like I've ever been besties with my bosses before, and James can at least acknowledge when he's being an ass.

"You're forgiven, Mr. Adler. Thank you."

He smiles a full toothy grin at me, and I nearly melt into the chair. How is this man so freaking handsome on top of being smart, rich, and apparently, kinda nice? God really does have favorites.

"I thought I told you to call me James."

"I thought I told you to call me Georgie."

"You got me there. In that case, *Georgie,*" he draws out my name and I feel myself go a little weak in the knees. Thank god I'm sitting. "What are your plans tonight?"

"Uh..." It's Friday, I should think of something fun so he thinks I'm cool and hip, but I'm a little stunned by the question. Why does he want to know what my plans are?! I can't think, so my mind has no choice but to settle for the truth. "I'm gonna drink some chardonnay alone in my room and do some writing. Why do you ask?" God, I sound like an idiot.

"Well, I'm a little jealous that my friends have gotten so chummy with you already. I was going to ask if you'd want to stay here, order in food and get to know each other a little better. Since I'm assuming you don't hate me anymore-" he winks, and I blush "-I was thinking maybe we could be friends? It's weird working so closely with a stranger, but as much as I want to know you, I don't want to take you away from drinking and writing. It's very Hemingway of you."

"Know me?" I ask, my brain zeroing in on those two words.

"Yeah, know you," he smiles.

If I thought I was stunned by him asking what my plans were tonight, him asking if I want to eat food with him and get to know him better in his office after hours practically has my jaw on the floor. I mean, this is the makings of a really steamy scene. If I were writing this, we'd be sitting on the floor, sharing something cute but vaguely phallic shaped, like french fries. I'd get a bit of ketchup on the corner of my lip and he'd lean over, wiping it off with his thumb. He'd trace over the line of my lips, staring at them like he wants nothing more than to devour me. He'd swallow hard, and my breath would hitch as I watched the muscles of his jaw working. I'd lean in slightly, a silent invitation, and he'd take it, crashing his lips into mine. Our tongues would dance together, fighting for control as he kicks the food out of the way, crawling on top of me, and before I knew it, his head would be between my legs, stroking-

My thighs clench together. *Jesus Georgie, this is an icebreaker meal with your boss, not one of your smutty, unpublishable books.*

"Georgie, you spaced out on me again," James says, giving my arm another pat that heats me from the inside out.

"Sorry, I was just deciding if I could ignore my word count tonight. Food sounds great."

Do you ever get that thing where you're convinced the people around you are actually mind readers? Because I swear James knows that I was just picturing the fictionalized us in my head in the throes of passion and I want to curl in on myself and die.

"Great, well just meet me in here when you're wrapped up for the day and we'll hang out."

Hang out, fuck me against the wall. We'll see where the night goes.

Oh my god brain, STOP BEING SUCH A HORNBALL!

"Sounds good," I squeak out, rushing the hell out of his office and back to my own desk. If I didn't know he could still see me, I'd smack my head into my keyboard and scream.

6

James

❧

"See, this is one thing I hate about California. Why is all the pizza so pretentious?" Georgie says, picking a piece of basil off her margherita slice and taking a large bite. She gets a little bit of sauce on the corner of her lip, and I watch as her tongue peeks out and swipes it away, absolutely mesmerized by the small movement.

We're eating on the floor of my office, and it's surprisingly not that uncomfortable. I ordered pizzas and a few different antipasti from my favorite Italian spot in North Beach for our "get to know you" date tonight.

Not date, meeting. Definitely not a date. If it were a date, I would've brought out one of the nicer bottles of red I have stashed in the bar cart under my window, but instead, we're drinking Diet Cokes with paper straws and I have to hold in a burp with every sip.

"It's not pretentious! It's just regular, traditional pizza."

"Exactly. I mean, don't get me wrong, it tastes good, but who puts a whole basil leaf on a pizza? Like, get over yourself, man," She says around another bite. She doesn't talk with her mouth full *perse,* but she also doesn't wait until she's finished swallowing to speak. It's unbearably cute.

"It's Napolean style pizza. This is how they make pizza in Naples" I tell her.

"I wouldn't know, I've never been, but thanks for the mansplain." She rolls her eyes but smirks at me, so I know she's just teasing. "I just mean, why can't I find any good American style pizza in this state?"

"You mean like Domino's?"

"No, not that stuff. Like New York style. Greasy, flimsy, cheese so hot it burns the roof of your mouth, smothered in crushed red pepper flakes and grated parmesan. That's the ticket." She pops an olive into her mouth.

"Next time I'll see if I can Postmates from Manhattan." I wink at her. We might not be on a date, but there's no harm in flirting a little, is there? I mean, I'm trying to show her I'm not an asshole. I might as well hit her with some charm while I'm at it.

"That's all I ask. So, what do you want to know?" she asks, taking a sip from her soda and leaving a light lipstick mark on the lip of the can.

"What do you mean?"

"I mean, you said this was a 'get to know each other' hangout, so let's get to know each other. What do you want to know?" I feel like an idiot, but I gotta admit, I didn't really think about this part. I spent my morning praying that Georgie would accept my apology and maybe my invitation to stay after work, and I spent my afternoon trying not to stare at her ass in those skinny black trousers.

I rub my hand over the back of my neck. "Honestly, I didn't think you'd say yes to this, so I didn't come prepared."

She makes a sound in her throat that's sort of like a laugh, sort of like a snort. "Okay then, Mr. CEO. I'll go first. Where are you from?"

"Here in San Francisco. I grew up in Bernal Heights with my aunt and my sister. You?"

"White Plains in New York. I moved here a few years ago."

"That explains the pizza."

"And the 'fuck around and find out' attitude." She winks.

I laugh out loud at that. "Damn right. You're so sugary, you're a walking cavity until someone pisses you off. I was scared for my life yesterday."

She laughs too, the sound sending shivers down my spine. That laugh is the best sound I have ever heard. I want to bathe in it, tattoo it on my brain, hang it in the Louvre.

"I was not that bad!" she argues, with a swat to my knee.

"Are you kidding? I had to schedule an emergency meeting with my therapist to discuss the trauma of it all."

"So things I know about James Adler so far - hates change and is easily terrified by women half his size."

"Exactly. It's my turn to ask a question."

"So ask."

I pick up a discarded straw wrapper and start to turn it over in my hands.

"Why San Francisco?" Don't get me wrong, I love this city, even with all of its problems, but most transplants come here to work in the tech industry, coding, developing, fancying themselves the next Zuckerberg, not writing.

"It's dumb, but I've always loved the thought of SF. I grew up watching Full House and I would get chills every time the camera panned over the city. I also was obsessed with the counterculture movement of the sixties, and being a writer, I kind of romanticized coming here and being an artist with a free spirit."

"Do you feel like a free spirit?" I ask.

"Technically that's your second question, but I'll let it slide. And yes, I do. Not all the time, like when I'm crying over my bank balance after my rent check clears or I'm avoiding screaming people on MUNI, but when I can take my laptop down to the Ferry Building or even over by Aquatic Cove and write by the bay, I feel like I unlocked something I yearned for growing up. I feel like I'm where I'm meant to be."

"There is something magical about this place. I've lived here my whole life so sometimes I forget, but anytime I leave the city and come back, I realize how lucky I am to be here, surrounded by history and nature and city life and technology. Everything that makes San Francisco what it is makes my heart happy."

I can feel my cheeks redden, but something about the way she ideates about the place I've called home for almost forty years speaks to my soul.

"Listen to you, waxing poetic over there. I think maybe you're the writer in this duo."

"No way, I think I stole most of that from a Tony Bennett song." She tips her head back when she laughs this time. I'll do anything to make her laugh like that for the rest of my life.

"Alright Adler, my turn. What's with the cats?"

I'd be embarrassed, but I knew this question was coming. It's usually the first thing people ask when they come into my office. I don't even hide the toys for meetings anymore. I have no shame when it comes to my stuffed cats.

"I have a ten year old cat, Lucifer. He's evil and he's my best bud. He can't stand my sister Jenn or Amy. I love him more than anything. Jenn gives me stuffed cats for gifts and they always come with a card that says something like 'Take the devil cat to a shelter and love me, I won't piss in your sister's shoes.' She knows my little Lucifer isn't going anywhere, but she keeps giving them to me anyway." I pull my phone out of my pocket, swiping to a photo of Lucifer sprawled out on my bed, stretching all of his toes.

"Ahh, so fluffy! And that explains the lint rollers!"

"Yeah, he sheds like crazy. I love him to death but I refuse to walk around wearing his fur. " She laughs and sighs as I show her another picture, this one of Lucifer laid across my lap like a newborn baby.

"I would love to have a cat, but I think my landlord would toss me on my ass if I ever brought one home."

"You can come meet Lucifer. He might change your mind about pet ownership."

"I'd like that." She smiles, and I try not to think about how she technically just agreed to come to my house sometime. I can see her curled up on my couch with a cup of coffee, lounging on my balcony and watching the fog roll over the Golden Gate Bridge, or tangled in my silk sheets, hair mussed and skin flushed pink, looking perfectly sated after I fuck her into the mattress. I bite the inside of my cheek and start running baseball statistics through my mind to calm my growing erection. She's reaching for another slice of pizza, seemingly unaware of the pain I'm in, and I take the opportunity to adjust my tightening pants while she's not paying attention.

"What's your favorite thing about writing?" I ask, and she takes a moment to ponder over her answer.

"Knowing that my characters are safe and happy. No one can hurt them because I won't let them. That's stupid, right?"

"Not at all, it makes total sense. They're like your children, they're yours to protect," I tell her. Truthfully, I've never thought about characters in a book being real, but I suppose if you're the person who created them, they can feel that way.

"What about you?" she nudges. "What's your favorite part about being a CEO?"

Lately? My assistant.

"If you'd asked me a few years ago, I would've said the thrill of being the king of my castle. Amir and I, we built this company from the ground up, and I'm immensely proud of it. I'm getting a little tired of the corporate monotony, though. I mean, you're with me all day, you know that 90% of my job is boring shit and putting out fires that never should have been started." I sigh, running a hand through my hair. "I don't know. I feel like an asshole, y'know? I've got everything I ever wanted and now it doesn't feel like enough. Sometimes I wish I could just step down and find a new passion."

I've never told anyone about these feelings, the way I don't enjoy my work anymore, how I truly don't care about most of what I do.

I miss being in the thick of it. I miss creating. I feel like I need a different outlet for the pent-up energy brewing inside of me. I've kept it all bottled up, but one meal with Georgie and I'm spilling my inner thoughts all over the place.

"Wanting to be fulfilled in life doesn't make you an asshole," she says with a small smile before ripping her crust in half and stuffing one piece into her mouth.

I reach over to her, taking her hand in mine. I only let myself enjoy the smooth feeling of her palm for a moment before I place the ring I fashioned out of the straw wrapper on her finger.

"Georgie." I wipe a fake tear from my eye. "Will you...be my friend?" She fans her face and squeals.

"Yes, yes, a thousand times yes!!!" We both laugh at my stupid joke, but she keeps the paper ring on her finger.

The rest of the meal speeds by as we play rapid fire question and answer with each other.

Favorite color?

Georgie, yellow. Me, black.

Favorite food?

Me, sushi. Georgie, chicken tenders.

Favorite TV show?

Both- The Office.

I found out that she's a December Capricorn, and being a Virgo myself I know that means we'd make incredible partners in crime.

It's all surface level shit, the kind of stuff that doesn't really matter but is fun to find out about someone new. I'm just glad she's willingly sitting here with me. I'll listen to her go on and on about the best way to eat a Philly cheesesteak all night. Apparently, you need to put mayo and fries on it- who knew?

It's almost seven when the pizzas are nothing more than a couple grease spots and stray pepperonis, and the Diet Coke cans are empty. We've been quiet for a few minutes while we take our last bites. I'm not ready for the night to end, but it seems I'm the only one. Wiping her hands on her pant legs and moving to her knees to stand, Georgie speaks.

"I should get going. I really do need to write tonight, and I have an early morning tomorrow." I want to keep her here, I want to keep her talking and laughing, but I can't think of a good enough reason to ask her to stay.

Please stay with me. I know you barely tolerate me but I think you're funny and beautiful and I want you to have my babies.

Yeah, that's not gonna fly.

"Sure. Let me just get this cleaned up real quick and I'll walk you to your car." I stand, grabbing an empty pizza box and our plates.

"Oh, that's okay, I didn't drive here. I'm gonna go catch the bus."

Look, I swear I think it's great that the city has reliable-ish public transportation, but the thought of Georgie taking the bus alone at night where anything could happen to her makes my skin crawl. Sure, it's summer and the sun is still out, but still.

"Just wait here a second. I'll give you a ride home." I rush out the words, and damn, do I sound like an idiot.

"That's sweet but really, if I run down, I can catch the 38R..."

"Please," I bite out, a tone just this side of harsh, "just, let me drive you home, Georgie."

She sighs, either sensing my desperation or realizing she's not winning the fight, and nods. "Sure, that would actually be great, thanks."

I realize I just spent the night trying to convince this woman that I'm not an asshole and then practically spit at her to follow me to my car, but what's done is done. Georgie collects her things from her desk as I throw out the trash from our dinner. I grab my jacket and messenger bag and lead her to the elevator down to our building's private parking garage. One thing I made sure of when we moved to this location is that all Streamline employees and guests would have free, private off-street parking, a luxury that's practically unheard of in the Bay Area.

We're silent in the elevator, but it's a comfortable silence. Like two people who do this everyday, eat a meal and then go home together.

Not that we're going home together. Georgie's going home and I'm going home. There will be no togetherness of it. None.

I grab my keys as the elevator doors open and hit the fob, the brake lights of my Jeep blinking in the empty garage.

"Hmm. I thought all you tech bros drove Teslas" Georgie muses as she makes her way to the passenger side door. I take a step in front of her and open it, offering her a lift up. She looks surprised by the gesture, but she takes my outstretched hand and lets me assist her. I'm not a "I need a big scary monster truck wheel" kind of guy, but I like that my Wrangler has an extra little height to it.

"Musk is a prick," I say, closing her door. I take extra care to not catch her clothes in the latch.

She's staring at me with a bewildered look on her face as I climb into the driver's side. I give her a silent "What?" look back.

"You're like, rich, aren't you?" I cough, because she's not wrong, but that doesn't mean I want to talk about it.

"I mean-" She cuts me off.

"Do you actually *know* Elon Musk? Like personally?" she asks, still looking at me as if I'm an alien from another planet. Unfortunately, he's hard to avoid in my line of work.

"Yeah, I do. And he's a prick. Put your address in." I hand her my phone with the Maps app open. She takes it and giggles.

"Hearing you say that makes me like you a bit more, Adler." She shakes her head while typing into my phone.

"If I had known that I would've started talking shit earlier, Hansley."

She hands my phone back to me as it connects to the car's Bluetooth, and Taylor Swift's "Anti-Hero" starts to play through my speakers while I back out of my spot and leave the garage.

"I also wouldn't have taken you for a Swiftie," she says, nodding her head to the beat of the music.

"I mean I've heard her stuff on the radio but never really got into it. But yesterday I was curious about the song you were performing in my kitchen-" She groans and covers her face, the embarrassment radiating off of her. I have to hold back from placing a comforting hand on her knee. "And I ended up listening to the whole Midnights album. It's amazing. I cried to this song last night."

My eyes are on the road, but I can feel her shocked face taking in my side profile. "You cried? To Taylor Swift? Which part?"

I point to the touch screen in front of us just as Taylor sings a lyric about life losing its meaning when the person you love sees the real you and leaves.

"I had to email my therapist about that particular lyric. It hit a little too close to home." She continues to look at me, but I can tell she's not judging me or thinking that I'm lying. She's just...taking me in.

"A certain Twitter-owning-billionaire hating Swiftie who buys me pizza AND goes to therapy? James Adler, will you marry me?" I throw my head back and laugh, trying to ignore the butterflies fluttering inside of me. My mind knows she's kidding, that the thought of Georgie, me, and marriage in the same sentence is outlandish, but my body doesn't seem to have gotten the memo.

"Set the date, sweet girl," I say, and she laughs too.

It's a short drive to Georgie's apartment, and for the rest of the trip we listen to the music and I secretly smile at the way she sings under her breath. I didn't look at the address she put into my phone, I just followed the directions, so when the voice is telling me that my destination is on my right, I'm not exactly happy with the street we're on.

I give her an uneasy look.

"Georgie, this is a really terrible neighborhood." I realize I sound like an elitist snob, but a lot of crimes occur around here. My stomach flips at the thought of Georgie ever being unsafe. She shrugs.

"It's really not so bad as long as you keep to yourself, and it's cheap. Well, cheap for the city, anyway."

"Right." I nod, completely unconvinced, but it's not like I can do anything about it. If it were up to me, I'd take her upstairs, have her pack a bag and come live with me in my penthouse with the 24/7 security, but something tells me she wouldn't be receptive to that idea.

"Let me walk you up," I say, jumping out of the car and hurrying to her side before she has a chance to respond.

"It's fine James, you really shouldn't leave your car alone unless you want your windows smashed in. The republicans on TV might exaggerate about the state of this city, but that is one stereotype that holds up."

I reach my hand out and grab hers. "I can buy a new car, I can't buy a new Georgie." Her eyes roam over my face, and I can see the slight lift of a smile forming on her beautiful red lips.

"Okay. But when you come back and your catalytic convertor is gone, don't think you're taking it out of my paycheck."

She lets me help her out of the car, and to my delight, she doesn't let go of my hand as we get to the door. She uses one key on two different locks and leads me up a stairwell to a second door marked 2A.

"This is me," she says, turning towards me. "Thank you for dinner, and for the ride, it was a fun night." The fingers of her left hand are still entwined with mine, the scratch of the straw wrapper ring I made for her grazing my knuckles. In this tiny alcove outside of her apartment, our bodies are so close, I can feel the heat of her breath on my chest as she looks up at me. I want to stay here all night and count the flecks of gold in her eyes. I step towards her, bringing us even closer, a whisper of air the only thing keeping our bodies from touching.

"I had fun too, Georgie," I say, angling my head in a silent question.

She lifts her chin in an answer, and my knees go weak. I take a calming breath before I go to lean in.

"Dammit," a female voice rings out between us. "I thought you were my Dim Sum." The apartment door slams shut as fast as it opened, breaking the trance and completely ruining the moment. Georgie drops my hand and steps back.

"Roommates. Can't live with 'em, can't pay rent without 'em." Her voice is breathless and nervous as she opens the door back up and steps in. "See ya Monday, James." I barely get out my own goodbye before the door to apartment 2A is shut in my face. I know she's just embarrassed that she got caught up in the moment, but shit. I really wanted to fucking kiss her.

I get back in my car-all windows and important parts still intact-and let out a frustrated "FUUUUUUUUCK".

Back at home, I sit on my couch with two fingers of scotch and my grumpy cat, willing myself to think of anything besides red lips and glasses and the sweet scent of vanilla sugar.

7

Georgie

"I don't think I've ever had *fun* doing cardio before. Usually I'm like a hippo on the elliptical just trying to survive." Rachel and I just finished up a 30 minute 90's pop ride at her favorite cycling studio, Spin Sync, and true to her word, we're now waiting for a table at Zazie. It's a French restaurant whose brunch menu I've been dying to try for months. Thankfully we both packed a change of clothes and got cleaned up in the locker room, because that workout was sweaty as hell.

"I told you! Kira's energy is just off the charts, she makes it so fun." Rachel wraps an arm around me while we wait. I've noticed she's very touchy-feely. She's always patting my arms or holding my hand. I don't mind, honestly I think I've been a little touch-starved the last few years. It feels nice to be held by another person, even in a platonic way.

"Kira is all energy baby!" I turn to see a five-foot blonde in half-up half-down pigtails skipping- yes, literally skipping- towards us. Rachel told me that she and Kira have been friends since the latter moved to San Francisco from LA three years ago, and now that I'm around, my presence at their monthly brunch date is mandatory. When I mentioned something about being broke, Rachel assured me that she was a spoiled trust fund brat and she'd take care of me. While Rachel and I both put on jeans and casual t-shirts, Kira changed from the skin tight bike shorts and sports bra she wore in class into a pair of black Lululemon leggings and a cropped hoodie. I can never pull off the athleisure look without looking like a slob, but Kira looks like a carefree fitness model.

"Rachel, party of 3?" The man at the host stand calls out, and Kira runs up, jumping as he gathers our menus.

"Just in time, I'm starving!!!" She bounces, and we follow the host to a table in the back of the small restaurant. Nestled in our corner, I groan, the smell of syrup and bacon overwhelming my senses. "I've been dying to come here forever," I say, picking up my menu as if I haven't read it online fifty times by now.

"OOH! Let me order for you!" Kira says, the southern twang in her voice peeking out over her excitement. I have to remind myself to ask her where that accent is from.

"It's my super power. Do you have any allergies?" Normally I would be averse to letting someone else decide what I'm going to eat- I'm not picky, but I'm not *not* picky- but something about Kira speaks to me. I've only known the woman for an hour, but for some reason, I already trust her.

"Nope, no allergies. I'll let you handle it," I say as the server brings over three oat milk chai lattes and the fixings for make-your-own-mimosas we ordered.

As it turns out, my instinct with Kira was right, because half an hour later, I'm absolutely stuffed full of the fluffiest scrambled eggs and most delicious gingerbread pancakes I've ever tasted. Our server pops the cork on our second bottle of champagne- all notions of adding juice to our glasses is lost at this point- as my new friend rattles on about her shitty ex-boyfriend.

"So not only did I find him in my living room doing lines off an escort's ass cheek, it turns out he's also fucking married with two kids. The whole time he's living two lives and I had no idea. Then I had to pay her after he ran off, and I couldn't even be mad at her! She was just doing her job. I mean seriously, fuck men!"

"And that is exactly why I don't date. Men do nothing but let you down, and I'm way too nervous to hit on women." I don't usually drop my bisexuality so casually, but the mimosas and the company have me feeling good.

"Ugh, Georgie. I wish I wasn't so straight. I'd wife you up immediately." Kira grabs my hand across the table.

"Oh Kira, I'd treat you so good. Damn your heterosexuality!" I laugh.

"Alright lovebirds," Rachel cuts in. "Speaking of men- you never told me what happened with the boss man yesterday, G."

"Oooh, workplace drama? Let me hear it." Kira's eyes widen as she takes another sip of champagne.

"Georgie screamed at her boss on Thursday and told him to get fucked to his face." Rachel says, picking a piece of bacon off of my plate.

"Oh my god will you stop?" I laugh, flicking an uneaten bite of toast at her while Kira tilts her head back and laughs like a hyena. We're definitely "those girls" at the restaurant today, but I could care less. I haven't had this much fun since...

Last night.

"I did not tell him to get fucked. I was mad at him for something and I let it be known. And for your information, he apologized to me yesterday."

"Excuse me? You yelled at James Adler at his own company and he apologized to you?" Rachel lets out a low whistle. "You must be lethal when you're angry, G."

"Wait a second, you work for James Adler? Streamline CEO James Adler? Top Ten Most Eligible Bachelors in the Bay Area five years running James Adler? That man is six foot six inches of hot, molten sex." Kira fans herself and I can't help but blush.

"I know. He's really gorgeous in person, too. Like, 'hard to focus' gorgeous. I'm almost mad that he apologized to me because at least when I thought he was an asshole I had something else to focus on besides his stupid, beautiful face."

"God, if I were you, I'd ditch the panties and spend my days 'accidentally' dropping things in front of him until he hiked my skirt up and plowed into me." I blush. Kira clearly has no filter, and I love it.

"There's more..." I say, sipping my drink. I'm gonna need a serious nap after this. Both of my friends' eyes widened. "He asked me to stay after work to get to know each other better, kind of push the reset button on our relationship. We sat on the floor of his office and talked for hours, and then he drove me home."

"Oh. That's...nice," Rachel says, her face wrinkling with disappointment. I think she was hoping for a more NSFW story from me. Rachel has been with her high school sweetheart, Brian, for almost ten years, she once told me she thrives off the excitement of other people's relationships.

"Okay, woman, let me finish." I roll my eyes.

"Did HE let you finish?" Kira asks, and I ignore her.

"He insisted on walking me up to my door. He held my hand to help me out of the car and didn't let go the entire time we walked up my stairs. And then when we were saying goodbye, there was this moment. I really felt like he was going to kiss me. He was staring at my lips and breathing kind of heavy. I wanted him to go for it, but my freaking roommate opened the door and killed the mood."

"Oh my god!" "What did you do?" they yell at the same time.

"I said goodnight and slammed the door in his face. What else would I do?" I drop my face into my hands, pissed at myself for running away. I don't even know if I wanted him to kiss me. Everything is feeling so weird and fast. All I know is that I definitely wasn't ready for that moment to end.

"Ugh, I want to murder your roommate. I should be hearing about the size of his dick and how many times he made you come, not about an almost fucking kiss." Kira fake-slams her hand down on the table. Seriously, you'd think we've been friends for years with the way she talks.

"So then what? Did he text you or anything?" Rachel asks.

"I don't think he even has my number in his personal phone. I was so annoyed. Not at him, but at the situation. Honestly though, it helped me break through some writer's block. I stayed up past midnight writing a really spicy scene between two characters I decided I've kept apart long enough." It's true. One thing I love about being a writer- working out my own sexual desires and frustrations in a Google Doc.

"Okay, I have to know before I beg you to read them." Kira looks me in the eye with a dead serious expression. "I've been burned before, so please tell me. Are your books 'I'd read it in public but maybe not at my mom's house' spicy or 'lock myself in my room with a glass of wine and fresh pack of batteries' spicy?"

I laugh- actually, it's more like a cackle- out loud. I think I'm in love with her. Then something weird happens. My stomach doesn't flutter. I don't get the urge to collapse in on myself (or vomit, whichever comes first). Kira is asking me if she can read my work, *and I want to say yes.* That has never happened to me before. Even when I was posting fan fiction anonymously when I was a teenager, I'd break into nervous sweats as soon as I'd hit 'publish'. Hell, I used to shake like a leaf turning in work in my creative writing classes. But right now, the thought of Kira wanting to read my words, my vibes, my world- it excites me.

"Honey, break out the Cabernet and AAAs, I'll email you some of my work when I get home."

8

Georgie

After brunch, Kira and Rachel wanted to go thrifting, but I wasn't kidding about needing that nap. Day drinking is all fun and games until you're 26 and nursing a hangover at 5pm. When I get home, I grab a Diet Coke can from the fridge, give a polite nod to Ashley (or maybe it's Ryan?) who's watching TV on the couch, and close myself off in my room. After I decide what piece of work I want to send to Kira and Rach for review, I slip out of my jeans and pull my bra off from under my t-shirt, sitting back at my desk.

I planned on getting some writing done today, since last night's work was all porn and no plot. You know what they say, write drunk, edit sober. I'm working on the third book in my interconnected standalone series. All set in a fictional small town, the first book is a nanny/single dad story, the second is a second chance, high school sweethearts to enemies to lovers, and this one is supposed to be a big city man finds love in the countryside, sort of like a reverse Hallmark movie, but I'm having trouble finding the chemistry without the tension. It was supposed to be a grumpy/sunshine trope, but both main characters are unraveling as total golden retrievers. I need to figure out how to up the ante between them.

I know what you're thinking- *Georgie, why are you putting pressure on yourself to write 5000 words of a story no one is ever going to read because you're too scared to publish it?*

Because all I ever wanted in life is to be able to call myself a writer. I went to college for creative writing. I started at community college to save money, and then scored an okay-ish scholarship that allowed me to attend The College of West Chester. I had to work my way through (not that that paid for tuition. Nope, I'm saddled with student loans like the rest of my generation). That meant I had to take less credits. It took me six years to earn my Bachelor's, and then I didn't have a single relevant job opportunity after graduation. I didn't have time to do internships or work for the school paper or do anything to build my resume besides my GPA. I was completely unhirable.

My diploma is nothing more than a $40,000 piece of paper. I didn't even bother framing it.

Since I was a kid, I've found solace in words. I kept journals where I'd create characters based on the people around me. The grumpy old man next door was secretly a spy working for the government, my fifth grade teacher was a big animal veterinarian who rode elephants on the weekends (I never said they were good characters). When I was a teenager and discovered One Direction fanfiction on Wattpad, it was over. I wanted to write love stories where everyone was smiling and no one was scared of their dad and they all got to live happily (and hornily) ever after.

When I was emancipated at 16 and was renting the cheapest room I could find in town- a half-finished basement with no windows and no bathroom door- I'd get out of school, go straight to my job bussing tables and seating cranky baby boomers at Applebee's, then come back to that tiny room and lose myself in the worlds I created. At the time, I was purely writing fanfiction and the occasional teacher/student after school romp in the classroom. (I know, I know, inappropriate, but I was a kid with a crush on my hot history teacher, sue me). I didn't even own a computer. Most of the stories were handwritten in notebooks and then typed up at that one computer in the corner of the library where no one could see the screen unless they looked really hard.

I'm just going to be blunt- my life back then was really shitty. I had no one, I barely had any money, my circumstances forced me into adult responsibilities way before I was ready for them, and I couldn't relate to the other kids around me. Writing was my escape, my home, my happy place. It still is, and even though I'm scared, I'm desperate for some kind of acknowledgment of my talent, because *I know* I'm a good writer. I pressure myself to keep writing, to keep working, to always have a backlog of ideas because I know in my soul, someday I'm going to nut up and release my work into the world, and someone will like it.

I'll do it, I swear. Just not yet.

Right now, though, the champagne headache is starting to kick in and those gingerbread pancakes are weighing me down. I decide to lay down for a bit, finally get that nap in, and revisit my document when I wake up. Maybe I'll dream up a breakthrough for my two nameless characters (why is naming them the hardest part?).

I flop onto my bed and snuggle up in my blankets, a small ray of sun peeking through my curtains. I close my eyes and go through my normal "I want to sleep" scenario in my head.

I'm in a hammock by the ocean. I sip from the crisp glass of water by my side. The glass of wine and sushi I had an hour ago has calmed me to my core, and my eyelids start to feel heavy. The sound of waves crashing lulls me away from the book in my hand. The sun is warm on my face as I sway back and forth. I close my eyes and start to drift off. Two strong hands wrap around my middle, and I'm enveloped by the scent of leather as I feel soft lips pressing a kiss to my temple.

Uhh...that's new...

Usually after I close my eyes and settle into the fantasy, I start to drift off. There's never been another person in this little sleep scenario of mine. I want to question it, but I know exactly who's hands and mouth have snuck their way into the oceanside hammock in my mind.

James Adler.

I groan into my pillow. I so do not want to be thinking about him right now, not after the humiliating moment last night when I actually thought he might kiss me. God I'm so stupid, holding on to his hand like that. He was probably just thinking of a polite way to tell me to let go, and I'm standing there practically puckering my lips at him like a cartoon character.

Sleep, Georgie. You can do this. *I'm in a hammock by the ocean, the sound of waves crashing around me as James plants light kisses on my neck, slipping his hand beneath my bathing suit top and tracing a circle with his fingertip around my...*

Jesus Christ.

I'm in a hammock by the ocean, the sound of waves crashing around me. The book I've discarded falls to the ground and the rest of the world fades into oblivion as James works himself in and out of me-

DAMMIT!

The pulse between my legs picks up. I know I won't be able to do anything, let alone sleep, if my pussy keeps throbbing with the need for release. I roll onto my back and slide my panties down my legs, tossing them on the floor. I need to sleep, and I can't get James out of my head, so I do what I gotta do.

What's that old saying? If you can't beat 'em, beat it?

I rub my hand down the front of my body, brushing against my hard nipples and snaking my hand down to my slit, already slick with arousal. I decided to move the fantasy to this bed (my imaginary hammock is my place, thank you very much). I close my eyes and swipe my finger over my clit once - twice- as I imagine James standing in front of me, no shirt, cock straining against his tight slacks, his eyes dark with lust.

He shoves his pants to the floor, gripping his rock hard erection through his underwear as he takes in the sight of me. He drops onto the bed, his knees on either side of my legs and presses his lips to my hot skin.

"You. Are. So. Beautiful," he says between kisses that work their way up my naked, needy body. His lips meet mine, and I wrap my legs around his waist, desperate to feel him against my center. "Tell me I can make you come, Georgie."

"Fuck, yes please." He dips his fingers between my legs, working my swollen clit with the pad of his thumb and teasing my soaked entrance with his fingers. He works my clit with delicious pressure, pressing down and pulling back, bringing me closer and closer to the edge.

"I need you," I say, pulling his throbbing cock out of his briefs and stroking it.

"I'm all yours," he answers with a kiss, lining himself up and slamming into me, hips bucking and skin slapping, relentless in the way he fucks me.

Sweat beads on my brow as I rub my aching nub furiously, chasing the orgasm I need so desperately, but it's not enough. I reach behind my head and pull out my trusty pillow- firm but soft with a jersey cotton cover- and bring it between my legs, mounting it. I slowly rock my hips and rub my dripping pussy across the cushion, the seam of the fabric working my clit.

"I'm so close," I breathe against his hard chest as he pounds into me, and then I'm no longer on my back. James flips us so that he's on his back and I'm on top, his cock never leaving my pussy as we roll.

"Ride me, Georgia. I want to see you come all over me baby." I can take him so much deeper in this position, and when I lean forward, my clit rubs against the base of him. I rock my hips on top of him, pulling myself closer and closer to release, when James leans forward and sucks one of my pebbled nipples into his mouth.

That image is my undoing. With one hand pulling the pillow tight against my pussy and the other covering my mouth to swallow my moans, stars explode behind my eyes and my entire body shakes as I come. I bite my tongue and move the hand from my mouth to my headboard, bracing myself as I continue to ride out the waves of pleasure. My body goes limp and I flop to my side, pulling the poor pillow out from between my legs and tossing the case over to my laundry basket.

"Thank you for your service and I apologize for the mess," I whisper to the pillow as I tuck it back in place behind the rest, giggling to myself in my post-orgasm euphoria.

I definitely didn't mean to sleep so long. It's 10:46 pm when I blink my eyes open and look at my phone.

Kira Riley has added you to the group "Pussy Posse"

Kira: Oh. My. God.

Kira: *Picture of shriveled up chocolate lady from Spongebob*

Kira: ^ that is my poor clit after reading that scene with the dad and the nanny in the kitchen *fans self* when he lifted her leg onto the counter and pounded her from behind. I came so hard I actually screamed. Thanks for the multiple orgasms, G

Rachel: Jesus Keeks *laughing emoji* I haven't gotten to that part yet, I'm still hot over the tension in the pool scene and they didn't even kiss. My panties didn't stand a chance. I guess that's why they call them one handed reads?

Georgie: *curtsies* I told you I would treat you good *wink emoji**girls kissing emoji*

Unknown number: The infamous Georgie joins the group chat! I'm Dottie, and I have no idea what you're talking about but I think I need in.

Kira and Rachel's praise of my writing made me laugh out loud, and I'm thrilled to be added to my first group chat that has nothing to do with school or swapping shifts. I've never had friends to be in a group chat with, let alone friends that are comfortable enough with me to tell me they've masturbated to my words. Maybe that should weird me out, but honestly, it gives me a sense of pride. I mean, I write romance. My goal is to make people feel good, right?

My stomach growls, so I pull myself away from the puddle of drool on my pillow (why are naps so drool-producing?) and tiptoe into the kitchen. Ryan and Ashley are both in their rooms. I have no idea if they're asleep or not but I have no intentions of waking them. I don't have the energy or the willpower to cook a proper meal, so I throw together a turkey and cheese sandwich with avocado and a generous glass of chardonnay and take it back to my room.

I plop onto my desk chair, feet resting on the edge of my bed, and throw on an episode of The Office on my laptop to watch while I eat. I'm trying to decide if I should try to pull an all nighter to write or eat 13 melatonin gummies and pass out until Monday morning when my phone lights up.

Unknown number: You'll never guess which Taylor song I just cried to

I don't have this number saved in my phone, but I know exactly who it is. My stomach does a flip. Why is he texting me? Was he thinking about me? Was he *thinking* about me? I save his number, which is annoyingly difficult since my hands decided to start shaking, and text him back.

Georgie: How did you get my number?

James: I had it in my work phone goofball. Now guess

Georgie: How many tries do I get?

James: Hmm...three

Georgie: Was it...Look What You Made Me Do?

James: ...

James: Yes...

James: How the hell did you do that?

Georgie: *shrug emoji* it's a secretly sad song hidden by intense production. If you read the lyrics like a poem, you realize how somber it actually is

James: I was all ready to tease you about how I understand t swizzle on a level you never will, and you cut me off at the knees.

Georgie: You're a grown man crying to Taylor Swift alone on a Saturday night and YOU were coming to tease ME? It's good that you're in tune with your emotions and all, but that's just sad, Adler.

James: *laughing emoji* who said I was alone, Georgia?

Oh god. Of course, he's not alone. It's Saturday night, he's probably on a date or something. Although it would be weird if he was on a date, crying and texting me...

My phone buzzes again.

James: I've got my emotional support demon

A picture accompanies the message.

Jaw, meet floor.

He sent an image of Lucifer laid across his lap, but as cute as the gray fluffball is, he's not what I'm focusing on. Leaning against a headboard surrounded by black silk covered pillows, James is shirtless. The camera is angled slightly so I can see his face, chest, and the cat on his lap, and it's a goddamn work of art. I can see every bump of muscle on his broad shoulders, the flex of his bicep holding the phone, every ridge of his 36 pack abs, I can even see the very beginning of that sexy as frick "V" guys get above their dicks when they work out regularly. I have never in my life been sexually attracted to a man's nipples, but his look so perfect, dark reddish brown and small, I'm aching to run a finger over them. I wonder if he'd like that.

His hair is mussed and his blue eyes are sleepy and happy, looking perfectly content. The image sends a whisper of desire down my spine. I find myself wishing I was Lucifer, spread out on his lap, waiting to be pet.

Jesus that's weird. This man is fucking with my brain.

Georgie: Looks like the guy is asleep on the job. You might want to vet the people you hire a little better.

James: I'll keep that in mind. What are you up to?

Georgie: Big night. I accidentally slept for like eight hours and now I'm eating a very belated dinner in my bedroom.

James: An eight hour nap? What brought that on?

Oh you know, just getting myself off to the thought of your naked body underneath me.

Georgie: Boozy brunch and too many pancakes. I'm watching TV and regretting all of my life choices

James: *laughing emoji* That'll do it. Send a pic

The butterflies in my stomach are flapping like crazy. He wants a picture of me, now? I spin around to face my mirror. My hair is in a messy bun, I have no makeup on, and the t-shirt I'm wearing with the cartoon pig taking a selfie captioned "InstaHam" has been fighting in the trenches since 2016, but honestly, I don't look *that* bad. I think I rock the sleepy look, and at least I'm wearing clothes, unlike mister "I just casually look like a Greek god while I chill in bed with my adorable cat".

I turn my camera into selfie mode, angling it the same way he did so he can see the glass of wine I'm holding on top of my thigh, right where my shirt ends. I think it's long enough that he won't realize I'm not wearing pants.

Georgie: I'm not alone either. I have my emotional support white wine

James: Haha, instaham. Cute :)

Is he calling my shirt cute, or me? No way I'm asking so I guess we'll never know.

James: I've never seen you without your lipstick on

Georgie: I don't usually wear it to sleep

James: Don't get me wrong, I like the red. It suits you. But I think no makeup Georgie is my new favorite.

Jesus. He's actually flirting with me isn't he? I'll have to screenshot this conversation and send it to the girls to be sure. I don't want to give any merit to the butterflies doing laps in my stomach if I'm misreading the situation.

Georgie: Good to know, with the way I've screwed up my sleep schedule today, I'll probably be too wiped on Monday morning to even look at a tube of lipstick.

James: I'm looking forward to it :) I'll see you Monday sweet girl

Georgie: See ya Monday boss

Oh. My. God. The texts, the almost moment in the hallway, calling me sweet girl...

Is it possible that James Adler might actually...*like me* like me?

I kind of hope so, because I think I'm starting to *like him* like him.

9

James

⸙⸺

"Jesus, Amy. Warn a guy!" I exclaim, snapping my eyes shut while handing baby Riley over to my sister-in-law.

"Grow up, James. Your niece eats from my tits. I'm not hiding them in my own home for your comfort." I peek one eye open and see that Riley has latched, so I'm safe.

"I didn't say hide them, I said give me a warning. I didn't know nipples could be that fucking big."

"Stop gawking at my wife's body, James," my sister yells from the kitchen where she's packing up the leftovers I told her I won't eat but she insists on sending home with me anyway. Before the baby came, my sisters and I would get brunch out at least once a month, but

83

now that Riley is here, we'll be brunching at home for the foreseeable future.

"I'm not gawking. I think my dick shriveled up and died at the sight of those monsters." A pillow hits my face and I laugh, impressed with Amy's ability to whack me and hold her baby to her breast at the same time.

"I'll still never understand how you two have worked together all this time without killing each other," Jenn muses, handing me a cup of coffee and passing a decaf to her wife. Amy and I are always like this outside of the office. We tease each other and bicker like siblings. Sometimes we like to gang up on Jenn and tease her too, but it's all in good fun.

"Because I am the picture of professionalism in the office. They don't pay me the big bucks for nothing," Amy says, and I avert my eyes yet again as she moves Riley from one breast to another.

"Don't think I forgot about the time you and Catherine wrapped my entire office in Christmas wrapping paper," I point out, sipping my coffee.

"We were trying to get you in the holiday spirit."

"It was April!"

"At least I'm creative. You put my wireless mouse in Jell-o. Seriously, stole that one right from The Office."

"It's a classic prank. Besides, what about the time you-"

"Okay, that's enough," Jenn interrupts us. Ever the moderator, she radiates big sister energy. "How's it going so far with the temp?"

"Fine. She caught on quick." I sip my coffee and set the mug on the table beside me. My sisters look at me expectantly. "What?"

"Fine? I had to listen to you bitch about me going on maternity leave for almost nine whole months! Two weeks without me and all you have to say is fine?" Amy scoffs, passing the baby over to Jenn to be burped.

"Yeah, well, turns out you're not that useful to me." I roll my eyes as another pillow hits the side of my head.

"Will you stop with the violence in front of our daughter, Ames? Jeez." Jenn pouts at her wife and Amy immediately melts, reaching over and kissing her, whispering an apology against her lips.

It's gross, cause it's my sister, but it's also incredibly sweet. Jenn and Amy have always had this amazing connection that you can't help but feel when they're together. For the first time in a long time- maybe even ever- I find myself craving that kind of intimacy with someone.

No, not just someone, a certain red-lipped assistant.

"You know me and Riley are still here, right?" I say, as I can see their kiss developing into a full on make out.

"Right," Amy coughs, pulling away. "Anyway, according to my spies, you're lying to us."

"Spies?" I ask, already knowing the answer.

"Catherine and I talk everyday. I know all about the way you've been treating that poor Georgie like shit and making her cry. Seriously, James, what the fuck is wrong with you?"

I run my hand over my jaw. "I didn't mean to be a dick to her. I was just keeping my distance. She called me out on it and I apologized. We made up, we're good."

"Why are you trying to keep your distance from someone you have to work so closely with?" Jenn asks, that annoying knowing gleam in her eyes. I stare at Riley, now fast asleep in my sister's arms, and I wish

I could switch places with her. She just sucks a few nipples and falls asleep, the dream life. And she doesn't have to answer to my sister, at least not until she starts talking.

Am I seriously jealous of a newborn?

"If you've been talking to Catherine, you already know why."

"Oh I know, I just want to hear you say it."

"She's cute." I shrug, keeping my eyes fixated on Riley and the way her little baby mouth moves and twitches as she sleeps. She has that new baby smell, the one that's kind of like a mix of baby powder and oatmeal, and I want to lean over and breathe it in. She is the first baby I've ever really been around, and I'm struck by how addicting her presence is.

"Oh puuuuhhhlease" Amy draws out dramatically, rolling her eyes so hard I'm amazed they don't get stuck like that. "I've seen rooms full of supermodels practically dropping to their knees in front of you, ready to suck the soul out of your billion dollar dick and you don't even bat an eye. Don't pull that 'she's cute so I must avoid her' shit with me."

I wince, not just at the crude language, but because she's right. I've had my guard up for thirty years, refusing to let a single woman get through to my heart. One look from Georgie Hansley, and I'm ready to rip the damn organ out of my own chest and give it to her to keep.

"She just…" I start, struggling to find the words. I've discussed my feelings with Dr. Patel, but talking to anyone else about these things feels impossible. My voice shakes as I continue. "Affects me. I don't know how to explain it. I saw her there, the beautiful mystery girl, and I felt a shift. It's like she rocked my entire world before she even said hello. She's so beautiful, I feel like I don't deserve to look at her.

She's smart and funny and she lights up every room she walks into. She adores Amir, she's incredible at her job, and when she was yelling at me for being an ass, I could tell that even though she's kind, she takes no shit and will stand up for herself. I'm just...enamored by her."

"Oh, James," Jenn gives me a sympathetic nod "you've got it bad, little brother."

"I really do, and it's freaking me out. I don't do the feelings bullshit."

"Have you talked to your therapist at all?" Amy asks, not looking so smug anymore.

"Yeah, he keeps telling me to remind myself why I keep my guard up and ask myself if it's worth missing out on something good, whether it's with Georgie or someone else. He says it's good that I'm even feeling these feelings for once."

"It is," Jenn agrees, "You've let what that woman did to us dictate so much of how you live your life." She hasn't called her 'mom' since the day she left us on Aunt Janine's doorstep. She's always been *that woman*. "It'll be good for you to open yourself to new possibilities."

"Yeah," Amy cuts in, "but you also have to remember that she might not like you back, and even then, you spent the last two weeks being a jerk to the girl-"

"Amy!" Jenn chastises.

"No, she's right. Amir told me the same thing. But I think I've made progress, at least on the friend front. I bought her pizza on Friday night and we texted a little last night. I feel like there's potential." I pick at a stray Lucifer hair that's threaded in my jeans, and I don't notice Amy reach across the coffee table and grab my phone from the cushion next to me until it's too late.

"Amy!" I lunge after her, but she's quicker than me, even after giving birth just a few weeks ago.

"Oh my goodness, James Alexander Adler, you are a flirt!" she squeals, scrolling through my phone. Of course she knows my passcode, being my assistant and all, though she rarely abuses the privilege. I drop backwards over the side of the couch, my back connecting with the cushions as I groan.

"What does it say?" Jenn asks, carefully running towards her wife with the baby in her arms. "Aww, you listen to Taylor Swift now?"

"Oh my God, James, you sent her a thirst trap picture!" I look up. Both of my sister's mouths are wide open.

"What? I sent her a picture of my cat."

"You sent her a picture of your bare-naked chest that your cat happens to be in," Amy says "And you asked her to send one back? Tell me now, did you guys sext? Cause I definitely don't want to read that." She covers her eyes and holds the phone away like it's covered in fucking cooties.

"Jesus, no, we did not sext."

"Aww, look at her, she is really cute!" Jenn croons. Even though it's just my sisters, the fact that anyone else is seeing that picture that was meant just for me causes my stomach to ache. It feels like an invasion of Georgie's privacy, not to mention I did unspeakable things to myself in bed last night while looking at it.

"She looks young. How old is she?"

I was dreading this part. "She's twenty-six," I tell them.

"Uh, hello cradle robber! You're way too old for her!"

"I'm older than you," Jenn reminds her wife.

"Yeah, by three years, not eleven. James, you were practically in college when she started kindergarten."

"Okay yeah, she's younger than me, but don't be weird. You're making it sound like she's a teenager and not a grown woman." I roll my eyes. I usually only mess around with women my own age, but I resent the implication that I'm somehow creepy for being attracted to another adult.

"You're right, I'm sorry. She's cute."

"She's gorgeous." I sigh. "So what do I do now?"

"You woo her!" Jenn bounces.

"Yeah, it's wooing time! Keep it professional at work, you don't want her to think you're taking advantage of her because of your position, but after hours, keep up the flirty texts. Invite her out with you and Amir and get Amir to go home early. OHH! You have the LA trip coming up, that's perfect! You can take her out on a date without her realizing it's a date and before you know it, you'll be taking her to pound town!"

"Jesus Christ," I mumble under my breath. "This has been...helpful, but you two are exhausting. I'm going home." I snatch my phone back from Amy and give each lady a kiss on the cheek before heading to the door. I'm halfway down the driveway when I hear my name being called from behind. I turn to find Jenn jogging towards me, wrapping me into a hug when we meet.

"It's okay to be afraid," she says, head pressed against my arm, "but it's also okay to let yourself fall."

I give her a kiss on the top of her head. "I love you, sis."

"Love you too, bro."

I've never really been the "Ugh, Mondays, am I right?" kind of guy. I love my job. Or, I used to, anyway. I work with my friends and a great group of people. I love my free time, but I don't let the prospect of a new work week get me down.

I'm not sure if "Sunday scaries" is the right thing to explain what I'm feeling right now, but I'm definitely nervous. I've already scoured my work phone for forgotten meetings, missed deadlines, anything that could be contributing to this feeling coursing through me, but it's pointless. I know exactly what's got my stomach flipping and my heart beating out of my chest.

I'll be seeing Georgie for the first time since I almost kissed her on Friday.

I may have told Jenn and Amy about the pizza and the texts, but there was no way I was letting them have that moment outside of Georgie's apartment. I can't help but wonder what would have happened if that door never opened. Would Georgie let me kiss her? Would she even want me to? Usually I don't make a move unless I'm 100% certain it's wanted, but around Georgie, I'm no better than a bumbling teenager. I don't know if anything I'm perceiving is real, or if I just want her so bad that I'm willing to believe anything.

It's 8 o'clock, and considering it's a rare warm summer night in the city, I decided to enjoy a beer or two out on my balcony, watching the headlights of cars driving back and forth over the Golden Gate Bridge in the distance. I open my phone and scroll through the short text thread from last night. I enlarge the selfie Georgie sent me, and zoom in on the spot where she held her wine glass against her leg. Last night,

I thought about how that smooth skin of her leg might taste, but right now, I'm focused on her hand gripping the glass. That hand that felt so soft and smooth in mine, small and warm and perfect. My own hand itches at the memory.

James: How's the sleep situation going?

I promised myself I wouldn't bother her again this weekend, hoping she'd reach out first, but I'm not a perfect person. I'm a Georgie addict, and I need my fix.

Georgie: Believe it or not, I slept through the night last night. A big glass of chardonnay and a couple melatonin gummies knocked me right back out

James: Ah, to be young

James: Glad to hear you got yourself settled

Georgie: You should be. If I didn't, I would be less than a pleasure to be around tomorrow morning

James: You're always a pleasure to be around

Three dots...three dots...three dots...

Georgie: So said all my of report cards in school 'A pleasure to have in class' aka 'quiet people pleaser I don't have to worry about', lol.

James: That's not how I meant it. I meant I enjoy your company, even when you're yelling at me

James: Especially when you're yelling at me ;)

Georgie: I already forgave you James, you can cut the flattery

James: Never gonna happen, sweet girl

Three dots...three dots...three dots...

Georgie: I have to ask...

Georgie: What's with the nickname?

I was afraid she was going to ask that. The partial truth is that she really is just sweet. The main truth is that my brain and my mouth are constantly fighting the urge to call her baby, and I had to think of something else. I think I'll go with the partial truth.

James: Because you're sweet. Your demeanor, your personality, your smile, you're like pure sugar for the soul.

James: Contrary to some of my earlier *ahem* behaviors, it's impossible to be anything but happy when you're around

James: If you don't like it, I'll stop

Three dots...three dots...three dots...

Georgie: Don't stop. I do like it

I breathe a sigh of relief.

James: I'll see you in the morning, Georgia :)

Georgie: I'll be the one with the coffee

I smile and fold my hands behind my head in the lounge chair, fighting the urge to kick my feet and giggle like a schoolgirl. Jenn was right. I have it so bad for this woman.

10

James

∞

Alright, new plan. I know, I know. The first one went so well, but I have faith in this one. Operation *Get As Close To Georgie As Possible Without Being A Creep* is in action. I got to the office early this morning so that I could unpack my shit and go for a walk around the block where I could *just so happen* to run into my assistant on her morning coffee run. I left my suit jacket in the office and rolled up my sleeves, wanting to show off a more casual side of myself. Plus, if there's one thing Amir has taught me about women in all his research, it's that they appreciate a slutty little forearm peepshow. Just like I thought, I timed it out perfectly. I hear the squeak of the 38R as it comes to a stop, the morning rush filtering out, some young workers donning Google backpacks and Salesforce t-shirts, a few older folks toting around little carts. Finally, there in the sea of people, I spot the curly golden brown locks I've been dying to sink my hands into.

Here in the soft haze of the morning sun and fog, Georgie looks even more beautiful than I've ever seen her. She's wearing a knee length gray dress and a long sleeved yellow cardigan. I can't see her feet, but judging by her shorter than usual height, I'd guess she's wearing flats. The neckline of the dress is high, perfectly modest, but I can still make out the round shape of her plump tits. She has on those damn glasses again, and even from here, I can see that she went without makeup, or at least left the lipstick at home. Her mouth is moving slightly, like she's lip syncing along to whatever is playing through her headphones. The light surrounds her like a soft halo, illuminating her in a way that threatens to bring me to my knees. I swear, she looks like an angel.

I'm leaning up against the building, directly in her path, but Georgie walks right by me. I've noticed that when she listens to music, she sort of disappears into it. In the car when I drove her home last week, in the kitchen where I caught her putting on her show, and even right now, she seems completely enamored by the sounds flowing through her ears. I catch up to her in three steps- my stride is much longer than she can manage in all of her five foot three inch glory- and tap her on her shoulder.

Wrong move. Georgie yelps, jumps, and smacks me with her tote bag. It was lighter than a mosquito bite, but it did catch me off guard.

"WHAT THE HELL?" she yells, ripping her headphones out of her ears. "Jesus Christ, you scared the shit out of me." The realization that it's just me hits her, and she presses a hand to her chest. She makes a dramatic show of catching her breath and I can't help but laugh at her a little. I didn't mean to scare her, but had I known her reaction would be this adorable, I might have considered it.

"I can see that." I chuckle, delighting in the way she rolls her eyes at my teasing. "I'm sorry. I got in early today and I thought you might appreciate a hand with the coffee run."

"Oh," she murmurs, glancing around at nothing in particular. "Um, it's okay. I can handle it." A person in an electric wheelchair heads in our direction, and I reach to place my hand at the small of her back and pull her out of their way. Even through the layers of fabric separating us, I can feel the heat of her skin warming my hand and tingling its way to my spine. I want her even closer, I want to wrap my other arm around her and pull her body against mine, but for now, I delight in the intimate gesture for a beat longer before I let her go.

"Ah, c'mon. I've been thinking about a pain au chocolat all morning." It's the truth. Rachel has fresh pastries from a French bakery in the Castro delivered every morning, and I could eat them until my blood was pure bread and powdered sugar. I grab her tote out of her hand and start walking. It's a move I haven't broken out since college, grabbing a girl's books from her so she'd have to follow me to the dining hall or wherever else I was trying to herd her, but it works. Georgie falls in step with me.

"Okay, fine. If you're going there anyway," she concedes like she wasn't already heading to Espresso Yourself at my side.

"Atta girl, let's get moving. Daddy needs a pastry." She playfully whacks at my arm as she giggles. I laugh too, and I move around her, making sure she's on the inside of the sidewalk and I'm the one closest to the traffic. I may not have girlfriends, but that doesn't mean I'm not a damn gentleman. When she settles into my side, I take the opportunity to slip my arm around her shoulder and tuck her into me. To the outside world, the action is friendly, just two pals enjoying a little joke between themselves. I know Georgie sees it like that by the way she keeps her hands to herself, letting me lean on her but making no moves to touch me back, not even a tilt of her head to the crook of my arm. Me? I don't know how I'm managing to get one foot in front of the other. She feels so good in my arms, like this is where she's meant to be, and I may have slowed my stride just a bit to prolong the walk, keeping her tucked into me for as long as possible.

From the moment we walked into the coffee shop, Rachel and Georgie have been chatting nonstop, but I notice something...*else* between them. Their mouths are saying one thing, but their eyes are communicating in that way only women seem to understand, widening and thinning at random, darting to random spots in the room as if to indicate- I don't know, something- like they're having two completely different conversations at the same time. I just sit back and watch until Rachel hands me the packages.

"Christ woman, this shit is heavy. You carry this everyday?" I make a show of letting the bags sag below my knees. They're not that heavy at all, but it's enough that I feel awful for making Georgie- and, quite frankly, Amy- do this alone.

"Yeah, it sucks but it's been great for the gun show." She cocks her hand into a fist and flexes her bicep, kissing the muscle the way professional bodybuilders do at competition, making both me and Rachel chuckle.

"Alright Schwarzenegger, we've got jobs to get to."

I motion towards the door and follow her. She peeks over her shoulder and calls out, "Happy hour at Wine Down tonight?"

I almost think she's talking to me, like she's decided that right here, right now would be the perfect time to ask me out for a drink, and it is. Anytime is the perfect time for Georgie to ask me out, but I hear Rachel respond from behind me.

"5:30, I'll text Keeks."

Well. That pops that balloon.

Back in the office, I help Georgie set up the coffee bar while the early birds start to filter in. We keep mugs, tumblers, spoons, and anything else one needs to make and drink a cup of coffee. Amir would prefer that we all drink out of disposable paper cups so that he could further avoid the taste of the "dreaded bean juice" - his words, not mine- but for the sake of the environment, I nixed that idea years ago.

"So how come I paid for my pain au chocolat, but I didn't see you whip out a card for that cherry Danish?" I nudge Georgie's shoulder, trying to make conversation. She's been quiet since we picked up the goods. Not silent, but timid.

"Probably because Rachel knows you're a rich white male and wouldn't miss five bucks." She nudges me back, and electricity flares through my every nerve ending. Warm vanilla fills my nostrils. It's subtle. I can't tell if it comes from her shampoo, or maybe a perfume, but my nose has trained itself to be so in tune with that particular scent that it overpowers the smell of the coffee and invades my senses.

"Still, the blatant favoritism hurts." I clutch at my chest, feigning an ache at the slight. She smiles, but it fades just as quickly as it came.

"During my first week here, I mentioned something to Rachel about her coffee being the best perk of this job. I told her I was used to drinking the cheapest coffee I can find on sale every week and that I usually skip breakfast all together to save money. She wouldn't let me leave until I picked something from the display case. I've tried to pay her but she won't take my money." Her voice is soft as she speaks, and I can tell she doesn't like accepting help. My heart throbs in my chest. I already knew she wasn't flush with money, but the thought of Georgie (or anyone) skipping meals to save cash pulls at my gut. I give regular, hefty donations to the city's food banks that help to feed hungry children, the unhoused population, and anyone else in the city who may need it, but that doesn't lessen the guilt of knowing I have so much and Georgie is struggling to scrape by. I really do my best to give back as much as I can, but I know it's never enough.

I clear my throat. "Well, that's nice. Rachel is a cool person."

"She is. I'm glad I met her." She closes her eyes and inhales deeply from the mug of coffee she poured for herself. I stare as a wave of euphoria crashes over her, her shoulders dropping and limbs loosening as she takes her first sip. I watch as every one of her muscles relaxes at once, enthralled by the way she loses herself in the moment. It's so simple, and yet incredibly erotic. I can't help but imagine other things that might loosen her up, but now is most definitely not the time for that.

"Your boyfriend looks pissed." She points to the window leading out to the bullpen of the office, where Amir is staring at me with his hand on his hip and a glare in his eyes.

I check my watch, and sure enough, we have a stockholder meeting happening across the building in twenty minutes, and we need to get there early to set up parts of our presentation. If there's one thing Amir hates more than coffee, it's me making him late.

"Shit. Why didn't you remind me?" I ask, grimacing as I chug the rest of my drink.

"I'm not on the clock yet, Mr. Adler." She winks as she sashays past me, and I don't even care that Amir can see me open mouth gawking at the way her perfect ass sways in that dress. He gives Georgie a fist bump and then plugs his nose, sticking his head through the kitchen door.

"Dude, tuck your fucking hard-on away and get moving."

I flip him off, but as soon as he turns around, I'm making an adjustment. No one needs to see my bulge this early in the morning.

The meeting went well. It was boring, most of our meetings are, but in a shareholder meeting, I'll take as little drama as possible, thank you. All of our numbers are trending upward, we're making progress on all existing projects, and we should be ready to roll out beta versions of our messaging technology before the end of year code freeze. Everybody's happy.

Georgie was in the meeting with us of course, taking notes and helping field questions with information from the master document she created. She was able to provide the answer to a particularly involved question from Warren Yates (one of our wealthiest, and therefore most important stakeholders) about one of our trickier project management platforms, and after, he pulled me aside to tell me he was impressed with her zeal.

Shit, me too. The woman is fucking brilliant. I know she's dedicated to her writing, but she has the goods to make it as an executive somewhere in this city. I'm pretty sure she can do my job better than I can at this point. Although, with the level of effort I've been putting in for the last few months, Lucifer might even be a better pick for CEO. Before we get pulled into a million different things, Amir and I are taking a post-meeting breather in his office.

"What'd you get into this weekend? You never texted me back," I ask, shooting the child sized basketball through the tiny hoop that hangs off the back door.

"I binged an entire six book interconnected sports romance series on my Kindle. I think I'm really into hockey now." I can see him scrolling through Amazon, looking at NHL gear.

One time, he read a series of cowboy romances and convinced me to try bull riding with him.

Never. Fucking. Again.

"That explains it. Here I thought you'd be chomping at the bit to find out about my dinner with Georgie." I was hoping he'd ask me about it all weekend. I wanted to talk about it with someone who actually *knows* Georgie, not just my sisters.

"Oh yes. How did your creepy 'lock her in my office after hours until she likes me' plan go?" He curses and ducks as I lob the toy basketball at his stupid head.

"It wasn't creepy, dick. It was nice. It was cool getting to know her better. It did nothing to help tamp down my crush, but I liked spending time with her."

"Well she did tell me you guys had fun, so it looks like you did a good job, man." He tosses the basketball back to me and I shoot it again. This time, it bounces off the rim and rolls to the other side of the room.

"She talked to you about it? What else did she say?"

"Nothing, just that it was a good time. Oh, and that the food was banging."

"She didn't say anything about what happened outside her door?" That gets his attention. He slams his laptop shut and bears into my soul with his intense gaze.

"What happened outside her door?" Amir is not a gossip, but he does love to collect information about others anyway. I shrug.

"I don't know, man. I walked her up from the car. She held my hand the entire way, like fingers intertwined and everything-"

"Is there another way to hold hands?" he interjects.

"Uh, yeah. Like palm hand holding." I try to demonstrate with my own two hands, cupping them and holding them up to show him.

"No one holds hands like that." He shakes his head.

"Plenty of people hold hands like that!" I counter.

"Little kids who have no finger dexterity hold hands like that, not adults."

"Christ man, do you want to know what happened or not?" I'm tempted to go over and flick him in the forehead.

"I do, I just don't appreciate your unnecessary details." He leans forward, elbow on his desk and places his chin in the palm of his hand. "Continue."

I roll my eyes, but I do as he says. "So we're outside her door, and she's thanking me for dinner, still holding on to my damn hand, and it felt like...something. The air was all heavy and shit. She was staring up at me and leaning her head, and I took that as a sign. I was moving in to kiss her, but her roommate busted through the door and ruined the moment." My heart rate picks up as I relive that moment. The way her hand felt so small and velvety smooth in mine, her little tongue peeking out to wet her plump lips, her chocolate brown eyes dark and dilated.

"Have you talked to her since?" Amir's voice brings me back to earth. I rub my hand over the back of my neck.

"A bit yeah. We texted and I helped her at Rachel's place this morning." I swear I see my friend's spine stiffen when I say her name. Interesting.

I'll file that thought away for the next time he decides to give me shit.

"I've got a plan. I'm just gonna keep trying to get close to her, spend some more time with her, try to get her to open up more to me."

"Sounds like you're on the right track, but you gotta step it up. She's a romance writer."

"What does that have to do with anything?"

"It means she's a romantic and has high expectations for her leading men. I can tell just by talking to her that her love languages are acts of service and words of affirmation. She wants to be seen and heard and appreciated, out loud."

"I just don't want to come on too strong. She's pretty independent."

"She's only independent because she's had only herself to depend on for so long. Just keep showing up, be around, offer her help and shit. She'll like it."

I really fucking hope so.

11

Georgie

After work, I decided to walk the few blocks from the Streamline office in the financial district to the cute little wine bar south of Market Street. It's unseasonably warm tonight, and I wore flats, so it was nice to stroll down the sidewalk packed with other people on their way home from work.

"G, over here!" I hear as soon as I open the door to Wine Down. It's a small place on the ground floor of a huge building, the kind of place you could easily walk right by and not notice, but it's cute. There's a large wrap-around bar, high top tables, and a tap where they pour different kinds of wine instead of beer. There's a table in the back corner where I can see Kira and Rachel waving me over.

"Hey!" I wave back and make my way to my friends. Kira bounces up and wraps me in a hug, and when she lets go, Rachel is bringing me in next.

Have I said yet how good it feels to have friends? Cause it feels really freaking good.

"I have a surprise!" Kira sing songs, and Rachel rolls her eyes.

"She hasn't stopped talking about this surprise since we got here ten minutes ago but she wouldn't tell me what it is without you. Here, we ordered you a chardonnay." Rachel nods to the bartender handing me a glass of wine.

"Thanks so much," I say, both to him and to Rachel. "What's the surprise, Keeks?" She ruffles through the black Lululemon belt bag strapped to her chest and pulls out three bracelets. They kind of look like the beaded bracelets kids make at summer camp, but also, sort of elegant. The colored "beads" are flat disks in muted pastel colors and soft patterns. Rachel's bracelet reads 'Rach', the one on Kira's wrist says 'Keeks', and mine is a simple 'G' with hearts on either side. It's an accessory that would be completely out of place at a wedding, but perfectly cute for day-to-day wear.

"They're friendship bracelets!!" she gushes, grabbing Rachel's wrist and then mine, sliding them into place. "I made them yesterday. Aren't they cute?"

"Keeks, this is so sweet! They look like a Dottie Lynn piece!" Rachel says, turning the bracelet over on her skin. Dottie Lynn is a very famous Instagram influencer. She has a few million followers, and while she mostly does lifestyle content, she had a jewelry collaboration with a sustainability-focused brand that went mega viral last year.

"That's 'cause I copied her." I throw her a wry look. "It's ok, we're friends. I thought I told you that? We went to high school together back in Knoxville and moved to LA together for college. We were on FaceTime last night making them together and planning for when she's in town this weekend. She's dying to meet you, Georgie."

Normally I'd be gushing about my sorta kinda "Six degrees of Kevin Bacon" brush with semi-fame, but right now I'm too focused on the burn behind my eyes. I blink and tears threaten to spill. I'm not hiding it very well, because Rachel puts her arm around my shoulders as she asks "Hey, you ok, G?"

"Do you hate it that much?" Kira pokes the top of my hand playfully. "You don't have to wear it. It's just a silly thing."

"No, it's not that. It's not silly at all. I just...I've never really had real friends. My mom died when I was young and my dad...he was not a good person. I had to grow up way sooner than I was ready to and then I had such a hard time relating to kids my age." There was no holding back now as the salty tears trail down my cheeks. "By the time everyone else was grown up too, I was so shy, the thought of talking to new people scared the shit out of me. I just...stayed alone. I feel like you two just fell out of the sky and into my lap and I'm just grateful for your company."

Rachel pulls me in even closer, wrapping both arms around me and squeezing tight. "Georgie, you're the one that fell right into our lives. You round out our little pussy posse. We love you." I can hear Kira cooing her agreement.

I laugh and hug her back, then reach for a napkin because your girl gets snotty when she cries. "You sure you're not just taking pity on the sad lonely dorky girl?"

Kira reaches across the table and laces her fingers with mine. "Georgie, honey, you made me come so hard I had to change my sheets. We're sisters for life." I give her a confused look before the realization of what she means sets in, and the three of us break out in laughter.

"Okay, enough small talk. What the hell was going on this morning?" Rachel turns to me, wiping a stray tear from my cheek as a cheese board is brought to our table.

"This morning?" Kira asks, eyes darting between us.

"Georgie here walked into my coffee shop with a certain CEO wrapped around her." I pull my bottom lip between my teeth as Kira lets out a dramatic "WHAT?!" that has the other bar patrons heads' swiveling in our direction. A coursing heat spreads across my face and down my spine. The truth is, I've thought of nothing else but that moment all day. I don't know how I got anything done when my mind was consumed with images of James waiting for me, taking me under his arm and walking in step with me to my morning errand. I can still feel the scorching heat of his thick bicep resting on my shoulder, like I was his to protect. I had to fight every instinct not to lean in and press my cheek against his pec.

"Honestly, I have no idea. I got off the bus and he was waiting there by the stop, said he wanted a pastry and would walk me to the shop," I tell them with my hands on my cheeks, trying and failing to hide the blush that's blazing through them.

"And how exactly did you end up in his arms?" Kira sips her rosé, eyeing me with a smirk.

"I don't know. He just sorta grabbed me and we walked together. It was nothing."

"It was not nothing, G! The man was holding you like precious cargo, and he didn't take his damn eyes off of you the entire time you were in my shop." I pop a piece of bread with blue cheese spread into my mouth and avoid her gaze. "Keeks, you should've seen it. He was staring at her ass like he had X-ray vision or something."

"OH MY GOD! Georgie, he likes you!" Kira squeals and does a little jig in her seat. I want to play it off, pretend they're being dramatic and continue acting like it's nothing, but the thing is...

It felt like something.

"There's, uh, there's more," I say sheepishly, grabbing my phone from my bag and pulling up our text thread. "We sorta talked over the weekend, too." Rachel practically breaks my hand with the speed and force with which she snags my phone from me.

"Let me see, let me see!" Kira bounces, and Rachel moves over to her side of the booth, where the two of them read through our text exchange with excitement.

"G, the dude is hardcore flirting with you," Kira says, her face twisted up in a wicked looking grin. I bite my bottom lip even harder this time.

"I kinda thought so, but I couldn't tell."

"Seriously? He might as well be wearing an 'I Heart Georgie' t-shirt!" Rachel says, pointing my phone back at me. "Lucky for us, though, it looks like he doesn't like to wear clothes." She winks and Kira fans herself as they stare at the same shirtless selfie I spent way too much time sneaking peeks of all weekend.

"Do you like him?" Kira asks, leaning in like she thinks my answer is going to be a secret.

"I mean…" I start. "He's sexy, for sure. And he's funny. We have some stuff in common-"

"Christ, G," Rachel cuts me off. "Just say it, you like him!"

I didn't think it was possible for me to blush harder, but I'm pretty sure I'm giving myself a fever right now. I don't like to give in to my desires when it comes to other people. I mean, I *am* a human, I get crushes. I just find that usually it's better for me to channel those crushes into my writing instead of facing my feelings head on.

"Yeah, I like him." The girls "woooo" at me and lift their glasses to cheers. I clink with them but continue. "He's my boss, though. And he's so much older than me and rich and way out of my league."

"Who cares?" Kira drawls in her southern accent while pulling her mop of blonde hair into a perfectly messy bun on top of her head. "It's not like you're risking your career. You're just a temp- no offense- it's not that serious. Get flirty, have some fun."

"Yeah, what's the harm in that?"

There's plenty of harm in that, actually. I don't really flirt. I've never been good at it. When I write a cute banter scene, I have time to think of what I'm going to say. I know how my characters are going to react. I know what the payout is going to be. In real life, I have no such safety blanket. My last (and really, only) boyfriend, Tom, happened completely by accident. We were lab partners in chemistry my sophomore year and I had no idea that he thought of me as anything other than the girl he shared a Bunsen burner with until he kissed me.

I was so caught off guard, I just stood there. He told me later it was like kissing a dead fish. Real charmer.

Besides, James Adler is not the type of man you flirt with for fun. He's the kind of man you fall for, head over heels. He's the kind of man who could ruin your life, and you'd thank him for it. He's the kind of man you give your entire heart to.

I don't know if I can take that risk.

Two hours and two more glasses of wine later, we're tipsy and happy and ready to go home. The three of us make our way up to the bar to pay our tabs.

"It's taken care of," the cute bartender says when I try to hand him my card. "All three of your checks are paid."

"Who paid them?" Rachel asks, a tipsy hiccup escaping her mouth. It's times like this I'm thankful for the availability of rideshares.

"Some guy called earlier wanting to pay for Georgia and her friends. Left a nice fat tip, too."

Kira and Rachel both turn to me, and yup, right on cue, there's that flush in my face again. Butterflies flutter in my stomach.

"You don't know that it was him," I say, although who else would it have been?

"Cut the shit, G. James is in luuuuuuuurrrve with you," Kira slurs, wrapping her tiny body around me from behind. We get outside and Rachel starts sing-songing, "Georgie has a boyfriend, Georgie has a booooyfrieeeend". Kira joins in and the two hook their elbows together and skip in a circle as they mock me. Thankfully, my Uber pulls up just then. I flip them the bird then blow them a kiss, and I watch them continue their hysterics as the car pulls away.

My phone burns a hole through my hand the entire drive home, but it isn't until I'm in the safety of my own bed that I gather the courage I need to send a text.

Georgie: You didn't have to do that

Three long minutes go by before I get a response.

James: Not sure what you mean

I know he's messing with me. No one else knew where I was going tonight with the girls besides him.

Georgie: *Staring eyes emoji*

Georgie: *eye roll emoji*

Georgie: *knife emoji*

James: Lol. Calm down killer.

James: It's no big deal, I treat Amy to after work drinks all the time.

Georgie: But she's your sister in law.

James: So?

Georgie: So it's different. I'm just your assistant.

Five minutes without a reply this time. It dawns on me that I've probably insulted him. He was just trying to do a nice thing and I'm fighting him on it. I start to type out an apology and a thank you (which I realize I never even said) when his message comes in.

James: You're more than just my assistant, Georgie. I want to make you happy.

I want to make you happy.

Mission accomplished, Mr. Adler.

Pussy Posse group chat

Georgie: SOS

Georgie: *screenshot*

Rachel: Oh, G *heart eyes emoji* we told you he likes you

Kira: You two are totally gonna fuck *eggplant emoji*x10

Georgie: Keeks! Lol

Georgie: ...

Georgie: *fingers crossed*

I wake up the next morning slightly hungover and still reeling from six little words.

I want to make you happy.

I can't remember the last time someone told me that. Come to think of it, I don't think anyone has ever said that to me. Certainly not either of my parents. I know for a fact neither of them cared if I was happy or not. Not even Tom. He did nice things, the occasional flowers or chocolate bar, but he never *told me* he wanted to make me happy. He never even told me he cared about me.

I want to make you happy.

His words ring in my head as I get ready for work. It's chilly today, so I'm wearing my black straight leg trousers and a black v-neck sweater that molds to my curves but isn't tight. I curl my hair and leave it down, and unlike yesterday, I swipe on my red lipstick and a bit of mascara. I decided to go with black ankle boots for shoes, and looking in the mirror, I really like this outfit. I'm fully covered, the cut of the sweater is modest enough to not show too much cleavage, but I look...kinda sexy.

I've never really thought of myself as sexy. Pretty, sure. Cute, yeah. Sexy? That's a description I haven't heard, but standing here in my all black outfit, I feel it. I look damn good, and I know it. I smirk at myself in the mirror, knowing that I feel good in my skin today, and because I know exactly where that sense of confidence came from.

I gather my things and head out, giving a polite wave to Ryan and Ashley, who ignore me as always. When I walk out onto the street, I'm greeted by none other than James Adler, leaning against the side of his black Jeep Wrangler, arms crossed against his broad chest and one leg propped up on the tire behind him. We must have had some mind-meld thing going this morning, because he's also dressed head to toe in black, but while my getup came from the clearance rack at TJ Maxx, his Brioni jacket and Tom Ford sleek button up scream elegance and style. I know that the Patek Phillipe watch on his left wrist costs more than some people's homes, but he manages to look perfectly casual (and seriously gorgeous) while he waits for me outside of my beat-up apartment on the wrong side of town.

James wasn't completely wrong the other day when he suggested I live in a bad neighborhood. This part of the city is well known for the petty crimes and drug use that happens on the streets, but like most places with a bad reputation, if you mind your own business, you'll be fine. And of course, not everyone on the street is a threat. There are a lot of unhoused people in San Francisco, partly due to the cost of living and partly because the year-round mild weather is appealing to people who don't have a roof over their heads at night. There were times in my life where I was so broke, I might have ended up in this city under different circumstances as well.

"What are you doing here?" I ask, gesturing towards him and the car.

"I'm picking you up for work. What does it look like I'm doing?" He smiles, holding his hand out to take my tote bag from me. I watch as he opens the back door and places my bag on the floor before opening the passenger side for me. Just like last Friday, he holds his hand out to help me up.

"You didn't have to go out of your way." I turn my gaze towards the inside of the car to hide the blush creeping up my face.

"It's not out of my way. I live in Pac Heights, you're directly in my way." He leans one arm against the top of the door frame and with the other, he gently cups my chin and pulls my eyes back to his. "Besides, I don't like you taking the bus. You ride with me from now on." My breath hitches as he shuts my door and makes his way to the driver's side.

I want to make you happy.

"Glad to see you got my telepathic message this morning," he says, buckling his seatbelt and pulling out onto the road.

"I- what?" I ask, looking over at him. His right hand rests on the center console, while the left grips the steering wheel. I watch as the large, masculine hand envelops the steering wheel, the morning sunlight shining through the windshield and highlighting the thick veins running from his fingers to the place where his jacket hides his forearm. He flattens his hand against the leather of the steering wheel, and I'm enamored by the way the small tendons flex as he maneuvers the vehicle into a left turn. The smooth, fluid motion shows a level of control over the vehicle that is borderline erotic. I wonder what kind of finesse those hands could work on my body.

"The matching ensembles," he draws out like "duuuuh". "Lucifer and I had to work really hard to send that message out to you this morning. There was chanting and a weird dance, and we had to walk backwards in a circle three times while meowing, but it looks like it worked."

Confusion and amusement cross my face at once and I choke on my laugh. "You're so weird, James."

"Yeah, but you like it," he agrees, gripping my thigh in his right hand and lightly squeezing. The small action lights my skin on fire, and a ripple of desire courses through my core. His touch lingers for only a moment before he pulls away.

"Yeah, I do."

12

James

⌿

Tuesday whizzes by in a blur of meetings and preparations for the CRM Universal Summit next week. The conference itself is always incredibly boring. Unlike some of the summits I actually enjoy attending, like Dreamforce, this one is more focused on marketing and sales, customer retention, and engagement. Typically we send some lower-level executives to show face and gather whatever information they find important, but I was called up as a keynote speaker this year. Yay me.

I have to say, my excitement for the event has ramped up now that Georgie is here. When I told her I hadn't gotten around to actually writing the speech yet, she offered to lend me a hand, as a "wannabe professional writer". Her words, not mine.

"I know I write fiction, but I did study technical writing as well as creative writing in college. I could be a good person to bounce ideas off of," she told me that morning as we picked up coffee. Funny, she didn't realize that she didn't need to convince me. I'd gnaw off my own leg for the chance to spend more time with her doing anything at all. We ate lunch with Catherine and Amir in his office (he ordered us Filipino-Mexican fusion burritos that are impossible to resist), and then spent the rest of the afternoon deciding on a theme and drafting the speech. Georgie in her element was a sight to see. I loved watching the crinkle between her eyebrows as she tried to find the perfect word or syntax to convey her message and the way her fingers fly over the keyboard like it's an extension of her own body that she knows as well as the back of her own hands. Watching Georgie think and brainstorm and write is incredibly fucking sexy.

"So, what's tomorrow's color?" she asks me as we walk through the garage to my car. She didn't fight me when I told her I'd be driving her home from work from now on as well. My new favorite part of the day is when she lets me take her hand in mine and help her in and out of my car. Her skin is like the softest velvet in my palm, and I realized this morning that she must put perfume on the pulse point on her wrist, because when I was leaning my chin on my hand during a call with some start up we're thinking of acquiring, I could smell the faint floral vanilla scent on the edge of my sleeve. I kept my head there for the rest of the meeting, inhaling her soft scent and willing my cock to stay down.

"Georgia, my sweet summer child, we cannot *plan* our colors. We have to just match each other through sheer force of will." I shut her door and move to my own side.

"Sheer force of will, huh?" She smirks over at me as she buckles her seat belt, and I allow myself to peek at the way it lays between her heavy breasts for just one second before I pull my gaze away.

"Exactly. You think of a color really hard, like harder than you've ever thought of anything in your life, and Lucifer and I will take care of the rest." I pull out onto the street, praying for some traffic or construction that will extend this time alone with her.

"Right, the chanting and dancing. I guess if it starts raining tonight, I'll know you guys messed up the moves," she jokes. I keep my eyes on the road, but in my peripheral vision, I can see her pulling her hair into a high ponytail, getting comfortable. It makes me wonder what she does when she gets home, if she takes off her bra from under her clothes in that contorted, acrobatic way women do. How does she unwind after work? I know she likes wine. Maybe she has a glass in the bath, reading her smutty little books and slipping a hand under the water and between her thighs.

Shit. I shift in my seat, angling my lap away from her. I haven't spent this much time hiding my erections since I was fifteen and my hot, hippie English teacher refused to wear a bra.

"Don't worry, lady. My cat and I are professionals." I love making Georgie laugh. It's a soft giggle that starts low in her stomach and works its way up and out of her cute mouth. Occasionally she lets out the tiniest little snorts, and it's a noise I would fucking die to hear twice. If I wasn't driving, I'd watch the way her chest rises and falls as she chuckles at my dumb joke.

I pull up outside of Georgie's building, and even though I still don't like her living here, it doesn't look as bad when the sun is still out. I know it's not cool for me to judge a neighborhood by its reputation, but I worry for her safety.

Honestly, I'll worry for her safety whenever she's not with me.

I round the car and grab her tote bag out of the back before opening her door.

"If you plan on walking me to my apartment every day, you're really going to be tempting the petty theft gods." She raises her eyebrows at me as I help her set her bag on her shoulder.

"Will you settle for me walking you to the door, at least?" She makes a show of looking like she's thinking about it, and I pull my lips into a puppy dog pout. She rolls her eyes, but her mouth breaks into a toothy smile as she laughs and nods her head. I place my hand softly on the middle of her back and guide her across the sidewalk.

"Thank you for driving me today, James. I really appreciate it." She gazes up at me, chewing on her bottom lip. Even in her heeled boots, I've got a good amount of height on her and she has to crane her neck for her eyes to meet mine. Just like last Friday night, we're standing close, no more than a whisper of a breath between us. I tuck my hands into my pants pockets so that I don't reach out and pull her soft body into mine.

"It's my pleasure, Georgie," I tell her sincerely. The pull between us is electric, the air charged with something that makes the hairs on the back of my neck stand at attention. I think I see a flicker of desire in her eyes, and I hope she feels this pull too. If she were any other woman, I'd take her and spin her, kissing and licking at her neck while grinding my erection into the curve of her ass, right here in the middle of the fucking sidewalk. I'd be lying if I said I wasn't tempted to do just that, I think she might even let me, but I want Georgie to develop real feelings for me. It would be so easy for us to give into the sexual energy pulsing between us, but if I want something more with this girl, I need to take it slow.

Instead, I lean in and place a chaste kiss on the apple of her soft cheek. The vanilla scent of her skin so close has me feeling drunk. Her cheek is hot against my lips. I can feel the blush creeping across it. She exhales, and her breath tickles my neck. I want to live here in this moment forever, but I let my lips linger just long enough to memorize the feeling of her on me.

"I'll be right here for you in the morning, sweet girl." I turn and head back to my Jeep, reveling in the feel of her. I play it cool and don't look back, but as I get in the car, I can spot her through my tinted windows, standing in her doorway, looking back at me with her fingertips touching the place my lips just were, mouth slightly open and chest heaving.

Yeah, that's the effect I wanted.

I stand in front of the row of shirts in my walk-in closet, trying to figure out what color Georgie is going to be wearing today. I think back on some of the things she's worn since I've known her. There have been a few repeats, but I haven't seen that sexy as fuck navy dress since her first week at work. She's bound to pull that one back into rotation today. Navy it is. I pair a crisp white button down with a blue Tom Ford jacket and trousers and pull the look together with dark brown

Hermes loafers and matching belt. I give myself a good once-over with a lint roller and head out.

Sure enough, half an hour later Georgie is walking up to my car in that delicious navy dress. Her heels are black, not brown, but I can let that slide. Her hair is swept up into a bun with soft curls framing her face. In her tortoiseshell glasses, she looks like a sexy librarian, imbedding a fantasy in my head that I didn't know I was into until now. I cock an eyebrow at her and wiggle my finger between us, pointing from myself to her and back. She throws a palm in my face, dismissing me.

"Don't even start, Adler. It's just a coincidence." I take that hand in my own as I open the car door for her.

"Deny it all you want, Georgia. Our minds are intertwined." I wink at her, shut the car door and we're on our way.

The day is more of the same. We set up the coffee bar, check emails, and go over my schedule. My morning is free of meetings, so we continue to work on my speech. It's pretty much finished- and mostly written by Georgie- so we spend some time working out the kinks and doing some light rehearsing. I'm not scared of public speaking, but I do feel more confident if I'm extra prepared. I may or may not be purposefully messing up at points to keep the session going, but I can't help it. I really love having Georgie working in my office with me instead of at her desk.

Around lunchtime, Catherine knocks on the side of my open office door.

"You guys hungry? Amir and I are busting out of here. I'm desperate for some fresh air." She's been working for two weeks on a resource efficiency issue in our finance department, and I know she's running herself dry.

"I could eat," I answer, standing and smoothing down the nonexistent wrinkles in my pants. Catherine looks over to Georgie.

"You coming?" she asks, and Georgie shakes her head.

"No, it's ok. I brought some pretzels to snack on."

It kills me that Georgie denies herself proper nutrition to save on money. There's no fucking way I'm going to stand for her skipping meals or calling a Snickers bar 'girl dinner' anymore.

"Not an option," I tell her, extending my arm towards the door. "Eating lunch with the executives is officially part of your job description. Let's go." I pull her out of the chair and stand behind her, placing my hands on her shoulder and start pushing. "March, march, march," I chant, walking behind her like a zombie to keep her moving in front of me. She and Catherine laugh as I walk Georgie like that all the way to the elevator where Amir is waiting for us.

The four of us walk right down the street to a little diner-esque restaurant that sits two doors down from Espresso Yourself. If I didn't know better, I'd think my coffee-averse friend was looking longingly into the window of the shop as we passed by. We order at the counter and I pay for everyone's meals. I would've paid for my friends anyway, but today I made a show of it, insisting I get the tab for everyone instead of singling Georgie out. The last thing I want is for her to think I see her as a charity case. There are four tables set up on the street outside of the building, and we grab one of them. Thankfully, Amir picks up on my silent pleas and pulls out the seat next to Catherine, allowing me to tuck in next to Georgie.

"So Georgie, we still haven't gotten to talk about your books. What do you write about?" Catherine asks, popping the lid off her water bottle. I can see her cheeks flush slightly, but she doesn't hesitate to answer.

"I like to write romance. I have this little small town world that I've built, single dad and the nanny, high school sweethearts getting a second chance, stuff like that. I like happily ever afters, so they're like Hallmark movies, but with spice," she says as a short man in a white apron places four plates on the table in front of us. I grab the one with the chicken tenders and slide it in front of Georgie before snagging a burger for myself.

"It's not just spice, Peaches. You write some serious smut. That single dad of yours has a dirty fucking mouth." Amir turns to Catherine while I try not to choke on my lunch. I didn't realize she'd let him read her stuff. "There's this scene where she's on her knees and he's fucking her throat. He calls her all these names like a greedy cumslut and his perfect whore. He makes her touch herself until she comes while she swallows him down. It's insanely hot." Catherine's eyes go wide and her jaw drops.

"Oh my god, Georgie. You're so quiet, who knew you had it in you? You have to let me read it!" Georgie's cheeks are bright red, but her smile is wide as she tells Catherine she'll email her some stuff.

The conversation moves on, but I, on the other hand, cannot. I clench my jaw and pinch the side of my thigh, trying to push down the arousal that is coursing through my veins right now. It was one thing to have a vague idea about what Georgie reads and writes, but to hear the filthy words she's put down on paper, it's fucking torture. Is that what she likes? Honestly, I've never been much for dirty talk since I've never cared that much about the women I sleep with. Sex is usually just a means to an end for me, but right now I want to know what it would feel like to bring Georgie to her knees by whispering dirty words against her skin. Amir senses my tension and hits me with a knowing wink and a chuckle. I mouth "Fuck you" back at him while I try to subtly adjust and turn my attention back to my burger.

The four of us smash our food down with the urgency of frat boys drunk eating pizza, it's that fucking good. Even though we're finished eating, we hang out and talk before going back to work. I'm fiddling with a straw wrapper while Amir is telling them about the new doorman in our building that keeps bringing deliveries to the wrong people. Georgie shivers beside me, and I don't even think before I'm pulling off my jacket and wrapping it around her shoulders.

"Oh, jeez. Thanks." She grins up at me while pulling the lapels closed around her chest. Shit, I like seeing her in my clothes. I like it a fucking lot.

"It's a good thing we're color coordinated. This could've been a fashion catastrophe." She snorts and rolls her eyes at me, turning her attention back to Amir. She makes a motion like she's cracking her neck, but I swear, I can see her brush the tip of her nose over her shoulder, like she's trying to catch a whiff of my cologne off the jacket. I bite back my smile. I hold up the straw wrapper ring to her.

"With a jacket that fabulous, you need a fine accessory." She sucks her cheeks in when she smiles, taking the ring and sliding it onto her finger.

On the walk back, I slow my steps so that Georgie and I fall behind Catherine and Amir. I don't say anything. I just want more time with her next to me, wrapped up in my jacket.

"Can I ask you a question?" She stops in the middle of the sidewalk to look up at me.

"You can ask me all the questions." She shifts her weight from foot to foot. Her hands are hidden in the sleeves of my jacket, but I can see her grabbing and bunching the fabric from inside.

"I can't lose this job." She breathes the sentence out like it's one word. I bunch my eyebrows together.

"That's...not a question."

"This," she gestures between us, "This...friendship. I know I'm only assigned to you for now, but if it got back to the agency that I've been...unprofessional in any way-"

"Georgie, there's nothing in the rules that says we can't be friends. You can be friends, or...more than friends with anyone in the company." Those particular words taste like tar on my tongue. "You're a contractor, not a Streamline employee. You're protected by your contract. I promise, I wouldn't pursue a friendship with you if it could negatively affect your reputation or income."

She lets out a slow breath.

"Thank you, James."

I pull her to my side and twirl a strand of hair between my fingers as we start to walk again.

13

James

I barely got to see Georgie for the last day and a half, despite our carpool situation. This morning she came downstairs wearing a pretty, long sleeved purple dress and her hair pinned half up, half down. Her eyes widened in delight when she saw my all black suit and button up, but her smugness was quickly tamped down when I lifted my pant leg, showing off my royal purple socks. This is going to sound like such bullshit, but ever since we started this little game, it's like I can feel Georgie's vibes surrounding me when I get dressed, like that ever-present pull between us is telling me what color to choose.

It really is like my mind is melded with hers.

Unfortunately, she was out of the office for most of the day. It was my fault, of course, I had a laundry list of things I needed her help with to prepare for our trip next week, but I still felt that hollow pit of sadness in my stomach every time I looked out my office window and she wasn't there. I got a brief glimpse of her around noon when she dropped off the salad I ordered from Sweetgreen online, (I ordered one for her too, my not so subtle way of making sure she eats today) but then she was gone again. I forced her to use Streamline's car service, because there was no way I'd be able to focus knowing Georgie was running around the city by herself.

I dropped her off at her place half an hour ago. Just like every other night this week, I walked her to the door and kissed her cheek before leaving. Unlike every other night this week, instead of going straight home and jacking off in the shower, today I dropped my car off at home and took an Uber to meet Amir for drinks.

"Macallan 18, neat." Amir pours from the bottle of scotch he ordered for us while I take my seat in the booth. Typically we hang out at places that are more low-key than the dark restaurant we're sitting at tonight, but every once in a while we like to blow some serious cash on overpriced scotch and steaks.

"Thanks man." I say, bringing the amber liquid to my lips and delighting in the delicious way it burns sliding down my throat. "Did you order food yet?"

"Yeah, the usual. That okay?"

"Of course."

"Good. Time to tell me how it's going with the girl." Unlike the other times Amir has pushed me on the Georgie issue, I'm fucking delighted to talk to him about it today. I tell him about the car rides listening to Taylor Swift and the matching outfit mindfuck. The dude squeals- actually fucking squeals like a schoolgirl- when I tell him about the kisses on her cheek. It's hilarious, and I love that my best friend is such a romantic. Our server drops off a feast of Caesar salad, Japanese wagyu, fried potatoes in truffle oil, and blistered shishito peppers, and Amir helps me brainstorm somewhere I can take Georgie while we're in LA that will set a romantic mood without being too over the top.

"So, is anyone on the horizon for you man?" I ask, indulging in my third glass of scotch. He shakes his head, picking a pepper off the almost empty plate. "No lucky lady getting brought back to the fuckitorium this weekend?"

Having lived with Amir for years, I'm well versed in his quirks. One of them is that he hates having sex where he sleeps. He says he can feel the "sex cooties" all over himself like bugs crawling on his skin. This led to me catching him several times fucking everywhere and anywhere in our dorms and apartments.

I still can't eat food straight off the counter, the memory of Amir's clenched ass imprinted on every surface I see haunts me. He and Eric Collins actually broke our kitchen table senior year, and I made him do my laundry for a month to make up for it. Now that he's an adult with his own place, he has a special room for sex. I call it the fuckitorium, like Troy and Abed's dreamitorium on Community, but, y'know, for fucking. I've only been in there once when he first finished fitting it out, and I'll tell you one thing, the man has everything he could ever need to show someone a good time.

"Nope. It's me and my hand right now."

It's rare for Amir not to have someone on his arm. Unlike me, he actually does do relationships. They just never seem to last very long. In between, the guy gets laid like crazy. I'm pretty sure he's slept with half the single people in the Bay Area at least once. I want to push him on it, but the way he's swirling the ice in his glass and avoiding eye contact tells me that he doesn't want to talk about whatever is keeping him from finding someone to warm his sex dungeon right now. I change the topic, and we finish off the bottle while we talk about the new Legend of Zelda game that just came out, just like we used to in college. After all these years and with all our money, we're still just two nerdy kids at heart.

An hour later, I make my way through my front door, stripping myself of my jacket and shoes, tripping over myself and impaling my hip on the corner of my breakfast bar. The scotch in my system has me lightheaded in the best way possible. I'm drunk but not inebriated, still full from dinner and the luscious cheesecake we ordered on a whim. I stumble into my bedroom, where Lucifer is lounging on our bed, stretched out on the black comforter like he's zooming through space. I give him a quick scratch under the chin before I whip off my belt and chuck my shirt and pants to the laundry bin.

There is a large ensuite bathroom attached to my bedroom. The tile floor is equipped with heating elements to keep the room warm, there is a towel warmer built into the wall that holds the fluffiest Turkish cotton bath towels, as well as two thick bathrobes. The bathtub is deep and wide enough to fit more than one person comfortably (not that I've ever shared it), and the standing shower is encased in marbled glass with adjustable sprays coming from every direction. I spared no expense in designing my entire home, but this room is my absolute favorite. I flip the switch that turns on the heated floors and reach around the glass wall to turn on the shower. I give it a second to heat up while I strip off my boxer briefs. The hot spray of water feels amazing pelting against my bare skin. My muscles immediately start to melt under the massaging mist. I give my hair a quick shampoo and condition while I soap up my skin, washing the day away. Soap runs off my body and down the drain while I let my mind drift to where it's been desperate to go all day.

Georgie.

I run my hand down my stomach before gripping my hardening cock, giving it a tight squeeze and tug. I've concocted plenty of fantasies starring my temporary assistant, but tonight I'm going with my favorite, the one with Georgie in my office, ass propped up on the corner of my desk.

She crosses and uncrosses her legs, giving me a peek of lacy white panties. I stand and force my thigh between her legs, spreading her as I capture her mouth with mine. She moans, and I explore her mouth with my tongue while she grinds herself on my leg.

I stroke myself faster, capturing the precum bubbling at my tip with my thumb and using it to lube the head of my cock.

I slide my hand up her thigh and under her skirt, teasing my way to her wet center. "Spread for me Georgia," She does, lifting her feet to rest on the edge of my desk, exposing herself to me. I have no fucking patience for teasing right now. I need to taste her. I drop to my knees, pushing her panties to the side and spreading her legs further apart with my hands.

I dive in, finding her swollen clit with my tongue immediately, flicking and sucking it before moving down to her tight hole, already dripping for me. I lap up her arousal, fucking her with my tongue and moving back to her clit. She fists my hair, pushing my face even further into her soaking wet cunt, grinding herself on my face as she comes for me.

I brace my hand on the wall while the other works my cock through my impending orgasm. My balls tighten as the pleasure builds at the base of my spine. I imagine the taste of Georgie's perfect pussy on my tongue as the white-hot pleasure explodes through me. I groan and curse as rope after rope of thick cum hits the glass wall and floor of the shower. I stand there on shaking legs, catching my breath as the showerheads wash my release down the drain. That particular fantasy always makes me come so fucking hard, I rarely make it past the part where I first taste her on my tongue.

I grab a warm towel and dry myself off before slipping naked into my bed. If you've never slept nude in silk sheets, you're fucking missing out. I set my alarm and plug my phone in to charge, ready to pass out in a slightly tipsy, post orgasm haze.

Something is missing, though.

My dick might be sated, but my heart is not.

I grab my phone off the nightstand. I need my Georgie fix before I can sleep.

James: You up?

Georgie: It's only 8:30...yes I'm up

James: Shit lol. I went out with Am tonight. There was steaks and cheesecake...and scotch

James: So much scotch

Georgie: Sounds like a good time.

Georgie: Should I worry about your ability to pick me up in the morning? ;)

James: Never. I take my chauffeuring duties very seriously.

James: What are you doing?

Georgie: Laying in bed, reading. You?

I type out an answer- laying in bed with the cat- but my fingers hover over the send button. I think I might still be tipsy enough to make a bold move here. Instead of sending the text, I click the FaceTime button next to her contact.

Fucking butterflies invade my stomach as it rings once, twice, three times...

"You know, you should give someone a warning before you video call them. I barely had time to hide my stuffed animals."

God, she is so fucking gorgeous. She's wearing a SUNY Westchester Community College T-shirt that, considering the way the fabric stretches across her ample chest, is a size too small for her. Even through the small screen of my phone, I can see she's not wearing a bra. Her hair is braided into two pigtails on either side of her head, with little wisps of hair framing her heart shaped face, not a stitch of makeup on her porcelain skin. She propped her phone up against something on the nightstand next to her and is laying on her side, head held up in one hand. I close my eyes for just a moment, willing myself to commit this image to memory.

"Ah, Georgie, you don't need to hide your furry friends from me. You've already seen mine," I say, rolling onto my back and sliding a hand behind my head. I've got my blanket covering my downstairs regions, but I catch Georgie taking a second glance at my bare chest.

"You wouldn't be saying that if you saw how old and tattered they are. What's up?"

"Nothing. I just didn't get to see you much today. It bugged me," I tell her honestly.

"Well, whose fault is that, boss man? You had me all over town today, running your errands like a maniac." She shifts and I can see the book she's reading on the bed in front of her.

"Excuuuuuuse me for having you do your job." I roll my eyes dramatically so she knows I'm joking. "What are you reading?"

She lifts the book to show me. It's blue with some cartoon drawings on the front.

"What's it about?" I ask. She blushes and presses her lips together- fuck, I love when she does that- then answers.

"It's a 'why choose' romance. The main character gets stranded way up north in Sweden by the Northern Lights and is rescued by three guy best friends. They all end up in a relationship with her."

"What, like she dates one, breaks up with them and dates another?" I wrinkle my brow as she giggles at me.

"No, like she's their girlfriend and they're her boyfriends. They're all with her at once."

Well consider my interest piqued.

"Do they all have sex with her at once?"

"Sometimes. Sometimes she's just with one or two of them, some-times it's all three."

"Do the guys have sex with each other?"

"Not in this story, but there's plenty of why choose books out there where two or more of the guys are queer and together as well. Amir lent this one to me. The author has written a few others like it, they're

132

fun." I refrain from making a crude joke about Amir's books and sticky pages.

"Is that what you want? Three boyfriends? It seems like a lot of work."

I mean, I'm genuinely curious. Like, when I watch porn it's stuff that I'm into. Is she reading porn about stuff she's into?

I'm not gonna pretend like the thought of sharing Georgie with anyone makes me feel sick. I don't kink shame, but I couldn't handle watching someone else's hands brush against her skin.

I don't know why I'm even entertaining these thoughts. As much as I want her, she's not mine to be jealous over.

"I don't know. It doesn't sound so bad. Three times the love, three times the connection, three times the tongue..."

"Christ, Georgia! Get your mind out of the damn gutter for once." She covers her mouth as she laughs, probably trying not to bother her roommates. I wish she'd move it, though. Her smile is my ultimate fucking vice.

"I'm just kidding. Besides, I can barely find one boyfriend, let alone three."

"Oh, sweet girl. I think finding yourself a boyfriend might be easier than you think. He could be right in front of you."

I watch as a hundred different emotions flood her face. Confusion, embarrassment, flattery, intrigue, and so much more flash in front of me as she realizes the implication of my words.

"Me, Georgie, me. I could be your boyfriend. I could take you on dates and hold your hand. I'd spoil the absolute fuck out of you, move you out of that dingy apartment and into my home- our home- where you belong. You would never want for anything. Everything I have, everything I am,

it would be yours. I'd spend my days learning every detail about you and keeping you safe in my arms. I'd spend my nights worshiping your body and bringing you endless pleasure. I would love you so fucking hard, Georgia Hansley."

Of course, I don't actually say any of that. Instead, I watch her twist her mouth up into a smirk and roll her eyes at me.

"You're drunk."

"You're beautiful."

She pulls her bottom lip between her teeth and casts her gaze down, but not before I catch that familiar glint in her eye, the one that confirms what I already know. She fucking feels this too.

"Get some sleep, Adler, I'll see you in the morning."

"Night, Georgie."

The screen goes black, and my heart grows in my chest. I roll over and snuggle up on one of my extra pillows, wishing it was Georgie's warm body pressed against me instead.

14

Georgie

I barely slept last night. I tried to go back to my reading, but my mind wasn't absorbing the words on the page. I turned on an episode of The Office, but the tension between season two Jim and Pam was too much. I tossed and turned, frustrated as hell, until I finally gave in and slipped my hand between my legs while sweet nothings echoed in my skull.

He could be right in front of you.

You're beautiful.

I want you to be happy.

Now I'm operating on just a few hours of sleep and both dreading and counting down the seconds until I see the face of the man who has invaded my every thought and dirty dream. At least it's Friday, so the day should go by quickly, and since I know there's no way James is going to be ditching his expensive suits for something more casual, I can take comfort in knowing the matching curse will be broken today. I threw on a pair of light denim, raw edge straight leg jeans and a plain white v-neck t-shirt. I threw my hair into a high ponytail but curled the ends to give it some bounce, and slipped my feet into my eight year old black Converse sneakers. Checking my watch, I know that James should be pulling up my street any second. I give myself a little slap on the cheeks to help wake myself up before I fly downstairs to see my man.

No. My boss. My friend. Not my man.

The delight on his face is sinister when I open the door to my building and spot him in his usual position, propped up against the side of his Jeep.

Fucking. Hell.

Sure enough, James is wearing a pair of light wash jeans with a simple white t-shirt that stretches deliciously across his broad chest. God has a sick sense of humor, because he's even wearing Converse. They're the Commes des Garçons Chuck Taylors, but still. The denim hugs his muscular thighs, and I know if he turned around, I'd be able to see the way they adhere to his ass like the skin of a peach that I'm desperate to sink my teeth into. My eyes trace over the thick cords of muscle and veins running through the forearms he has crossed in front of him, and I notice one dark freckle on the crook of his right elbow. I'm tempted to go over there and run my tongue over it. James Adler in a suit is delicious eye candy. James Adler in jeans is a hot, fiery orgasm that starts in your spine and explodes through every nerve cell in your body, leaving you breathless and boneless and desperate for another shock of pleasure.

I feel my sex throb against the lace of my panties and try not to openly pant at him.

"Do you have cameras in my room or something?" I ask as I approach him. He laughs, and his icy blue eyes twinkle in amusement.

"I'm telling you, my Georgie senses have just been tingling like crazy lately." He tosses me something and it takes me a moment to realize it's his car key.

"You wanna drive today, killer?" He asks, and I shake my head. "What? You're not afraid of the big bad Rubicon are you?"

"No," I shake my head again. "I don't have a driver's license." He chuckles and puts his hand on the small of my back.

"Just don't get pulled over, and you'll be fine." I sigh and put the key fob back into his hand.

"I don't know how to drive, James. No one ever taught me." His jaw flexes and his cheeks turn a pink tint with what I hope is embarrassment and not pity. I really hope he doesn't ask me to elaborate. I don't want to get into the fact that I had no adult in my life to teach me before I was old enough to get even a learner's permit. He only pauses a moment before opening the passenger side door and holding out his hand to help me up.

"I'll take you out to Treasure Island one of these weekends and teach you if you'd like. We can take one of my smaller cars." My heart flutters and I hurry to get into the car and shut the door before he can feel the sweat accumulating in my palm. Why is the thought of this man teaching me how to drive a car so sexy? Even just him offering has my head spinning. No one has ever offered to teach me how to drive before.

I squeeze my thighs together to try to ease the dull ache growing between them. I turn the song playing through the car speakers up louder and start to quietly sing the lyrics, trying to indicate that I'm too into the music for conversation right now. Really, I don't think I can properly string two words together with James sitting next to me, looking so delectable. I definitely don't think I can handle whatever might come out of his mouth this morning.

He might be right in front of you.

You're beautiful.

I want to make you happy.

Thankfully, Rachel had a lot to say to me today about the newest season of *Love Is Blind*. By the time we got to the office, we were swamped with speech practice and last minute travel preparations. It's nearly noon, and James and I haven't exchanged a single word that wasn't work related. We're sitting in his office on either side of his desk. He's reading through his speech one last time while I confirm the vehicles that will be dropping us off at SFO, as well as the pilots that will be chartering our private flight to Los Angeles.

That's right, James has his own freaking plane.

I mean technically, he shares it with Amir for business purposes, but still. The man has a whole ass plane! My only flight experience so far in my life has been the budget airline I took here where I was squished between two very smelly men for six and a half hours, so I'm pretty damn excited. He even gave me a company card to buy some new clothes for the conference. I tried to refuse it, but he said it was a perk of the job.

"What's for lunch today Georgie?" James asks, spinning a pen between his fingers as he sways in his swivel chair.

"Uhh, you tell me. Decide on something and I'll make the call." I don't want to just assume that he's including me in his meal plans, although he has bought me lunch every day this week.

"Nah, we're not ordering in. Did you get all the confirmations you needed?"

"Yep, we're all set to go for 5 am Monday."

"Perfect. Let's blow this pop stand." He stands and tosses a balled up piece of paper into the trash can like it's a basketball.

"What?" I ask, confused as he shuts my laptop and pulls me to stand with him.

"It's Friday, we've got nothing left to do. Let's get out of here, go do something fun." I follow him out of the office and to my own desk, where he grabs my bag and starts throwing some of my stuff back into it. "James, it's only noon. There are still people working. We shouldn't just...leave." He tilts his head and raises his eyebrows at me before he lifts himself up onto my desk and stands, facing the bull pen.

"SCHOOL'S OUT, KIDS!" he shouts through cupped hands. "If you want to stay till five, go ahead, but I'm getting a head start on my weekend and I suggest you all do the same." There are a few "whoops" and claps from the office as James jumps down, and I can't hide the grin on my face when he interlocks his fingers with mine and leads me to the elevator.

"I can't believe you've only been down here once!" James says for the third time since he parked the car at Fisherman's Wharf. He led me right over to Alioto's restaurant where he ordered us the freshest and most delicious fish and chips and Dungeness crab cakes I've ever tasted. We eat out on the sidewalk, watching the early afternoon fog roll over the bay, casting Alcatraz in a gray murkiness.

"It's touristy! I didn't want to be 'that girl' who moves to a new city and only hits the most famous spots." I shrug, and our forks clank together as we both go for the last bite of crab cake. He pushes it towards me without a word. I have honestly eaten better than I have in my whole life since starting this job. Even though it's a Friday afternoon, there are fewer visitors to the spot today than I remember there being the last time I was here. It was a Sunday and it was so crowded, I almost had a panic attack.

"Pier 39 is touristy. The wharf is beautiful. Tell me you've at least taken the cable car."

I scrunch my face up as he throws his head back in dramatics.

"Georgia Ann Hansley, you've lived in San Francisco for how long and you still haven't ridden the fucking cable car?!"

"My middle name is Marie you weirdo. And it's eight freaking dollars! I could take the bus four times for that much. It's extortion."

"Georgie Marie Hansley. I like that. And I like this," he says, reaching over and lightly tugging at the end of my ponytail. The small touch sends a shiver down my spine. Thankfully, a breeze comes in from the bay and conceals my reaction.

"Damn, I knew you'd get chilly. C'mon, let's go get you a sweatshirt before the real fun begins." He takes my hand in his and leads me to the souvenir shop on the corner, where I let him pick out a light pink hoodie with an outline of the Golden Gate Bridge for me, and a "Property of Alcatraz" zip up for himself. Outside of the store, I slip the hoodie over my head while James bounces around like a little kid on the first day of summer vacation.

"What are you so excited about?" I tease, poking him lightly in the stomach. Even through the layers of clothes, I can feel the hard contours of his abdomen against my fingertips. The man is a brick wall, and I wonder what that brick wall would feel like lying on top of me. He wraps his hand around my own again. I don't think I'll ever get used to the delicious feeling of his large, lightly calloused skin linked with mine. The straw wrapper circling my ring finger that he gave me over lunch scratches at my skin, but I refuse to take it off. I don't know why James is always making me these little origami rings, but I've saved each one of them in a jar in my bedroom like they're a secret love letter or something.

"Follow me!" he says, pulling me across the street and towards a building backed up against the bay. The sign is red and white, it looks almost like an old-school circus advertisement, and it reads 'Musée Mécanique'. I can hear the faint chime of bells and whistles as we get closer.

"What is this place?" I ask James, who's still pulling me along like a child leading his mom to the mall Santa Claus.

"It's like an old school arcade. They've got shit in here that's over a hundred years old." We enter, and James goes immediately to the nearest coin machine, feeding it twenty dollars and watching as eighty quarters spill out. In front of us is a marionette doll with a mop of red hair. Someone must have put a coin in its slot, because the mechanical gears are pulling at its strings while it laughs. It's creepy, but also vaguely familiar.

"This is where Mia brings Queen Clarisse in The Princess Diaries!" James tells me as he gestures for me to accept the handful of quarters he's shoving at me. Right! That's where I know this creepy doll from! I love that movie! I've seen it a hundred times and several more since I've been living here in the city. How have I never thought to seek this place out before?

"You've seen The Princess Diaries?" I ask, cocking an eyebrow at the man in front of me.

"Of course, it's a classic. Now let's go." He leads me through the maze of old pinball machines, nickelodeons, and 80's style arcade games to a figure of a grappler with his arm cocked, ready to wrestle whoever is brave enough to sink a quarter into him.

"Oh my god! Julie Andrews plays this game in the movie!" I squeal and grab my phone out of my back pocket to take a picture of the machine.

"I know! Do you want to go first?" I widen my eyes at him. I remember how much Clarisse struggled with it in the movie. I don't think I'm ready for that humiliation.

"You go. I'll watch and critique your technique." He throws his head back and laughs before sliding a quarter in the slot. I watch as he sets his elbow on the worn mat and wraps his hand around the fake wrestler's. He has a serious look on his face, eyes squinted and lips slightly pursed. I can't tell if he's trying to amuse me with his dramatics or if he's genuinely ready to take this sucker down. A bell chimes and the arm starts to move, pushing James's down at first, but after a short second, James pushes back, taking the mechanical arm all the way to the other side, besting his inanimate opponent. He wipes his hands together and lets out a low whistle.

"Piece of cake. Your turn." He places his hand on the small of my back and guides me into place in front of the machine. I take a deep breath and shake out my arms, preparing for battle. I point two fingers at my own eyes and then to the chipped paint ones on the game in that "I'm watching you" manner.

James reaches down and slips another quarter into the machine, and the words he says under his breath are so low, I'm sure he didn't intend for me to hear them, but I did.

"You're so fucking cute."

Butterflies erupt in my stomach. It's amazing how this man is able to bring me to my knees with the simplest of things.

The bell chimes and the mechanical arm starts to move. I grind my elbow into the mat and push against the machine. My hand is reddening from the force of my grip on the lever and a bead of sweat forms at my brows, but still, I make no progress. In less than ten seconds, the damn fake wrestler has taken me down.

"That was rigged!" I pant, shaking out my now sore right hand as James laughs at me.

"Nah babe, you just have noodle arms." He wraps his arm around my shoulder and pulls me into his side, leaning down and bringing his mouth close to my right ear. "It's ok, I like them."

We spent two hours exploring the museum. We played basketball (James absolutely annihilated me, I blamed his height), skee-ball (I crushed him, he blamed his height) and Pac-Man. I watched the hundred year old moving dioramas in awe (although some were more than vaguely racist- looking at you, Opium Den) and was even shocked when one of the nickelodeon things in the back featured real life early twentieth century naked lady porn ("I can't even tell you how many quarters I lost to this one when I was a kid" James told me as I gasped against the ancient viewfinder).

"There's one thing we have to do before we go!" he says, leading me towards the back entrance of the building. "Ta-da! Get in!" He opens the curtain to a photobooth, and how could I possibly say no to that smile? I slide onto the bench and James follows, pulling the curtain shut behind him. He's so large and the booth is so small, he has to wrap his arm around me and crush our thighs together in order to fit comfortably. He pushes a five dollar bill into the slot and starts scrolling through our frame options.

"Best Friends"

"Luv U"

"Mwah!"

"Hawt stuff!"

"Let's go with this one," he says, picking the third option. "The little cartoon mouths match your lipstick."

"Sure." I swallow. My heart rate picks up and I try to steady my breath. Being this close to James, inhaling his leathery, masculine scent, feeling his firm leg against my own, the heat of him radiating through me, it's too much. Desire pools in my core and sweat trickles down my neck. I thank god my hair is in a ponytail, otherwise there would be no hiding the frizz that would no doubt be forming on my hairline.

"3...2...1..." the voice in the machine counts down, and I manage to smile up at the camera, matching James's wide, toothy grin.

"Ok now a serious one," he says, propping his chin up on his free fist. I tap my fingers against my mouth and squint like I'm thinking as the flash goes off.

"And now silly." He crosses his eyes and sticks out his tongue, while I touch my own to the tip of my nose.

I was sure there were only three pictures to be taken. The images on the outside of the photobooth showed strips of three, so I was taken aback when the voice started to count again.

"3..." I let out a surprised 'oh' and quickly try to think of a pose.

"2..." I feel James's hand cross our melded bodies, cupping my chin and pulling me towards him.

"1..." He brushes the tip of my nose with his, and I can hear the click of the camera go off just as he places his lips against mine. It's a soft, searching touch, our skin barely connecting. It's like he's using the pressure of his lips to ask me if this is okay. I answer with my own, pressing my mouth harder against his and placing a hand on his chest. Goosebumps crawl across my skin and fire burns in my chest as we move against each other. If anyone were to open the curtain, this would look tame, but I can feel the sparks of lust exploding between us burning my flesh. After a moment, I feel his tongue lick at the seam of my lips. I can't hold back the breathy moan that escapes as I open for him, giving him access to further explore my mouth. It's a tender movement, the way the tip of his tongue meets mine, teasing and tickling. He tastes so warm and delicious, like mint and something heady. When he nips at my bottom lip, I squeeze my thighs together for the second time today, desperate for relief from the arousal coursing through me.

I practically whimper when he pulls his lips away from me, his hand still cupping my cheek and pressing his forehead to mine.

"You have no idea how long I've wanted to do that." Still catching my breath, I say nothing.

"Will you go for a walk with me, Georgie?" he asks, eyes searching mine hopefully, like he's afraid of my answer. I nod again and let him lead me out of the booth. He grabs the two photostrips from the printer and points them towards my purse. "Keep these safe for us?" he asks, and yet again, all I can manage is another nod as I grab the pictures and tuck them into a zippered pocket. He takes my hand and leads me outside, where we walk along the edge of the water.

"Are you ever going to talk to me again?" He nudges me teasingly, but I can tell by the tone of his voice that he thinks I might be upset. I squeeze his hand in mine and he squeezes back.

"As soon as my mind catches up with my lips, I promise."

We walk in a comfortable silence for a few minutes, taking in the view of the bay and the Golden Gate Bridge in the distance. I focus on tamping down the nerves surging through my body as I try to come up with the perfect follow up line to the hottest, most perfect kiss of my entire life.

Instead, I say this.

"Do you *like me,* like me, James?"

Yeah, real smooth.

He stops his feet and looks down at me. I'm fighting the urge to throw myself over the edge of the fence and into the freezing cold bay when James stops and backs me up against the wall of the pier building, caging my body in with his own. Between his arms and the walls of the building I feel trapped, but I have no desire to escape.

"Yeah, sweet girl. I like you like you." He captures my mouth with his again, harder and more desperate this time.

I moan against his mouth.

He growls back at me.

His fingers dig deeper into my skin.

I open my mouth wider to him.

His tongue slips in, tangling with mine. I'd say we're like teenagers, but his movements are way too skilled for that comparison. His tongue massages mine, while his lips continue to hit my own with that beautiful, perfect pressure. The kind that avoids grossly overpowering me but still leaves me knowing I'll be feeling it tomorrow.

One of his huge freaking hands stays gripped on my hip, and the other moves up my face and then wraps around my ponytail, fisting it and angling my face up to him. The new position grants him access to the sensitive flesh of my neck. He drops his lips to the fluttering point of my pulse and bites at it. I let out a pained gasp that is quickly followed by a moan as he soothes the spot over with his warm, wet tongue. I have to move to my tiptoes to reach my arms around his neck, but I don't care. I need to hold him or my knees will give out.

"Are you this fucking soft everywhere?" he mutters against my neck.

I know we're alone back here, but it still feels so erotic to be making out so brazenly in public. It feels like anyone could walk by and see us seconds away from tearing each other's clothes off. Our lips meet again, and James pushes a knee between my thighs while he caresses my tongue with his own. In this position, I swear I can feel the hardness in his groin, and another spike of arousal shoots up my spine.

I'm so turned on. I'm ready to let go of any shame I'm holding onto and grind my jeans-clad center against his broad thigh when we're interrupted by the sound of yelling.

"The fuck is wrong with you dude? You fucking smell like shit."

"Please, I'm just trying to sleep."

Still holding my body against his, I can see James pull away from my mouth to peer around the corner to find the source of the noise. I don't have to look to know what's going on. Someone's trying to start a fight, and I need to get the hell away from it. My head is already dizzy from the kiss, but I can feel the fog taking over my skull.

You're safe. No one is going to hurt you.

"Stay right here," James says as he sets me down and rounds the closed ticket booth next us.

"James," I gasp, wanting to pull him back, but he's moving too fast. I want to run. I need to run. I can't have one of my episodes right now, not in front of him. I'll just run to the car and text him from there, telling him where I went. Yeah that's good. Run.

Run.

Move your feet.

But I'm glued here. I can't move. I hear James's voice.

"Everything okay here?"

"I'm just trying to sleep."

"You shouldn't even be here. Get a job, you fucking loser," the first man spits his vitriol and bile rises in my throat. I take a step, but instead of heading towards the parking lot, I move to the corner and peek around the side of the building.

There's a man lying on the ground, his head resting on a full shopping bag while another hovers over him, looking at him like he's the dirt on the bottom of his shoes. James is a few feet away still. I want to call out to him, but I don't want to attract attention to myself.

No one is going to hurt you.

"Hey man, the guy is just trying to get some rest. He's not bothering anyone." James says in a calm but cool tone, one I've only heard in meetings when he's trying to prove someone wrong without being a dick. Blood trickles into my mouth from where I've been biting my lip so hard. The standing man ignores James, and in a heartbeat, lifts his foot and smashes it into the laying man's face. I wretch as I try to keep the contents of my stomach inside where they belong.

"Woah, dude, chill the fuck-" James is cut off by a punch to the face. The man is a few inches shorter than him, and definitely skinnier. James's head barely moves as the guy lands his blow, but I can see he's fucking pissed. I gasp as I watch him cock his fist back and make contact with the man's nose. Blood spurts out, and the sound of bone crushing bone is enough to send me over the edge.

Shit shit shit.

What do I see? Red faced anger.

What can I smell? Blood, so much blood.

What can I hear? The crush of fist against bones.

I double over and vomit, tears falling from my face as I get sick on the sidewalk.

I'm lost in the haze. I can't see, I can't hear. I'm back there again, bleeding and crying on the floor of the grocery store. I think I feel footsteps coming my direction, and I sob.

Don't hit me. Please don't hit me, I'm sorry, I'm so sorry.

My legs give out beneath me, and the world goes black.

15

James

My mind is still reeling as I get Georgie into my car and help her buckle her seatbelt. I have no idea what the fuck just happened. Georgie's mouth on mine, a douchebag harassing someone, a punch to the face, Georgie falling to the ground next to me. I couldn't give less of a shit about the fucker I had just knocked out cold hitting the pavement. I dropped to my knees and pulled Georgie's limp body into mine, patting her cheeks to try to wake her. I tried to be as gentle as possible. She opened her eyes, and as soon as they met mine, she turned and retched, puking for what looked like the second time. I pulled out my wallet and tossed a few hundreds to the poor guy who got his face kicked in. I wanted to make sure he was okay, but I also knew I had to get out of there before the other son of a bitch woke up and called the cops on me, so I scooped Georgie up and power walked us to the car.

We've been driving for 15 minutes. I have no idea where to go or what to say. Georgie is in the passenger seat silently crying and shaking. I had tried to hold her hand, but she tensed at my touch. It fucking kills me, especially since before she passed out she was begging me not to hit her. I hate myself for putting her in a position where she'd think that would ever be a possibility.

"Are you sure I shouldn't take you to the hospital? Or even urgent care?" I ask her again at a stoplight, and she shakes her head. "Do you want me to take you home then?"

She looks over at me for the first time since she woke up on the ground.

"Can I come meet Lucifer?" I let out a breath I didn't realize I was holding. That's something I can definitely do for her.

"Of course," I tell her, turning on my left blinker and driving towards my place. "He loves getting visitors."

He actually hates everyone but me and Amir, but she doesn't need to hear that right now.

The elevator from the underground garage in my building goes straight up to my floor, so thankfully I don't have to pass anyone in the lobby with a split lip and a shaking woman with vomit on her clothes in my arms. I press the "PH" button and Georgie shakes her head.

"What?" I ask.

"I just keep forgetting you're rich," she tells me. I know Georgie isn't like the people who have tried to get close to me for the wrong reasons since I made my fortune, but it's still a relief to hear her say things like that. It's more proof that she sees me for me, not my wallet.

The elevator door opens and I lead her to my front door. It opens right into my kitchen, filled with stainless steel appliances and top of the line cookware. We walk past it and into my living room. I press the button on the wall that opens my blinds, and the room is washed with sunlight. Georgie walks past the huge couch and 85 inch TV mounted to the wall and turns her attention to the windows. My balcony wraps around the perimeter of the penthouse, but this side boasts my favorite view. Even from inside, you can see the Golden Gate Bridge, the beautiful hills of Marin County and Alcatraz. On a fogless day, you can even spot Treasure Island and parts of the Bay Bridge.

"Quite the view you have here," she muses, and I watch her take it in.

"It's not bad. Lucifer likes to lounge in this particular sunbeam." I point to a ray of light on the floor that stretches out over the area rug in the middle of the room. "I can go find him for you if you want."

"Actually," she pauses, pressing her lips together. "Can I... can I take a shower?" I'm a fucking idiot. I should've offered that to her right away, or at least showed her where she could brush her teeth. She was puking in the street twenty minutes ago, she probably feels disgusting.

"Of course. Do you want me to wash these clothes for you? I can give you something to change into." She nods, and this time she doesn't flinch when I take her hand in mine and lead her to the bathroom. I could have gone the other direction and taken her to my guest bathroom, but mine is so much better.

I flip on the heated floor and reach under the sink, pulling out a fresh toothbrush and placing it on the ledge. I show her where the warm towels are and how to operate the various showerheads.

"Don't worry about changing the settings however you like them, it's easy to get them back," I tell her. She has her arms crossed over her chest as her eyes flick around the room.

"It's like a spa or something," she says, running a hand on the marbled glass of the shower door. I let out a low laugh. That was exactly my point.

"I'll go grab some clothes for you, stay here." I go to my closet and pick out some sweatpants and an extra soft Kiton black t-shirt. I know these are going to dwarf her, but at least the drawstring of the sweatpants should help them fit a little better. I plan on telling her to leave the clothes she's wearing outside of the bathroom door so I can toss them in the laundry for her, but when I reenter the bathroom, she's already stripped and wrapped up in one of my towels.

Jesus. Fuck.

She's holding the towel tight across her body, which pushes her tits up perfectly. All of my towels are extra large, but even so, the edge of the fabric hits her thigh two inches past decent. Her creamy skin glows in the soft light of the room, and I realize that in just three steps I could have her in my arms and my hand between her legs.

I shake the thought loose from my head. She was just sick and passed out in the street less than an hour ago for fucks sake. I silently tell my libido to stop being a pervert and avert my eyes to the floor.

"I'll just leave these here for you," I tell her, setting the fresh clothes down on the counter and scooping her discarded ones up.

"Thank you, James."

I give her a curt nod and leave the room while I still have control over my body. I wait until I hear the water come on before heading to the other side of the house to the laundry room. I've never actually used this room before. It's been a long time since I've done my own laundry, usually delegating the task to my housekeeper, but it's not rocket science. I find a detergent pod and toss it in, followed by Georgie's clothes. It didn't hit me until now that I hadn't just been holding her jeans and the souvenir shop hoodie, but her bra and panties as well. A pink cotton thong stares up at me from the drum of my washing machine, and all the blood in my body rushes to my groin.

Georgie is going to be going commando in my clothes. Nothing between her silky skin and the fabric of my t-shirt. No barrier between my sweatpants and her bare center.

I switch the machine on and close the lid before barging into the nearest bathroom and turning the water on as cold as it will go. I don't know how long she's going to take in the shower, but I do know that I can't jerk off with her here, it's fucking disrespectful. I quickly strip and jump under the waterfall of iciness, letting the water pelt my skin and calm my aching cock. It takes a few minutes to get it down to half mast, and that'll have to do. I towel off and get dressed. I lure Lucifer out of hiding with one of those nasty cat Gogurt treat things, and the two of us wait for Georgie on the couch.

Half an hour later, she emerges. Even though she's dressed head to toe in black, the lingering pink tint of her skin from the warm water makes her look like an angel. Her wet hair is braided and tucked over one shoulder. She tied the front of the t-shirt into a knot so it doesn't hang over her figure, and she had to roll the waistband of the pants over a few times so that the bottoms don't drag so low on the floor. She's fucking stunning.

She smiles when she sees Lucifer curled up on my side. I expect him to hiss and run away, but he just watches as she slowly approaches him with an outstretched hand. He sniffs at it for a moment, and then gives her the headbutt of permission. She squeals and starts scratching him behind his ears, doing that weird baby talk thing people do to animals. Part of me is shocked that Lucifer is allowing Georgie his time of day, but she's so fucking perfect, of course my demon spawn ball of fur loves her too.

She plops on the couch next to us and rests her head against the back of it. I reach over and twirl the end of her braid around my index finger.

"Do you want to tell me what the hell happened back there?"

16

Georgie

I've never experienced anything as luxurious as James Alder's bathroom. I never want to leave. I was pleasantly shocked when I pulled out a towel and found it warm and fluffy, so different from the scratchy pink towels I bought on sale a few years ago. The shower sprayed hot water with perfect pressure from a million different directions, and dried bundles of eucalyptus adorned several of the heads, coating the room in a natural form of aromatherapy that overtook all of my senses. I briefly considered climbing into his giant bathtub instead, but I wanted to get clean more than I wanted to relax. All of his soaps and shampoos were in glass bottles without labels, so I don't know where he buys them, but the familiar scent of leather and sandalwood bloomed in the steamed room and dizzied my head as I lathered my body. Even his toothpaste tastes expensive, like sweet mint and green tea.

Don't even get me started on his clothes. From the second I slipped the cashmere and cotton t-shirt over my head I knew all other fabrics would be ruined for me. I had to roll up the sweatpants a hundred times so I wouldn't trip over them, but even they felt silky smooth against my flushed skin. I hope he thinks they look cute on me. After embarrassing myself like I did right after he admitted he liked me, I'm desperate to know that he still thinks I'm pretty. Believe me, I knew exactly what I was doing when I wrapped that towel around my body, knowing he'd be back to the bathroom and see me in it. I didn't miss the way his jaw twitched as his eyes raked over my bare legs. That felt really good.

I throw my hair into a quick side braid and leave the bathroom. I find James and his cat curled up on his black couch. I wonder if he lint rolls the furniture as often as he does his suits. The ends of his dark brown hair are damp and slightly curled, and there's no longer dried blood on his knuckles. I'm secretly thrilled to see he has on a black t-shirt as well, but did he have to go all out with the gray sweatpants? Does he realize that's like, the sluttiest thing a man can wear?

"Do you want to tell me what the hell happened back there?" he asks as I sit opposite of him and stroke Lucifer's furry little head.

No. I really don't. It was humiliating. I haven't had an episode like that in public since I was a teenager. After spending months in police stations, courtrooms, and therapist's offices rehashing the tale after the incident, I never want to talk about it again. I usually explain away my parents in a nonchalant "we're not close" way, and people don't push it. Family can be a touchy subject, and thankfully there haven't been many people in my life wanting to pry.

"Your place is amazing," I deflect as Lucifer stands and stretches before settling onto my lap. James looks dumbfounded at the little cat's actions. The sun shining in from the floor to ceiling windows casts a warm, late afternoon glow over the room. The deep-seated sectional we're sitting on feels like a cloud underneath us. The TV on the wall looks like it belongs in a movie theater, not a living room. He has modern looking art adorning the walls, and coffee table books that span a variety of interests, from Steve Jobs to Montblanc, to one that just says "HUMANS". A record player sits to the side, next to a larger version of the bar cart in his office at work. I wonder if he'd let me play my *folklore: the long pond sessions* vinyl here.

"Thanks, I spent a lot of time deciding on exactly how I wanted it. My childhood home never really felt like home, you know? I shared a room with my sister when we were kids and my aunt did her best with us but nothing was ever homey. When Amir and I lived together, that was fun, but you know he has a lot of particulars. There was always something I couldn't do or have so that I didn't set off his sensitivities. This is the first place that was ever just mine." He cracks his knuckles as he speaks, the same way he did when he apologized to me for our tumultuous first weeks together. I think that that little movement is his tell that he's being vulnerable. I don't think he's comfortable sharing about his childhood either.

Sitting here in his home, in his clothes, heart still heavy from the events of the day, I realize something. It's clear that my body calls to James, based on my attraction and ever present arousal alone, but I think my soul calls to him as well. I want him to tell me everything.

I want to fix the parts of his heart that still ache for his younger self. I want to be a safe haven for him, somewhere he can lie his head. I want every single piece of him. And if I want those things, I have to be willing to give them. I close my eyes and take a deep breath.

"Lisa and Craig Hansley. Those were my parents. They never wanted me. They hated each other. I don't know how they were in a room long enough to conceive, but somehow they managed it. My mom's parents pushed them into marriage when they found out she was pregnant. I think she would have rather had an abortion, but I honestly don't think she had the option at the time. I was born, she started to drink and she never stopped. Then there was my dad. My dad was angry. Volatile. A molotov cocktail tossed into a crowded room every second of the day. They fought constantly. I can't tell you how many times I watched them come to blows in front of me. They never hid it. Not even when he started hitting her.

"She died when I was ten. Drunk driving accident, wrapped her car around a tree. Thankfully, the only person she killed was herself. I wasn't sad. I didn't miss her. I barely knew her. She was always at a bar or out with friends, probably avoiding my dad's fists. She was always drunk. She rarely talked to me. She never hugged me. She never tucked me in at night. She hated me. She resented me for being born. I remember being at her funeral, adults coming up to me to ask if I was okay and trying to soothe me, but nobody realized that I was fine, if not a little numb. All I could think was 'At least the house will be quieter now.'

I feel James's eyes on me, but I keep mine on the cat in my lap.

"I'm sure you can imagine that my dad wasn't any better on the affection front. I knew he didn't love me. He never said it, but I knew.

With Mom gone, I was even more of a burden. I tried my best to stay out of his way as much as I could. I'd go to school during the day and walk as slowly as I could home from the bus stop in the afternoon. I'd do my homework in my bedroom and sit quietly at the table on the rare occasion that he made dinner. As long as I kept my head down, he mostly left me alone, until something pissed him off and he needed an outlet for his release."

I see James's fist clench on his thigh and I wince.

"It started with spanking. I had always been spanked when I misbehaved, but the blows came more frequently after Mom died. Then there was the pinching. It sounds stupid, but he'd pinch me so hard I'd have bruises on my stomach for weeks. By the time I was a teenager, I was being kicked and punched in my middle so often my entire belly was permanently black and blue."

I feel a tear prick the corner of my eye, but I keep going.

"The worst of it was when he caught me kissing another girl. We were at a park, and he drove by and saw us. Turns out he wasn't so cool with the bisexual thing, and he took it out on my kidneys. He was smart. He never hit me where anyone could see. No one ever knew. No one suspected anything. I never tried to tell anyone at school because I had no idea what would happen to me. I was afraid he'd find out I told on him and kill me. I kept to myself, kept my head down, and started counting down the days until I turned eighteen and could leave. Then, one day when I was 15, we were at the grocery store."

My breath hitches. I hate this part so much. James leans forward and places his hand on mine.

"I don't remember exactly what he said. Something about the cereal I picked up making me fat. He was always taking verbal jabs at my body. He told me often how disgusting I looked to him. I never reacted to his insults. I never gave him the satisfaction, until that day. I don't know what possessed me, but I muttered 'you're an asshole' under my breath. I didn't think he could hear me."

The tears are actively falling now.

"It was the first time he hit me in my face, and he had the audacity to do it in public. He broke my damn nose and left me there on the grocery store floor. I woke up alone in a hospital bed surrounded by police and child protective services." I paused as I tried to choke back my sobs. "Long story short, he was arrested, there was a long legal battle, and a judge granted me emancipation on my sixteenth birthday. I've been on my own since then."

He squeezes my hand and I lift my gaze. I gasp when I see tears staining his cheeks as well.

"I hit that guy. That's what triggered you," he says, and I nod.

"Violence of any kind triggers me. I can't watch action movies or boxing without getting woozy and nauseous, but I haven't had an episode like today since I was a kid. It was the-" I swallow, the memory of the afternoon inciting another wave of nausea to roll through me. "It was the sound your fist made when it hit his face. I've had night-mares about that sound for years."

"Christ, Georgie. I'm so fucking sorry."

"You didn't know. You were just defending someone who needed help and got caught up in a stupid mess. That guy hit you first. I knew something bad was going to happen. I should have never followed you over there."

He urges Lucifer off of my lap and pulls me into his own.

"Don't you dare blame yourself for today. I scared you, Georgie. I fucking scared you and that kills me. I'm not an angry guy, I think you know that. I lost it when that dude took a swing at me. I was afraid he might come after you next and I couldn't let that happen. I promise you, sweet girl, you will never see that side of me ever again, I swear." He presses his forehead to mine and wipes a tear away from my cheek.

"I was scared, but not of you," I whispered. "I don't think I could ever be scared of you." He sighs before pulling my lips to his. It's featherlight, just a whisper of a kiss, but it ignites my desire for him anyway. He moves his mouth to place another soft kiss, this time on the tip of my nose.

"Will you stay here tonight?" he asks, and my eyes widen. "Not like that. You can stay in the guest room. I just...I feel like I need you close after today. I would feel better if you stayed here with me."

My stomach sinks. I wish he did want me to stay *like that*, but I guess I get it. Crying and sharing childhood trauma after puking in the street doesn't exactly scream "pillage my body, Daddy".

"Only if we can order dinner. I'm starving."

17

Georgie

~❧~

Two hours later, the mood is thankfully much lighter. We're both stuffed to the brim from Tosilog burritos and pork loaded nachos, arguing about the movie we just watched.

"But Andy stole that opportunity right out from under Emily's feet. She was harsh in the beginning, but Emily fucking earned the Paris trip."

"Andy didn't steal anything! Emily couldn't go and Miranda used it as an opportunity to pit them against each other," I explain to him *again*. "And besides, I think we can both agree on who the actual villain in this story is."

"Nate!" we say at the same time.

"Exactly. So stop woman-shaming and move on with your life."
He smiles at me from his side of the couch, the kind of smile that
reaches his eyes and causes them to shine the brightest turquoise hue
I've ever seen. We cuddled a bit while we watched the movie, but when
he criticized a certain part of Stanley Tucci's performance, I made a
dramatic showing of moving to the other side of the sectional. Stanley
Tucci is a national fucking treasure and I will accept no slander. Now,
watching him look at me like I hung the damn moon, I want to crawl
back into his lap and never leave.

"Come on, I wanna show you something." He grabs a blanket from
the back of the couch before taking my hand in his and leading me to
the balcony door. I follow him through and audibly gasp at what I see.
If I thought James's view was incredible during the day, it had nothing
on his view at night. He'd shut the blinds when the sun began to set,
so this is the first time I'm seeing it. The cool summer night is wrapped
around us and casts the bay in dark shadows. A million tiny sparkles
twinkle on the water as it flows. To the left, the Golden Gate bridge
glows a soft orange color, and the headlights of cars passing over it are
like tiny shooting stars. To the right, remnants of thick fog roll over
the island of Alcatraz and inland over the city. The angle from here
perfectly hides the taller buildings of downtown San Francisco, except
for the illuminated top floors of Salesforce tower.

"Jesus, James. This is what you get to see every night?" I look
around in awe as he nods. He turned on a string of twinkling lights
that gives us just enough of a glow to see each other without detracting
from the night around us. Soft music starts to play through speakers
I can't see, 'Butterflies' by Kacey Musgraves.

"The balcony wraps all the way around, so I get a city view if I want it. I prefer this side though." He takes my hand and pulls me in, wrapping his arm around my waist and swaying to the music.

"I never would have pegged you for a country music guy, Adler," I say, wrapping my arms around his neck and looking up at him. He's so damn tall, I'm going to invest in some super high heels for the sake of my neck muscles.

"Oh yeah, but only the women. I don't care about a dude's truck and light beer obsession. Kacey, Reba, Dolly. Oh! Andt Shania. Those are my girls." I smile, thinking about James rocking out to '9 to 5', driving up the coast in his Jeep.

A breeze passes over us and I shiver, suddenly feeling cold down to my bones.

James grabs the blanket from behind us and wraps it around my shoulders.

"Come here."

He sits down on one of the oversized lounge chairs laid out in a row and pulls me down into him. We settle into a comfortable, silent snuggle. Him on his back, arms wrapped around me as I nuzzle into his broad chest, the ultra soft fleece blanket helping to shield us from the chill of night.

"In spite of all the shit, I had a really great day with you, Georgie," he says after a few minutes, burrowing his nose into my hair and kissing the top of my head. I sigh out my agreement and hug him tighter, savoring the warmth of his body and the smell of his skin.

I don't know when I fell asleep, or for how long, but I wake up to gentle kisses on my forehead and fingertips tracing my arm.

"Let's get you to bed, baby." I yawn and follow James's movements as he lifts us out of the chair and takes us back into the house.

"Come on, I'll get you set up." I let him lead me down through the living room and down a hall in the opposite direction of his own bedroom. I feel like this might be a terrible idea, but I stop short anyway.

"You okay?" he asks, and I shake my head.

"I don't want to sleep in the guest room." I tell him, and his face falls with disappointment.

"Oh, um, not a problem. I'll get some shoes on and drive you home." He drops my hand, but I grab his right back.

"Can I stay with you?" Realization dawns on him and the corner of his lip curves up. He lifts my chin with one finger.

"That depends. Can you be a good girl and keep your hands to yourself?" My tongue peeks out and swipes over my lips, and arousal pools low in my stomach.

If there's one good thing my parental neglect and need for validation gave me, it was a praise kink.

I nod- a lie, my hands are itching to touch him all over- and he gives me an approving wink before turning and taking us the other direction to the master suite. He lets me use the bathroom first, washing my face and brushing my teeth before he takes his turn.

Unlike the rest of the house, the size of his bedroom is relatively modest. Either that or the floor space is dwarfed by the huge bed covered in black silk sheets and matching lush comforter in the middle of it. That thing has got to be bigger than a king. It's the kind of bed you see in those really high class gangbang pornos (not that I've ever seen one of those...). Now that I'm here, I'm kind of frozen. It feels like that scene in Talladega Nights when Ricky Bobby doesn't know what to do with his hands. James comes back into the room, fiddling with the Patek Phillipe on his wrist. He gestures towards the bed.

"Go ahead, get comfortable." He sets his watch on the left bedside table, so I assume I should lay on the right. Normally I'd take my pants off first, but seeing as I still don't have any underwear on, I should at least pretend that I want to be modest right now. I climb in, basking in the luxury of the silk on my skin. Today has been a whirlwind of seeing how the other half lives. Everything James owns is understated but still drips money. I lay my head on the pillow and it's so perfectly soft and firm, I could cry. I turn to ask James where he bought this incredible bedding and how many years of saving it would take me to afford it, but my words get caught in my throat.

James is standing with his back to me, facing the open door leading to his closet, pulling the black t-shirt over his sculpted torso. The little muscles at the base of his spine twitch as he pulls the shirt over his head and tosses it in what looks like a rich mahogany chest that I assume is his hamper. I watch the backs of his muscled arms flex as he pulls at the drawstring, and my eyes drift lower as he pushes the sweatpants over his hips. Clothed in tight black briefs, James's ass is a work of art. Round and tight, he could probably crush a freaking walnut between those cheeks. And those two little dimples right above the waistband of his underwear, I want to crawl over to him on my hands and knees and lick them.

"Like what you see?" My eyes must have been burning a hole in his behind, because he didn't even have to turn to catch me gaping at his peachy bubble butt.

"Yeah," I breathe out. There's no point in lying. He chuckles and grabs his phone off the nightstand. "Need an alarm for anything?"

"Uhm. I have a spin class at noon, but I'll probably wake up before then," I say, letting go of any shame I held on to while I let my eyes glaze over his chiseled abdomen. The man was clearly sculpted by God himself. I've seen the way he eats, and I can't imagine the hours in the gym it takes him to maintain that perfect physique.

"Can I come?" He slips under the covers and turns to me.

"I-what?"

"Can I come to your spin class? I've always wanted to try it."

The idea of working out next to The Rock's little brother clouds my mind in unease, but it's overshadowed by my desire to be close to him.

"I'll text the instructor and see if she has an open bike for you." I roll over and type out a quick message as James turns off the light. As I set my phone down, I feel James's large body move in behind me, wrapping himself around me like a koala on a eucalyptus tree. I instantly melt into him, relishing in the way his hard body feels pressed against my softer one.

"This okay?" he asks, pressing soft kisses in my hair.

"Yes."

"Good." His hand slides over my stomach and finds the hem of my shirt- his shirt. He slips under, palming the expanse of my middle and rubbing small arches with his thumb. I let out a small sigh and try to move, urging his hand to move further towards my breast, but he pulls me in tighter.

"James," I whisper, and I feel his hot breath on my ear.

"Goodnight, Georgie." Seriously? My core aches with arousal, and I can feel the hard press of his erection against my ass. He has to be just teasing me. There's no hiding how much he wants this. I move again, pushing my backside against the swell of his cock, desperate for any type of friction, but this time, he pulls away.

"What did I say about keeping your hands to yourself, Georgia?" he says, seamlessly grasping both of my wrists in one of his large hands.

"Technically, that wasn't my hands." I quip, embarrassment flooding my cheeks.

"Not tonight," he says. It feels like he's holding himself back from me on purpose.

"But...you're hard," I state the obvious. He lets out a long sigh before rolling on top of me and pinning me to the mattress with his hips. I moan at the delicious pressure of his arousal on my center and try my best to grind myself against him under his strong hold.

"I've been hard ever since you walked into my fucking office that first day, Georgie. I've never wanted anyone like this in my life, and it's driving me crazy. YOU drive me fucking crazy. I want to keep you in this room forever. I want to tie you to this bed and never let you leave. I want to wring every single ounce of pleasure from your body until you're nothing more than a breathless heap beneath me. But I'm not fucking you tonight. Not like this. Tonight I...I need to just hold you, alright?" His voice cracks on the last syllable. "Will you please just let me hold you?"

Realization dawns on me that today wasn't just tough for me. I had an episode and he had no idea what was happening. Even worse, he thought he caused it. He spent the entire night taking care of me, but he needed comfort too.

"I need that too," I tell him honestly. "Please, I won't be able to sleep without your arms around me." He cups my cheek with one hand and places a soft kiss on my lips before unpinning me and resuming his koala position against my back. I fell asleep in his arms that night feeling warm and truly safe, possibly for the first time ever.

"I'm telling you, I'm gonna be fine. I might be old, but I still know how to workout, little girl."

"I know you exercise. I'm just saying, Kira's pretty tough." I woke up this morning to James softly stroking my back, a homemade vanilla latte sitting on the nightstand next to me and a text message from Kira informing me that she has space in class for him today and that she has the perfect playlist to drive him wild...whatever the hell that means. Keeks is a bit of loose cannon, and that makes me nervous.

Not that I've had time to focus on pre-class nerves when I'm trying not to eye fuck the man next to me. James looks fucking incredible in his sporty clothes. It's simple athletic shorts and a sweat-resistant t-shirt, but every new facet of James's wardrobe I've discovered over the last few days makes me weak in the knees. He drove me home this morning so I could change, and I couldn't help but blush when he took in my outfit, swallowing hard as his eyes raked over the short, black bike shorts I'd chosen.

"I think I can handle her." Famous last words. We walk into the building and I show James where to check in and get his cycling shoes. I lead him into Studio B, where I see Rachel and Kira's friend Dottie occupying the first two seats in the front row.

"Dottie, it's so good to meet you in person!" She leans down from her bike to hug me. We FaceTimed her at the bar on Monday when we found out she was visiting. Kira really wants us all to hit it off, and Dottie is so lovely, I don't think it'll be a problem. I release her, and James sticks his hand out to shake.

"James Adler. I think we met at that Instagram symposium last year," he says, saving me the trouble of trying to introduce him. This is my boss, who is also my friend, whose bed I slept in last night while I fantasized about him fucking me stupid? Not a great option.

"Right, it's good to see you again." The lights dim and the production assistants urge everyone to find their bikes and clip in. Spin Sync does live productions of their classes that people can take at home with their own Spin Sync bikes, or using their app. I hop on my bike, Rachel on my left and James on my right, and the crew instructs us to start pedaling and clapping. The cameras roll as Kira enters the room like a celebrity, punching her fists in the air and high fiving students as she makes her way to the bike in the center of the room. The PA counts her down and the feed goes live.

"Welcome to hell, Spin Sync!"

An hour later, I'm still catching my breath from the intensity of that class. Kira put together the ultimate 2000's pop and hip-hop playlist. The girls and I had a great time riding and dancing to throwbacks from The Pussycat Dolls and The Black Eyed Peas, but nothing about that class was easy. I was so sweaty by, like, the third song that I had to take my shirt off and use it as a makeshift fan. I really did do it because I was hot, but when I caught James mouthing "you're killing me" while staring at my bouncing breasts in the mirrored wall in front of us, I felt a bit of pride in my accidental sex appeal.

I might have made a point to lean into it. The music definitely helped. When Get Low came through the speakers, the whole room roared and started to sing. It was the perfect song and perfect environment to do a little bike dancing and show off my assets. Every time Lil Jon told us to get low, I'd swing my hips as much as I could and lower my chest to the handlebars. Doing so squeezed my breasts together, and I could feel James's eyes burning into my skin. I guess he fell below the beat of the music because Kira called him out, yelling at him to pick up his speed. I couldn't tell if the red on his cheeks was from the exertion, being called out, or the sight of my cleavage.

A few songs later, it was Thong Song by Sisqo.

Yeah, Kira knew exactly what she was doing. She had us standing and riding the bike during the chorus, and with a little choreography queue she had us all bouncing our asses on the seat to the beat of the music.

I thought James was going to draw blood, he was biting his lip so hard.

Kira finishes up saying hi and taking pictures with the other students in the class before she bounces over to us. She doesn't blink twice at the grown man panting at her feet.

"What'd you think?" she asks him, nudging his leg with her foot.

"You..." he chokes out, still catching his breath. "are...fuck-ing...evil."

"I know, right?" She smiles and kicks him harder this time. "Get up, boss man, you're embarrassing yourself." I look away to hide my laugh. It was incredibly cute to watch that wall of muscle fall to pieces under Kira's watchful eye. I tried to send him a silent signal '*I told you not to underestimate her.*'

"Georgie!" he cries out dramatically, "I've fallen and I can't get up!" He reaches his hands out to me and I grab them, helping lift him to his feet. Well, help isn't necessarily the right word. He definitely did all the work himself, but his insistence on my assistance was undeniably adorable.

The five of us make our way out of the studio and into the lobby. Kira, Dottie, and Rachel are talking about where to go to eat, and James pulls me two steps aside.

"I'm really not going to see you until Monday?" he pouts.

"I told you, we're doing a girls day sleepover tonight, and then tomorrow I really need to pack for the conference. I've been so busy getting you ready I haven't thought about myself."

"Fine." He sighs. "You better send me at least three selfies a day between now and then, or I'll lose my mind. And use the card I gave you to treat your friends to lunch and shopping today. Whatever you ladies want, go nuts." I laugh and shake my head.

"I don't think HR will be too happy with me trying to expense my girl's day, Adler." He looks down at me like I have two heads.

"That's my personal AmEx, Georgie, not a company card. I want you to use it. I won't be happy unless I see my statement at the end of the month and have to clutch my pearls at the balance." He grabs at his neck for dramatic effect.

"I can't...I'm not gonna spend your money..." He cups my chin with his thumb and forefinger.

"You will, and do you know why?" he says, low enough for just me to hear. "I want, no, I need to give you everything you've ever wanted. It's primal, this urge I have to provide for you. You spending my money, giving in to your every desire? Fuck, just the thought of it is making me hard." He turns his attention to my friends.

"Ladies, you're not to pay for anything today. Georgie has my card and she has been instructed to use it and abuse it. Food, shopping, entertainment, buy an elephant for all I care, just have fun." Rachel and Dottie seem to share my skepticism, but Kira jumps up and down and claps.

"Hell yeah, thanks boss daddy!" I roll my eyes at her, but inside, I'm squealing. I have never been spoiled by anyone in my life, and even though taking his card makes me feel a little weird, the fact that he *wants* to spend his money on me lights me up inside.

"There. Go have fun, and I'll call you later, sweet girl." He leans in for a hug, and I recoil.

"James, don't. I'm still all sweaty and gross."

He looks me up and down, taking in the perspiration coating my skin, considering my words. I'm hoping he'll take the hint and settle for a high five or something, but instead, he grabs me roughly by the waist and pulls my sweat slicked body flush against his own. He dips his head to my collarbone and tickles my skin with his tongue, dragging it lightly up my neck to my earlobe, where he nips at me and says "You taste as incredible as you look."

I inhale a sharp breath before he places a chaste kiss on my lips, so different from the hot, dirty display he put on just a moment before. A rush of arousal floods my core, and I'm ready to ditch my friends and spend my day riding him instead.

"I'll talk to you later, baby," he says with a brush of my cheek, then turns and walks out of the building before my mind catches up with the moment.

I look over to my friends, who are all staring at me with wide-eyed disbelief. My skin is hot, and it has nothing to do with the cardio session we just had. Dottie speaks first.

"Oh my god, I think that just got me pregnant."

18

Georgie

"So, what all are we looking for?" Dottie asks, linking her arm in mine as the four of us walk into Neiman Marcus. After we showered and changed at the studio, we had lunch at a tapas bar nearby. Rachel and Kira agreed with her that it's better to shop for clothes after you eat, because you'll know how the pants are going to feel when you're full. I filled the girls in on the events of yesterday while we ate, leaving out the fight and the part where James and I shared his bed. After Kira's comments about the photobooth, ("You should have climbed into his lap and rode him like a carousel horse. THAT'S a photo strip I'd pay to see.") I wasn't ready for her opinion on his neglected hardon.

"Well, we've got three days of meetings with a business casual dress code, so I guess a few blouses, maybe some new pants and shoes?" I answer, already intimidated by the perfume and cosmetics section that we're snaking through.

"And what about after the conference?" Rachel asks, picking up a sample bottle of Baccarat Rouge 540 and sniffing, then recoiling at the smell.

"Like when we get back to the city?" I ask, feeling too out of place to start manhandling the samples myself.

"G, she means when you get back to the room, and you inevitably end up climbing that man like a tree. What color panties do you want him peeling off of you?" Kira comes up behind me and squeezes both my ass cheeks, causing me to yelp and laugh.

Right, duh. I don't know about panty peeling, but I don't think I want to pack my old InstaHam sleep shirt. Maybe we should go look for some fancier pajama options.

"Keeks, keep it in your pants. Let's start with a sexy little power suit and heels and we'll go from there." Dottie wrangles us to the elevator.

An hour later, I have an arm full of silk blouses, blazers, skirts and pants. Dottie really has an eye for this kind of thing. I never would've picked half of these pieces, but everything she brought into the dressing room has looked amazing on me. Rachel has been the shoe fairy godmother, finding the perfect mix between professional and sexy in everything she slid on my foot.

Kira has yet to give up on the lingerie hunt.

"I'm thinking see-through lace bra, tiny thong and a garter belt and stockings to show off your sweet ass," she says, slipping a pair of strappy light pink Jimmy Choos onto her feet. "Or maybe go old school and get one of those sexy as fuck silk slips that your hard nipples could poke a hole through. He's like almost forty, right? I'm sure he appreciates a throwback."

"Keeks," I sigh, exasperated. "It's a business trip. I'm telling you, I don't need lingerie."

She rolls her eyes. "G, you're hot. Your body is insane, don't you want to doll it up? Look like sex on a curvy as fuck stick when he tears your clothes off?"

"No." I put the shoe I was trying on back in its box and nod to the saleswoman, letting her know I'll take it.

"Why not?"

"Because he doesn't want to get my clothes off." She's gonna break her optic nerves if she rolls her eyes any harder.

"Oh puh-lease, the man looks at you like-"

"The man had his chance last night and he turned me down!" I shout, cutting her off. Dottie and Rachel look back and forth between the two of us. "I slept in his bed with him. He was hard as a rock, and when I tried to make a move, he told me he wasn't going to fuck me. It was humiliating." I drop down onto the seat and put my head in my hands. I know that his explanation made sense last night, but with Kira shoving the idea of sex down my throat, I've been second guessing myself. I don't think I can handle another rejection.

"Okay, relax G. Tell us exactly what happened." Dottie rubs a hand down my back. I drop my head into my hands and tell them everything, falling asleep on the balcony, asking to stay in his room, the way he rolled on top of me and pressed himself into me. Jesus I want him to do that again.

I feel my friends move in close. I open my eyes, Dottie is sitting on my left, Kira on my right, each with an arm wrapped around my waist. Rachel is knelt in front of me with her palms on my knees.

"Georgie, you know we love you, but you're an idiot," Kira says, kissing the side of my head. I shoot her a dirty look.

"She's right," Rachel says, and now she's on the receiving end of my death glare. "James wanted you last night, he literally said so himself. He just didn't want to take advantage of you in a vulnerable moment because he likes you. Trust us, every single person in the room this morning could see how far gone that man is for you. He was just trying to respect you." I don't know when the tears start to fall.

"I wanted him to disrespect me, for fuck's sake!" I laugh, exasperated. "I don't know. Everything is changing so fast. I got so used to being on my own, I was good at it. Now all of a sudden I have this job where people actually talk to me, I have you guys, I have James and whatever is going on between us. It's confusing. I feel like I'm starting to depend on him- on all of you- and that makes putting myself out there so hard. I don't want to get rejected again." Dottie wipes a tear off of my cheek.

"Babe, the man rubbed his boner on you. He spent half the class today staring at your tits. He licked your fucking neck in front of all of us. Believe me, he's not gonna reject you." Kira squeezes me close. I sigh.

"What do you want, Georgie? Do you want to feel sexy, to show James how much you want him? Make him eat his heart out? Or do you want to keep yourself guarded?" Dottie asks, and I shrug.

"No. I want to feel sexy. I want him to look at me like I'm sexy. I want him to fucking want me as badly as I want him." A devilish smile creeps across her face.

"Then let's go find you a dress he can't help but rip off of you."

19

James

The service I hired to take us to the airport arrived at 5 am sharp. I wanted Georgie to come spend the night with me last night, but she told me she got a burst of inspiration while she was packing and wanted to retreat into her writing cave. I missed her, but I love how passionate she is about her work, both the amazing things she does for me and her *real* work. She must have stayed up late, because as soon as we got her bag loaded into the back of the SUV, she fell asleep with her face against the car window. She didn't even bother to gloat that for the first time in a week we're not matching.

I did get to see and talk to her for a bit after our workout date on Saturday morning- a workout date that almost brought me to my knees. The class was hard, sure, but so the fuck was I. That girl Kira played nothing but old school bump and grind songs. I could barely keep my eyes off of Georgie as she danced and writhed and sweated on the bike next to me. During the third song (Hot In Herre by Nelly...seriously? Could she have picked a hornier song?!) I watched as Georgie whipped her shirt over her head, revealing a v-neck black and gold sports bra and continued the ride with beads of sweat running down her bouncing tits. I seriously thought I might fucking die.

True to her word, she sent me several selfies from various dressing rooms (much to my dismay, she was clothed in all of them), and she took a dinner break with me last night. I ordered us both Chinese food to be delivered to our separate homes and we ate sesame chicken and egg rolls together over FaceTime. She told me about how starstruck she was actually spending time with Dottie, but also that she was the cutest sweetheart and she wants to carry her around in her pocket all day, whatever that means. I would say the girls did a good job spending my money (you know I was keeping tabs on my account to make sure they were using it), but they barely put a dent in what I expected.

I was just happy to see Georgie in good spirits after Friday. Every time I pictured her crying on my couch, my stomach lurched. I couldn't believe all that she had gone through. You would never guess that the walking ray of sunshine had such a dark past. I was seriously tempted to track down her piece of shit father and kill him with my bare hands, but I meant what I said. I'm not a violent person. What happened on Friday was in self-defense, and I will never, ever let Georgie see me put my hands on another person again.

We pull up to the tarmac and I see the flight crew ready to help us onto the plane. When Amir and I were buying this beast, we knew we'd want to go with a big model because part of the fun of having a private jet is showing it off. The plane we went with seats 15, has two private cabinets with single seats and desks, as well as a small room in the back equipped with a queen size bed. My favorite part, of course, is the bar. I don't care if it's before 6 am, if I'm in the air, I'm having a drink. I brush my hand down Georgie's arm, trying not to startle her.

"Wake up, sweet girl. We're here." She rolls her neck lazily and yawns as she opens her eyes. She smiles at me for a moment before noticing the plane out the window.

"Holy shit that's yours?" Her jaw drops. I know she doesn't care about my money or what I can buy with it, but it's hard not to be impressed the first time you see a private jet in person. I lean in and kiss her cheek, still warm from sleep. She smells so amazing. I loved it on Saturday morning when I woke up wrapped around her and she still smelled like me from my shower, but later that night when I was alone, it was her warm vanilla scent that I wanted on my pillow. I'll have to figure out what products she uses on this trip so I can stock up on them for her at my place.

"Come on, it's even better on the inside."

Two of my favorite people, Jeff and Annie, are our attendants today. They greet us at the bottom of the stairs while the driver helps stow away our luggage. I watch in amusement as Georgie takes in the magnitude of the jet. She's slack jawed at the lush cream-colored leather seats, the mahogany desks and tables, and the opulent bar.

"Screw my apartment, I'm moving in here." I let out a loud laugh and point to the back.

"There's a bedroom back there. I can have Annie set it up if you want to go back to sleep." The flight crew have joined us, puttering around and getting the cabin ready to go.

"Oh, that's ok. It's a short flight, I should stay awake. Where do I sit?"

"I want to be a gentleman and tell you to sit wherever you want, but I usually sit here." I gesture towards my favorite seat on the left side of the plane by the window. "Which means you have to sit there." I point to the chair directly across from it. I move into her and wrap my arm around her waist. "When we get to our cruising altitude, you can get into my lap," I murmur into her ear and she scoffs away from me, but not before I feel the shiver wrack through her body.

Jeff brings us drinks- a scotch for me, water for her- and in a few moments, we're off the ground and on our way. After takeoff, I watch as Georgie dozes in and out of consciousness. When she is awake, her eyes flit between me and the door to the bedroom I showed her.

"It's not too late to go lay down, baby. You've got at least forty minutes." I reach forward and brush my thumb over her knee. She's wearing black leggings and a light pink sweater that hangs off her shoulder. I know it's new because I saw it in the background of one of her dressing room pictures from the weekend. I fucking love seeing her in shit I bought for her. I wasn't lying yesterday. Spoiling this woman, providing for her, it turns me on.

"I'm fine, really. If I sleep any more I'll wake up totally cranky," she says, but I catch her looking towards the bedroom once again. It dawns on me what's going on in that head of hers.

"Ask the question, Georgie."

"Hmm?" she purrs, avoiding my gaze.

"You want to ask me a question, so ask it." She sighs and looks down at her hands in her lap.

"Have you ever...have you joined the mile high club in this thing?" she asks quietly. She's so guarded, so much like myself. I know it kills her to ask that, to all but admit the feelings she has for me while acknowledging the jealousy she feels towards the women who came before her. Little does she know, they all evaporated into dust the moment I laid eyes on her. There is only Georgie. There will only ever be Georgie.

I lean forward and unbuckle her seat belt, pulling her up and into my lap. The flight attendants are in their private crew cabin and won't come out unless we call for them, not that I'd care if they saw me holding Georgie like this. I want the world to see it. I want every single person to know that she's mine. I take her chin in my hand and answer.

"No, not on this plane or any other one." It's the truth. I can see her try to hide the relief washing over her. I wonder how she'd react knowing she's the only woman I've ever brought back to my home, let alone shared my bed with. "Amir, on the other hand.." Her eyes go wide.

"NO! Amir has," she drops her voice to a whisper, "*fucked* someone in there?" I chuckle, but the word "fucked" coming out of those sweet red lips has my pants tightening.

"In there, out here, in the bathroom, the cockpit." She gasps. "A pilot and his female copilot took a real liking to him on a trip to Chicago, and the three of them made good use of that little space when we landed."

Her jaw drops.

"He just...he's such a sweetheart! I can't imagine him-"

"You know the kind of books he likes to read, sweet girl." I give her a playful poke on the side of her thigh. "He might look cute and innocent, but the man is a hornball. Next time you see him, ask him to tell you about his 'special room'." I twiddle my fingers into air quotes with my free hand before brushing a lock of hair out of her face.

"You're so beautiful, Georgie." She closes her eyes and leans her hand against my cheek. I want to live in this moment forever. She feels so warm and soft on top of me. Her skin feels like silk against mine. In the warm, pink glow of the rising sun, she's luminous.

"Would you ever have sex up here?" she asks, tracing the seam of my collar with her fingertips.

"Maybe...if they changed the sheets." Her giggle is the sweetest sound I've ever heard. "Are you propositioning me, Georgie?" I cock an eyebrow at her.

"No," she says flatly, and I don't believe her for a second.

"Hmm. Too bad." I press my lips to hers and drink in the taste of her, savoring every lick of her tongue against mine, every soft breath and moan, the feel of her arms wrapped around my neck. We're like that until the pilot announces that it's time to prepare for landing, moving between lazy, languid kisses and watching the California coast pass by underneath us. I feel her absence the second she moves back to her own chair, and I miss her even though she's only two feet in front of me. She's taken up a permanent space under my skin, like a tattoo, and I'm never going to let her go.

20

Georgie

As soon as we land in LA, the morning flashes by in a blur. We take a car to the hotel where they let us check in early, since the entire place is pretty much sold out for the conference. We're sharing one suite with two rooms. It's apparently the arrangement he and Amy usually have for work trips, and I have no issue with it. I'm desperate to share a bed with him tonight, but I unpacked and changed in the second room anyway. After what happened in his bed a few nights ago, I've resolved to letting him take the lead. If he wants me, he can take me, but he has to be the one to ask.

Walking around this space, I was even more grateful for James's generosity, because my straight from Target clothes would have definitely stood out against the smartly dressed people in this hotel. The girls really were a huge help in finding me some business appropriate but still cute things. Dottie in particular put together the outfit I have on right now- waist high black trousers that fit snug against my hips and ass and flair out into a slightly wide leg at the bottom, a silk (REAL SILK!!!) bright white blouse with long sleeves and a bow tied loose at my chest, showing off the slightest peak of cleavage, and white pumps with a cut out on the inner edge of each of my feet, and a certain shade of red lacquer bottom. And of course, I swiped a coat of my emotional support Ruby Woo on my lips.

We had two events on opposite sides of the hotel to endure before James's speech at noon, and between the running around and the early morning wake up call, I was actually afraid that I was going to fall asleep while he talked. Not a good look for an assistant (or a potential girlfriend). Thankfully, as soon as James walked on stage, looking so devastatingly handsome in his stark black suit and perfectly styled hair, I perked right up. I've heard this speech a thousand times- hell, I wrote most of it- but still, I hang on to his every word. I love watching him in CEO mode. He absolutely commands the room. His stature, his passion for the industry, the tone of his voice, it's intoxicating. He complained about this speech for weeks, yet up at that podium, he shines.

He ends the speech to a standing ovation, and with a polite nod and acknowledgment of their applause, he makes his way off the stage and out the back door. I gather up my iPad and bag and follow after him.

"You were amazing!" I exclaim at him in the empty hallway, holding my hand out for a high five. He grabs it and uses it as leverage to pull me into a hug instead.

"You're amazing. You did most of the work, I just said the words." He squeezes me a little tighter before pulling away, linking his fingers with mine.

"Well you said them really good." He laughs, and I swoon. I fucking love that sound.

"It was hard to concentrate. I kept wanting to look over to you, and every time I did, you were mouthing the words along with me."

"I was not!" I insist, although it's completely possible that I was.

"You were, and it was fucking adorable." He pulls me to his side and kisses the top of my head, and we head to a lunch meeting on the other side of the hotel.

Five incredibly long hours later, James swipes the card that lets us into our suite. I drop my bag on the floor and flop on the couch.

"I know you're a nerd and everything, but I gotta say, your field of work is so freaking boring." Seriously. How am I expected to go through another day of deployment strategies and coding languages? It's rotting my brain.

"I'm with you there, sweet girl. I don't know how much more of these things I can take." He spots me cuddling up with a throw pillow and pats my leg.

"Don't get too comfortable over there, Georgie. I'm taking you to dinner." My stomach growls, but I groan.

"Can we just order in room service? I'm so tired." I cuddle into the couch further. This is the kind of couch you take *that* nap on. You know, the one where you pass out for hours and then wake up in a puddle of drool with pillow imprints on your cheeks wondering what year it is.

God that sounds so good right now.

"Absolutely not. I'm tired too, but we don't have much time here. Go get changed, we're going out." I groan louder when he physically lifts me off the couch and onto my feet. "Come on, you're 26, boot and rally, baby!"

"Gross. Can you at least tell me where we're going so I know what to wear?" I slump and walk at a snail's pace to the second bedroom.

"I'll text you the website. Get a move on." I shriek when he pats my ass and quicken my steps before shutting the door in his face. I hear his laugh through the door, and I can't fight my smile. I might be truly exhausted, but I'm excited. This is technically our second date. I mean...I think. He didn't say Friday was a date, but we slept together. That implies date type activities.

True to his word, James texted the link to the restaurant. It's a rooftop situation, and a quick check of the location tag on Instagram tells me that I should dress up. I look into the closet and pull out the dress my friends helped me choose. It's an Amanda Uprichard number, black silk that clings to my curves and hits me right at mid thigh, sleeveless a high collared neckline with a keyhole in the back, showing the thinnest expanse of my skin, and long bow tied around my left hip that dips below my knee. Thankfully, Keeks also made sure I bought the tiniest thong in the lingerie department, because this thing would definitely show off all of the panty lines.

I keep my makeup simple- the red lip speaks for itself against this dress- and pull the pins holding my hair back out. It still looks pretty good even after running around all day. I clean up a few spots with my curling iron, especially the strands that frame my face. I spritz my pulse points with a touch of perfume and slip my feet into a pair of black heels with straps on the toes and around the ankles.

I take one last look at myself in the mirror and smile. I look sexy, like really sexy. Even better, I *feel* sexy. I snap a mirror selfie and send it to the group chat. My girls are on it immediately.

Pussy Posse

Georgie: -*image*- what do you guys think?

Rachel: GASP! G, you're fucking HOT!!!!

Dottie: Georgie, that dress was absolutely made for you!! Beautiful!

Kira: If the CEO doesn't fuck you tonight, I will *fans self*

Georgie: LOL! Wish me luck ;)

I tuck my phone into my clutch and open the bedroom door. I catch James's side profile as he runs a lint roller over his sleeves. I guess his fear of Lucifer's fur on him defies distance. He's got on the same black trousers as earlier, but he's switched out his suit jacket for a sportier black blazer and matching black button up. I love him in a monochrome look. It makes him look sleek and dangerous, a total contradiction to his sweet and goofy personality. His hair is longer than when I first met him. Still short on the sides, but the longer strands on top end in loose curls that I yearn to run my hands through. He skipped the shave, and his scruff takes his face from disgustingly handsome to absolutely devastating. I clear my throat since he still hasn't noticed me standing here.

He turns, and I swear, it's like a moment from the movies. I watch in slow motion as he glances up and falls back into a double take. Fire burns behind his bright blue eyes, and I feel it scorch my skin as he drinks me in, starting at my feet and dragging his gaze up my body, slow and deliberate. When he finally meets my eyes, I watch the muscles in his throat work as he swallows. Fuck, I want to walk over there and lick that neck.

"Ready?" I ask, breaking the silence stretched between us. I watch as he looks me over one more time, wetting his lips. The air is thick, and I feel the sexual tension between us stretch until it's ready to snap.

I've never wanted anyone like this in my life. You drive me fucking crazy. Yeah, well, the feelings mutual, my dude.

"Georgie, you are so stunning. I can't believe I'm lucky enough to have you on my arm tonight." Heat floods my cheeks, and he steps towards me, taking my left hand in his and wrapping the other around my waist.

"Let's get out of here before I do something really stupid." His normally bright eyes are dark with lust, the gray rings lining his pupils more prominent than I ever see them. I nod and we head out the door, secretly wishing he would've chosen stupid tonight.

21

James

∽

"How high up is this place?" Georgie asks me as we ride the elevator to the restaurant I chose for tonight. I could give a fuck about food right now. The only thing I'm interested in eating is my girl's sweet pussy. When she walked out in that scrap of black silk, I knew I was in fucking trouble. It took all of my willpower not to throw her down on my bed and fuck her senseless, but I promised her a date, and a date she will get. I give her hand a light squeeze while I clench my other fist. Patience, man.

"73 floors. It's the highest open-air bar in the western hemisphere." I've been here before with Catherine and Amir, and the views are insane.

"Jeez. Good thing I'm not afraid of heights." The elevator door opens and we're met with a hostess who leads us to our corner table by the fire. We tuck in and I order us a bottle of Moet.

"Going right for the good stuff, huh?" she teases.

"We're celebrating. Champagne is necessary." I wish they had something better than this cheap crap, but it will have to do for now.

"What exactly are we celebrating?" she asks as the server pops the cork and fills our glasses.

"Us, Georgie. You and me, here together. Don't you think that's worth celebrating?" I watch as the blush creeps up over her cheeks. The sun is setting behind her, illuminating her into a gorgeous golden pink glow. The honey brown curls framing her face get caught up slightly by the breeze that comes with being so high up. I let my gaze fall down for just a moment to where her dress has ridden up just slightly, giving me a better view of her luscious thighs. She pulls her bottom lip between her teeth.

"I think it is. Cheers." She clinks her glass with mine. I watch as she lifts the flute to those red lips and sips. She closes her eyes as the bubbly beverage meets her tongue, and I'm finding myself incredibly jealous of the glass. The lightest imprint of red lipstick sticks to the rim of the glass, and I can't help but think about the other places I've fantasized about seeing those marks.

I clear my throat and mentally shake the dirty images out of my head.

"So what do you think of the view?" I ask her, gesturing to the skyline around us. She looks around, considering.

"It's nice. I think I like yours better though. I prefer fog to smog." I smile at the memory of her in my home, on my balcony, in my arms.

"Yeah, well, as a born and bred San Franciscan, I have to agree. We're programmed from birth to hate everything about LA. Although it is nice to lie on beach in something other than a parka every once in while."

She snorts and shakes her head. "It's funny how regional rivalries form. It's like in New York, we're supposed to hate New Jersey. I don't have any strong feelings towards the state, except you can't make a freaking left turn anywhere. But if someone from the city asks, it's fuck Jersey."

"I've never been to New Jersey, but I did once hear it described as the armpit of the country." She tips her head back and laughs, and I take in the way the collar of her dress stretches across her neckline. I want to peel it away and run my mouth over her flesh. I grab her hand and slide the straw wrapper accessory I fashioned onto her ring finger. I've become addicted to the look of my origami rings on her hand.

We order and chat while we wait for the food to arrive. She tells me about the breakup scene she wrote over the weekend and how it made her cry for her characters, and I tell her about the program I wrote in college that could take in the attributes you feed into it and match you with like people on campus, basically a rotary phone version of Tinder.

During dinner, we revert to telling embarrassing stories about ourselves and our friends.

"So I walk in, and I can see him- *ahem*- making love to himself. I slammed the door, but not before I realized he was holding my fucking French textbook."

"Not your textbook!" She smacks her hand over her mouth.

"Apparently he was very into one of the stock models. I let him keep it, and I got a C in the class." She laughs again while she takes a bite of her salmon. I love watching Georgie eat. I love the feeling of 'I put that smile on her face'. Call it what you want, feeding my girl strokes the hell out of my masculinity boner.

"Poor Amir. He must've been humiliated." She shakes her head.

"Nah, he was fine. He tells that story himself. And besides, we lived together for more than a decade. He's caught me with my dick in my hand a time or two as well." I don't miss the way her pupils dilate when I mention my dick. I smirk and give her a wink. Her cheeks flush pink, and I try to catch a peek of her legs, to see if maybe she's squeezing those thighs together, but we're interrupted by the server asking if we're ready for dessert.

I want dessert alright, but it's nothing this dude can bring me.

I look to Georgie. "The truffle cake is pretty amazing," I tell her.

"Actually," she smiles, "I kind of had other plans for dessert, if you're up for it, that is. I know it's been a long day."

"Let's do it." I don't even ask what it is. Wherever Georgie Hansley goes, I will follow.

"Absolutely not. Georgia, no!" After I paid for dinner, Georgie gave me an address and I ordered us an Uber. I don't know how she found a dive bar hosting a "Cookies, Cake and Karaoke" night in Santa Monica, but I was perfectly content to sit back and watch the LA wannabe pop stars sing and feed Georgie cake off my fork. I was not prepared to be yanked away from my plate of German chocolate and snickerdoodles and pulled towards the stage.

"Oh come on, you have to!" she says, tugging the sleeve of my shirt. I wrapped my jacket around her shoulders earlier while we waited for the car, and she's still swimming in it, looking fucking delectable.

"I absolutely do not," I protest, but I let her drag me along anyway.

I'd rather jump into traffic than sing karaoke, but I'd also rather gouge my own eyeballs out with a rusty spork than say no to Georgie.

"It's gonna be fun, I promise."

"I can assure you it will not. What if I don't know the words?" I'm still fighting as we walk on stage and in front of two mics and a full band.

"That's what the screen is for, you dork."

The band starts the opening notes of "Man! I Feel Like a Woman!" by Shania Twain, and Georgie immediately pulls her mic off the stand and starts to twirl. Like the day I caught her in the kitchen, the music lights her up. She sways her hips and raises her arm above her head, smiling as she twirls around the stage. She's not a particularly talented dancer, but the passion behind her movements is palpable. Thank god she starts the first verse, because watching her, I forgot what we were up here for.

I hate to admit it, but this is fucking fun. We sing the chorus together, and I really get into the second verse. I definitely tossed a little attitude into the 'best thing about being a woman' line. My heart fluttered a beat when Georgie sassed her way through the instrumental bridge, grabbing my hand and spinning into my arms.

Neither of us are great singers, but the crowd here doesn't seem to care. Georgie and I put on a damn good show. They've gone wild for every brave soul that has gotten on this stage tonight, but they go absolutely apeshit for us. People are on their feet, whistling and clapping and chanting "Encore!"

"Let's do another!" Georgie squeaks, basking in the praise from the room. Her hair is a little out of place and she has a slight sheen of sweat from the dancing. She's never looked more beautiful, she's fucking glowing.

"Yes," I agree "But I get to pick the song." She "eeps" and wiggles her way out of my jacket, tossing it to the side of the stage. I move in and tell my choice to the band. The drummer programs the song into the computer, and they start to play.

When Georgie realizes we'll be singing Dancing Queen by ABBA, she screams like a "woo girl" in a bar and starts to spin around. We sing together, dancing and putting on a dramatic show for our audience. I nearly combust when she rubs her back to my front while singing "You're a tease and you turn him on". Yeah, forgot about that horny little lyric. She tries to show me how to do the hustle while we sing, and I trip over my own two feet. She moves into the classic disco point instead. THAT I can do. I've never felt so fucking happy, holding and dancing with my girl, making memories. The way her joy lights up the room makes my heart beat hard in my chest. I know in this moment, that I would give my dying breath just to see Georgie smile.

22

James

We stay out longer than we probably should, considering what time we woke up this morning, but after our performances, the night really took off. We watched person after person pull off some pretty great vocal performances and ate about fourteen thousand cookies each, determined to try them all. Georgie nodded off for a moment in the car back, but by the hotel lobby, she caught a second wind. She practically skipped through the lobby and buzzed in the elevator.

"And that guy doing Whitney Houston!" she laughs as I open the door to our room and let her in. "I swear he was rubbing his nipples through his shirt."

"Oh yeah. The man was really feeling himself." She throws her head back laughing at my accidental pun, and I step into her, placing my hands on her lower back and pulling her body into mine. She's so fucking soft, she feels amazing pressed against me. I didn't want to straight up ask her to share my room with me tonight. I wanted to see how the night went and let her make the decision, but right now, the thought of her closing the door and going to bed without me makes me sick.

"I had so much fun tonight, Georgie," I tell her, and she wraps her arms around my neck.

"I did too." She tilts her head up to me. I take my thumb and brush her bottom lip with it.

"Miss these," I say, barely above a whisper.

"They're yours," she breathes, and I groan, capturing her mouth with mine. I start slow, basking in the delicious pressure of her lips on mine and her hips in my hands. The warmth from her mouth spreads throughout my body, igniting sparks of pleasure in every nerve from my fingertips to my toes. I need more, more, more of her. I let my tongue slip out, licking against those beautiful red lips, hopeful that she'll let me inside.

She moans, low and soft, the sound vibrating against my lips and sending a wave of lust shooting down my spine. She opens up to me, her little tongue meeting my own stroke for stroke. I feel her hands move from my neck and up into my hair. She tugs at the strands, and my cock aches harder in my pants.

God knows how long we're like that, making out like two desperate people who can't keep their hands to themselves.

I mean, that's exactly what we are.

Her fingertips roam through my hair, then back down, where she brushes soft strokes against the sensitive spot at my hairline. My own hands stay firm on her hips, gripping her tight. I'm terrified that if I move, I'll lose the moment, but I'm fucking aching to touch her. I swallow my fears, and my hands twitch before I start tracing lines from her delicious hips, back up the side of her soft belly, stopping only just before they meet the underside of her tits. I'm lost in her lips and her body and the warmth of her skin. My cock strains against the zipper of my pants, and I feel like I'm fucking dying. I need more. I slowly lower one hand down over her hip to the top of her thigh, hoping to grab onto the hem of that *fucking* dress she's wearing, but she pulls away.

"Are you going to touch me?" Georgie asks. That look on her face, it's heady. Glassy. Lustful.

She's turned on.

The low light from the lamp in the corner casts a soft glow on her lovely skin. God, she's so fucking beautiful. I lean down, drop my face to her shoulder and plant a tiny kiss to the side of her neck. She shivers.

"Do you want me to touch you, sweet girl?" I ask, my voice low against her sensitive flesh.

She gasps, a breathy, needy sound that I'll be jerking myself to the memory of for the rest of my life, and whispers "Please."

One word. One quiet plea, and I lose all fucking control. I kiss her lips again and then spin her so that her back is pressed against my chest. "If you want me to stop," I whisper against her neck, "say the word. You hear me? Say the word and I stop."

She whimpers, pushing up on her tiptoes and pressing her plump ass against my aching groin. Even in those sexy heels, she's still a tiny little thing compared to me. I feel like Sasquatch trying to feel up an otter.

"Answer me, baby," I warn.

"Yes. I say stop and you stop," she says, slowly and sinfully grinding her ass against me.

"That's my good girl," I croon, brushing her hair off of her back and over to one side. I stare at her bare shoulder, loving the sight of the goosebumps that have erupted over her skin. I find the zipper at the top of her high neckline, and I tug at it.

"This ok?" I ask and she sighs out a yes.

Slowly, one tooth at a time, I pull the zipper of her dress down, the fabric pooling against each of her curves. I follow my fingers with my lips, peppering hot kisses against her sweet skin. She even tastes like vanilla, how is that possible?

"Fuck," I say, pushing the tight dress over the curve of her ass and letting it drop to her ankles. I help her step out of her heels and then rise back up against her, pawing at her breasts like an animal.

"All night," I growl, lightly biting the skin where her neck meets her collarbone. "All night, you had nothing under that dress holding your beautiful tits in?" I suspected as much with that tiny dress, but I can't help but taunt her a bit anyway.

"I-oh- the straps would have shown," she whimpers as I roll her tight, hard nipples between my fingers. I give them a light tug, and she lets out a breathy noise.

"You like that, sweet girl?"

"Yes, oh my god yes." She throws her head back against my chest and moans when I pull a little rougher this time.

"Sensitive little thing, aren't you?" I tease in a low voice. She looks over her shoulder and up to me.

"Can I take your shirt off?" The question sounds so fucking cute on her lips, I can't take it.

"I think I'll die if you don't, Georgia."

She turns, and with shaky hands, she starts to work the buttons of my shirt. Her fingertips feel like fire against my bare chest, and I'm ready to let her set me ablaze. She frees the last button, and I help her to shrug it over my shoulders and toss it to the side. Her rock hard nipples brush against my bare chest as she sheepishly reaches down to fiddle with the button of my trousers.

I can't take the way her shy movements make me smile. She's so goddamn cute. I tug at my belt, pulling it loose.

"Go ahead baby, you can take those off too."

Her cheeks are flushed, but she does as I say, snapping open the button and pulling at the zipper. I place my hands over hers as she pushes the pants over my hips. I take a second to slip off my shoes and step out of the pool of fabric, and then I'm pulling her back into me, my black boxer briefs and her tiny white thong the only things between us.

I lean down to kiss her again, but she shifts her face at the last second, and I catch the corner of her mouth.

"What's wrong Georgie?"

"Nothing. I'm just...I'm nervous."

I pull back, cupping her jaw in my palm. Physically, I'm ready to explode, but mentally, I'm preparing for her to tell me to stop.

"Good nervous. You're just so gorgeous, I have butterflies." She looks me up and down with those big brown eyes and her red lips curl into an excited smile. I'm nervous too. I've wanted her for so long it hurts. Now she's here and ready for me and I'm fucking done waiting. One hand slides under her ass and the other grips her waist. I scoop her up and she wraps her legs around my waist as I carry her into the larger bedroom, tossing her right into the middle of the bed. She shrieks in surprise and then giggles as I crawl on top of her. I lean down and kiss her, desperate to capture that sweet sound in my mouth, and then I trace my lips lower.

I continue my path down to her full breasts, biting and soothing each pebbled nipple with my tongue. Georgie squirms underneath me, raking her fingers through my hair. The scratch of her nails on my scalp sends shivers down my spine. I continue to kiss my way over her stomach, then nipping and licking at her hips.

I find my way further down and grip her thick thighs, spreading her open for me.

"Jesus, Georgie. Look at you," I breathe, taking in the wet lace covering her core. "You're soaked, sweet girl. Is that all for me?" I lightly trace my finger up her seam and she whines, arching into my touch. I groan and wrap my hand around the pathetic piece of fabric. I pull at it, ripping it off in one piece and tossing it to the side. She yelps when the lace bites at her skin.

I pull her in closer and marvel at the sight of her beautiful cunt-wet, puffy and pink, like a flower coated in morning dew. She's freshly waxed and completely bare, not at all what I was expecting from my shy girl but a welcome sight nonetheless. She's so wet she's leaking down her thighs, and her clit is beautifully swollen, begging for my attention.

I'm out of my fucking mind with lust. My girl- My Georgie is here, she's perfect, and she's mine.

23

Georgie

Life is crazy. Two days ago, I was arguing with my friends in a La Perla changing room, insisting that I did not need the Brazilian wax or the $215 thong Keeks was waving in my face, and now that thong is shredded on a hotel room floor, while my boss stares at my naked body like I'm a gazelle and he's a ravenous lion. I watch him move between my thighs, taking in the sight of me, and I feel exposed and raw.

Not in a bad way though...in an incredibly erotic way. The way the muscles in his jaw twitch as he takes in my bare core is so arousing, and I'm trying to think of something sexy to say when he dives in, burying his face between my legs.

"You don't have to-" I start, his tongue laps at my slit and cuts my sentence short. He wraps his hot lips around my clit, and with one gentle suck, my back is bowing off of the bed.

"James!" I gasp, and I can feel the vibration of his chuckle against my pussy.

"I-" I pant, "I asked you for this. Let me do something you like." I move to reach for him, but he wraps his huge hands even tighter around my thighs, holding me in place. I'm definitely going to be bruised tomorrow.

He looks up at me from between my thighs, his eyes dark and full of lust, lips already coated in my wetness. I nearly come apart from the sight alone.

"Do you have any idea how many times I've thought about this, Georgia?" he growls. "How often I've fucked my fist, fantasizing about your scent, your taste? Sweet girl, if you think me licking this perfect cunt is anything but a selfish act, you're out of your goddamn mind."

He moves one hand up to my stomach, pushing me further into the bed and holding me in place, the other spreading me as far as my legs will go. He nuzzles back into my pussy and inhales, mouth not quite making contact and mumbles, "Fucking heaven."

He teases my entrance for just a moment, and the liquid heat that has been pooling in my stomach for weeks starts to boil over.

"Please..." I choke on a whisper, and then he's fucking me with that hot, sinful tongue. The tip of his nose rubs against my clit, giving me that sweet friction that I'm desperate for. My eyes snap shut and my hands find their way into his luscious brown locks, clawing to pull him even closer. A bead of sweat slips down my chest between my breasts, and that familiar feeling – the one I've only found in my own company, quiet nights at home with nothing but my fantasies- starts to build. It tingles through my toes and up my legs, and I'm gonna... oh god I'm gonna...

Fuck. I'm gonna lose it.

"James," I breathe, the orgasm that I thought was building moving further and further out of my reach. "This might...I might not...it might take a while."

I nearly cry out in desperation when he pulls his mouth away from my center and looks up at me. In the low light, the glisten of my arousal on his lower face looks downright dirty, so fucking sexy.

"Take as long as you need, Georgie. Forever. I'd be a lucky man to spend every moment of my life right here with my mouth on your tasty little pussy." I swear I see him wink before he lowers his head right back where I want him. My eyes roll to the back of my head as he focuses his attention on my clit, his tongue pointed and working perfect circles around the swollen nub. I don't have a second to fall back into self-doubt over whether I'll be able to finish before I feel it, one long finger sliding into my pussy. I moan, overcome by the sensation, and then his finger curls. He starts to gently work a delicious spot inside of me that I've never been able to find on my own, the ministrations of his tongue on my aching clit never slowing as his finger fucks me. Just as I think *this is it, it doesn't get any better than this*, he adds a second finger into my already too tight hole. Fire burns at the base of my spine, my breath grows ragged, and he hums against me. I feel the vibration everywhere, and then I'm falling.

The sound that leaves my mouth- I'm not even sure it's human. My thighs tense around his head as my orgasm rips through me. Pleasure runs through every nerve end and my pussy throbs under his tongue. I fist the sheets, needing something to hold onto to keep me grounded. I'm grinding against him, bucking and writhing without a care. I just know I fucking *need* this, need him. A tear escapes and rolls down my cheek while I- god I'm *still* coming. I can't tell if its one everlasting orgasm or multiple in a row, my mind is so clouded by overwhelming pleasure. James's fingers are still inside me, working my sensitive inner muscle, but he's moved his mouth off of me. His large hand cups my pussy, the heel of his palm grinding into my clit as I ride out the waves of euphoria on his hand. Through the blissful haze and the cries of my own moans, I can hear him praising me.

"That's it baby, such a good girl coming for me."

"Look at you making a sexy little mess all over my hand."

"Yes, sweet girl, keep going, keep coming for me."

I have no idea how much time passes. Seconds, minutes, hours, before the aftershocks slow down and my body relaxes into the mattress, before I remember who I am, where I am, and who I'm with.

I open my eyes and look down at James, still nestled between my legs. He smirks, the sound of his fingers leaving my pussy obscene, absolutely pornographic, and he crawls his way up my body. Leaning on one elbow, he taps my lips with those beautiful fingers that were just fucking me so perfectly.

"Open," he whispers, and I oblige, dropping my jaw and sucking him in. It's dirty, so fucking filthy, licking my own musky release from his skin, but that doesn't stop me from rolling my tongue over his fingers over and over again and moaning at the sensation.

"You taste that, baby?" he asks, and I shiver. His voice is husky and masculine and so fucking sexy. "You taste how perfect you are? I'm never gonna get enough of you." He pulls his fingers from my lips and replaces them with his own, gently licking into me.

"James," I breathe against his mouth. "That was...I've never..."

"I've never seen anything more beautiful. I fucking love the way you come." He works his lips up my jaw to my ear, leaving hot, wet kisses along the way. At the same time, he gently rocks his erection against my side.

"Yes, no...but like, I've never...oh god it's embarrassing." The red on my cheeks starts to feel less like a post orgasm high and more like a mortifying confession of my ridiculous secret.

He stops his nibbling, angling my jaw so that I'm looking straight into his gorgeous blue eyes, and runs his stare over my face inquisitively. "What is it, sweet girl? What have you never done?"

"UGH!" I roll my eyes and bring my hands over my face. I want to burrow into the freaking earth. I mean, the freaking irony of being a romance writer and getting embarrassed talking about sex, especially with the person I'm sort of in the middle of having sex with.

"I've never come like that. Hard. Or, god. Ever. Not with anyone else in the room at least. No one's ever gone down on me before."

He's quiet, and I can feel his gaze permeate my skin despite not being able to see his face through my covered eyes. He sighs, and I can feel his breath hot against my ear.

"Well baby," his voice vibrates my skull in the best way, "I plan on eating out your pretty cunt over and over and over again, so get used to it."

24

James

I'm not gonna lie, her admission shakes me to my core, in both good and bad ways. On one hand, it makes me fucking irate that she has lived 26 years with no one getting between her legs and taking care of her the way she deserves. On the other, the fact that I'm the only one who's ever gotten to taste her, that mine is the only tongue she's ever come on? Shit. That feels fucking good. Like, puff out my chest, throw her over my shoulder, take her back to the cave and ravage her, good.

Unfortunately, though, it means I have to ask a tough question. I pull her earlobe into another soft bite and whisper.

"Are you a virgin, sweet girl?" A sad laugh leaves her mouth.

"No," she breathes. "I mean, not really."

Uhh...what?

"Georgie, baby, at the risk of sounding like an asshole...what the fuck does 'not really' mean?"

"It means...I've had sex. Or, rather, someone had sex with me." My nostrils flare at the implication, anger smacking into me like a brick fucking wall and burning my skin. I know she senses it because she quickly backtracks.

"Not like that! No, oh no. If you're defining virginity as male/female penetration, then it was my ex-boyfriend, it was consensual, it just wasn't good." She lets out an exhale and rolls her eyes. "I slept with him because I thought I loved him, but it felt like he never cared. He definitely never bothered to make me finish, but that was the least of it. Intimacy, connection, we never had any of that. It was always just a race to his orgasm. I never even faked it, and he couldn't care less. After we broke up, I kind of figured, what's the point? If sex wasn't good with someone who supposedly cared about me, I wasn't going to bother trying with someone who didn't. I mean, I hooked up with a girl a few years ago but she turned out to be a curious straight girl who had no intentions of touching me back, so I don't count that. When I say not really, I just mean it's been...a few years since I've dated...or hooked up. My virginity might have grown back." She says that last part with a little chuckle, but it does nothing to tamp down the fire burning in my chest.

How could anyone get the privilege of having this angel in their bed and not take the time to worship at her altar? Who wouldn't want to hear the cooing sounds she makes when kissed on her collarbone, learn the way her hips roll when she's seeking friction but is too shy to ask for it, feel the vibration of the fucking moans that leave her tiny red lips as her release washes over her? Fuck. I've had her for what, an hour? I haven't been inside her yet- hell she hasn't even touched me yet- and I'm already fucking addicted to her. I don't want her to think I pity her, not when she's laying here baring her body and her soul to me, but I can't say nothing.

"Georgie, I don't want to dwell on the past, but I have to tell you that that's fucking unacceptable. You're a goddamn goddess, and you should be treated like one. I need you to know that you're my number one priority. Out there," I point to the door, "but especially in here." I rub a circle on her cheek with my thumb. "You come first, metaphorically and physically." I wink, and she finally breaks back into that beautiful Georgie smile that I'm so obsessed with.

I kiss her forehead and let the silence settle over us, giving her a moment to regain herself and nuzzle into my chest. My heart would be perfectly content to lie here with her in my arms for the rest of the night.

My cock, on the other hand? That bastard can't stop thinking about something she said earlier.

"You uh... you said you'd never had an orgasm with someone else in the room. That means you only come when you're alone, is that right Georgia?" I ask, pushing a honey brown curl out of her face.

"Oh gosh." The red flush on her cheeks is so fucking cute, I have to stop myself from leaning over and biting into one like a ripe honeycrisp apple. Here she is in my arms, naked and still dripping release between her legs, and yet she's so fucking shy. She tries to turn her head away from me, but I cup her jaw and pull her back.

"What do you do?" I ask, kissing her lips softly.

"What?"

"When you're alone. What do you do? How do you make yourself come?" Her eyes widen, but she's not getting out of this one that easily. I drop my hand from her jaw to her side, teasing a line from her hip to her breast and around her hardening nipple.

"Do you play with your clit? Do you use your fingers to fuck yourself? Or maybe you have a little toy hiding in your nightstand that you pull out when you're horny?" She avoids my eyes, but I can tell from the way she's clamping her thighs together and ever so slightly wiggling that my questions are having the effect I want on her.

"Answer me, sweet girl." I push. "Tell me how you make your pussy feel better when it aches."

She closes her eyes and lets out a long breath.

"My... fingers. On my clit. I usually just rub until. Yeah. And-" She stops herself short, sealing her lips shut. Her eyes grow wide like she can't believe she let that one little word slip.

"And what?" I ask. She shakes her head.

"And what, Georgia. Tell me."

She runs her tongue over her lips nervously, eyes finding a spot on my chest that is suddenly very interesting to her. "I have a...pillow," she whispers, the last word barely audible and I groan. My balls tighten and I grip my cock through my briefs, *hard.* The pain is the only thing keeping me from blowing in my pants at the image of this sweet, sexy woman, naked in her bed, riding her pussy against a pillow, maybe pulling those perfect, tight nipples between her fingers.

My jaw clenches and I swallow hard. "Show me," I tell her.

"Show you what?"

"I want to see how you get yourself off. I want to see the way you hump your pillow." I grab her, rolling so I'm on my back and she's on top of me. I help her straddle a leg on either side of me. "But I want you to rub yourself on my cock instead."

She looks down at me, biting her lip and still blushing, her skin pink from the apples of her cheeks to the swell of her tits. I know she's shy, reserved. She's given me so much already, maybe I shouldn't push her any further tonight. But fuck. I don't think I can go another second without seeing this girl come apart on top of me.

"I-"

"Shh," I cut her off, and with my fingertips pushing into her beautiful, thick hips, I grind her up and down over my erection- painful and threatening to bust out of my boxer briefs.

"Use me, baby. Be a good girl and use my cock to make yourself come again." She's hesitant, but only for a moment. Then, her hands are on my chest, her hot pussy rubbing against my length.

I run my hands up to her chest, teasing and tugging her dusky pink nipples.

"Shit, that's it, Georgie. Look at you, so fucking sexy riding me."

Fuck. I don't think I've dry humped anyone since college, but I know that it never- *never*- felt like this. She starts slow, timid even. With a little encouragement from hands rocking her, she finds a perfect pace that has me needing to think really unsexy things to keep from coming before she does. The weight of her is absolutely delicious pressure against my pelvis. Her thighs squeeze the sides of my ass cheeks in a fucking mind blowing way I've never felt before as she grinds down against me.

"Such a good fucking girl you are, Georgie. Taking all that pleasure and making your pussy feel so goddamn good." The sexiest moan escapes her lips, her mouth forming a perfect "O" that has me imagining them wrapped around my shaft, sucking me dry. Shit, she's so fucking hot.

"Fuck, you're so wet, baby. I can feel you soaking all the way through my briefs. Look at how perfectly you ride me, your pretty tits bouncing in my face. Such a sexy little minx. Fucking made for me, Georgie." I'm absolutely blinded by the feeling of her body on mine. I have no idea what the fuck I'm saying, if it makes sense or if she can even hear me. All I can think about is her and the friction and how badly I need to feel her come on top of me. Her pulsating pussy pulls at the fabric holding me in, and the head of my cock peeks out, red and angry and desperate for release. I shudder when her slick wetness meets my bare skin.

"James!" The sound of my name on her tongue is so goddamn beautiful. "James, I think I'm gonna-" I move my hands back down to her hips and dig into her flesh, bringing her even fucking closer to me. Her hard nipples scrape across my chest and I nearly combust.

"Come, Georgie. Come all over my cock. Let me feel it sweet girl." Her head falls forward and her hair joins her tits at the 'tickling my chest' party. The front of my underwear is absolutely soaked as I feel her cunt convulse on me. I grind her through it, watching as she writhes. She shudders and gasps, and I can't hold back any longer. White hot pleasure hits my spine like fucking lightning. With this gorgeous woman rubbing her spasming cunt all over me, I let go. My head lulls back and I come with a roar, eyes snapping shut and every muscle in my body seizing. Hot, thick ropes of cum coat my stomach and hers. I don't care that I should be embarrassed. I don't care that I just busted in my pants like a fifteen year old with no control. All I know is Georgie, her beautiful face, her sweet, shy demeanor and the way her pussy feels leaking all over me. I know I'm fucking ruined.

Her chest falls against mine and I wrap my arms around her sweat slicked middle. Neither of us seems to care about my cum on our skin as we shutter through the aftershocks of pleasure together. I work to even my breath, still trying to return to earth after the strongest orgasm of my life. I smile and whisper into her hair.

"I bet your pillow never felt like that."

She laughs and buries her face further into my chest. I kiss the top of her head and tell her I'll be right back. I head to the bathroom to change my underwear and run a washcloth under warm water.

When I come back out, Georgie is practically asleep, eyes heavy with exhaustion. She didn't even bother to move away from the wet spot on the sheets. I bring the washcloth to her skin and clean her release from between her legs and my own from her stomach. She shivers under my touch.

"Are you cold, baby?"

She nods, and I reach over to my suitcase, pulling a soft hoodie out of my bag and slipping it over her head. She's like jello in my arms, loose limbed, flushed and sated from our escapades. I pull her to the dry side of the bed and wrap my arms around her, snuggling our bodies together under the thick comforter.

Her breath is slow and even. I have no idea if she's still awake, but I whisper to her anyway.

"You're my *best* friend."

25

Georgie

Warm skin, sandalwood cologne, strong arms. I can't think of a better way to wake up than with James Adler wrapped around me. I blush, remembering our activities last night, how good he made me feel, not just physically, but emotionally. Coming with him- coming on him- it was the most intimate and erotic moment of my life. I snuggle closer into his bare chest, loving the way his smooth skin feels on my cheek when suddenly, I get that sinking feeling that happens when you know you've gotten too much sleep.

I roll over and see the time on the old school hotel clock- 9:32 am.

"SHIT! James, wake up!" I say, pushing at his arms.

"Whaaaat?" he whines, pulling the blanket over his head.

"My alarm never went off! We have to get up, we're so fucking late!" I scramble to get out of the bed, but he reaches out and pulls me back.

"It made the noises but I turned it off." He still hasn't opened his eyes.

"Why the hell did you do that?"

"It was terribly loud."

"Jesus James. What about the conference? You've got three meetings before noon-" He cuts me off by rolling on top of me and pressing his forehead to mine.

"Fuck the rest of the conference. We're skipping it. Now come back to my arms and cuddle me. We've got another half an hour before they bring our breakfast up." He rolls us back over, pulling me snug against his chest and tucking us back under the blanket. Call me a bad feminist, but this man's ability to toss me around like a ragdoll is incredibly hot. Technically, it's my job as his assistant to get him where he needs to be on time, but if he's willing to skip the hours of boring lectures that I don't give a shit about on the calendar today, I'm not going to fight him.

I don't know if James fell back asleep when we snuggled back up, but I laid there listening to the beat of his heart and watching the rise and fall of his chest in the shadows of the dark room until room service knocked.

He threw on pants and got the door while I opened the curtains to let some light in. I'm sliding back under the blanket when he places the tray down on the foot of the bed, careful not to tip the takeaway coffee cups.

"I went with bagel sandwiches, I hope that's okay." He tosses me a foil wrapped sandwich and crawls back into bed next to me, both of us sitting cross legged against the headboard.

"When did you order this stuff?" I ask.

"I called down last night after I wore you out." He smirks and nudges my leg with his own. I feel the embarrassment starting to creep in, but I shove it aside. Last night was amazing. I'm not going to let myself feel weird about it, about allowing myself to bask in the pleasure he so willingly offered me.

I unwrap my sandwich, expecting some sort of fancy LA hotel avocado concoction, but instead I find an everything bagel slathered in cream cheese with strips of bacon peeking out of the sides.

"How did you guess my bagel order?" I ask, genuinely perplexed. We've shared a lot of meals in the last few weeks, but bagels have not been one of them.

"I didn't guess," he says, taking a big bite of his own bagel. His looks like onion with ham, egg, and cheddar cheese with some sort of aioli. "You got that a few weeks ago, remember? Amir had them brought in?"

I just stare at him, taken aback.

"What?" he asks.

"Nothing, it's just... I'm surprised you caught that. I remember that day, and you seemed pretty pissed off at me. In fact, I don't think you said two words to me." He laughs, and now I'm even more confused.

"Oh I caught it, sweet girl. You wore your glasses that day."

What the hell do my glasses have to do with my bagel order? He reads the confusion on my face and cups my chin.

"I wasn't pissed, Georgie. Your glasses, it was the first time I saw you in them and you looked so..." He closes his eyes and sighs. "I was so fucking turned on, baby. I had to avoid you because if I didn't, I would have really embarrassed myself."

That makes me laugh out loud. This grown ass man ignoring me all day because of an inconvenient boner. It's hilarious and incredibly flattering. He does that adorable pouty face I'm starting to adore.

"Don't laugh at me, Georgie. I was in serious pain." Now I'm freaking wheezing.

"You should've gone home and taken care of it," I say between fits of giggles, and his face goes red.

"I mean...I do have that private bathroom in my office..."

"JAMES!" I shriek, flicking his rock hard arm. "Did you jerk off *while we were at work?!*"

His face scrunches as he winces and nods. "Twice."

"James Theodore Adler. Are you telling me you touched yourself to the thought of me? TWICE?! I never!!" I gasp and clutch at my nonexistent pearls.

"First of all, Georgia Marie, my middle name is Alexander. Second of all..." He leans in and nips at the spot below my earlobe "I've gotten myself off to the thought of you more times than I can count. You're my dream girl, my living fucking fantasy. You're the only goddamn thing my cock responds to. Up until last night when you rode me like a queen, the best orgasm of my life was in my office bathroom, picturing you on your knees, looking up at me through those cute little glasses and swallowing me down." My breath hitches as he plants a hot, wet kiss to my cheek, jaw, then neck. I shiver. Who would've thought that would turn me on so much? Why do I want to drop to my knees and beg him to make the fantasy a reality right now?

"Finish your breakfast, then we're going to the pool. If my intel is correct, Kira made sure you bought a bathing suit that would absolutely fucking ruin me, and I want to see you in it."

Dammit, I should've known those two were in cahoots. The only person that wanted James inside of me more than me is Kira. Speak of the devil...

Pussy Posse Group Chat

Kira: * video message *

Kira: Someone is going a little viral from my Saturday morning class. Georgie took a page out of Willa Ford's book because that girl wanted to be bad

Rachel: HOLY CRAP G. The way you whip your hair while you mouth the words, you're a freaking sex pistol.

Dottie: James looks like he wants to jump off of his bike and mount you in front of everyone

Kira: I told you the playlist would drive him nuts. You turned my studio into a softcore porno.

Dottie: Please tell me you finally gave that poor boy some relief?

Georgie: * smirk emoji * I think we both woke up feeling quite satisfied this morning

Kira: I'm officially adding pimp to my resume

James had called down and booked us a private cabana by the pool, which ended up not being necessary. The majority of the hotel guests

are attending the conference that we are so blatantly skipping, so the pool was empty, but it was nice either way. When we got down here, I took off my swim cover, and James fake passed out at the sight of me. It's a one piece, but it doesn't leave much more to the imagination than a bikini. It's a soft pink halter top that ties behind my neck with a deep v cut that goes all the way down to the top of my belly button. The sides are cut high on my hips, which makes the bottoms of my butt cheeks peek out, and my entire back is exposed.

"You make it impossible to keep my hands to myself," he said, brushing his knuckles along my sides. I told him he'd better behave himself, but I think I would've been perfectly fine if he'd stripped me bare and taken me right there in the open.

It's insane. I've always been a little insecure. I accepted a while back that I'm just a curvy girl. My stomach is always going to be soft. My face is always going to be round. My hips are always going to be full, finding jeans that fit will forever be impossible. Just because I accepted it, though, doesn't mean I don't worry about others accepting it.

Tom was my only real relationship, and even he was indifferent about my body at best. Sure, he loved my big boobs, but he'd make off handed comments about the snacks I ate or the days I skipped the campus gym. I really didn't think anything of it at the time. I had become highly skilled at letting men's opinions about my body roll off my back after growing up with my father.

James is the first person I've been with who seems to like my body unapologetically. I can see it in the way he looks at me. His eyes roam everywhere all at once, like he's trying to drink all of me in. I can feel it in the way he touches me. Last night, his hands and mouth were everywhere, not just my breasts and between my legs. It was like he couldn't get enough of me, like he was trying to memorize every single inch of my skin. I'd never felt so...cherished.

Of course, James looks fucking devastating in his black swim trunks. I swear, every time I see his bare chest, I have to hold myself back from licking each contour of his chiseled abs. We've spent the last two hours relaxing in these lovely lounge chairs that sit in the shallow end of pool so our bodies are partially in and out of the water. I've realized that James and I have that kind of comfortable silence that I've never experienced with anyone else before. We've talked, but mainly we've just laid here together, quietly reading and sunbathing, occasionally holding hands (and if I'm being honest, watching droplets of water and sweat drip down James's skin out of the corner of my eye).

"Mr. Alder, your fruit and charcuterie platters are ready in your cabana when you are, sir." Our personal server, Matthew, leans over, refilling our lemon waters. He was assigned to us with the cabana, and he's been a gem about keeping us hydrated. The only problem is that he keeps calling James 'Mr. Adler' despite his insistence that Matthew use his first name.

"Thanks Matthew. I think we'll head in there now." James helps me up and wraps a towel around me before leading me to the cabana, where Matthew explains all the different meats and cheeses arranged for us.

"Is there anything else I can get for either of you at the moment?" he asks, and I shake my head.

"This is great, Matthew. If you wouldn't mind drawing the curtains and giving us some privacy, that would be amazing." James smiles as he pops a piece of prosciutto in his mouth. I thought he'd pull a chair out for me, but he sits and yanks me into his lap instead.

"Of course, sir. The call button is right over here by the refrigerator if you need me." He closes the curtains and leaves us alone with our snacks in the shade.

"I hate to say it, but it feels good to be out of the sun," James says, spreading some soft blue cheese onto a piece of bread and handing it over to me. I've noticed that he does that whenever we're sharing foods. He's always giving me bites, like he's trying to make sure I'm eating. It's incredibly sweet.

"That's not very native Californian of you, Adler," I tease.

"Hey, I'm a San Franciscan first, Californian second. This body is built for 55 degree weather and June gloom, baby." He pats his stomach for emphasis and I can't help but laugh at the goof.

"I hear you. I do love me some Karl the Fog, although he wreaks havoc on my hair." He holds out a piece of watermelon to me, and instead of taking it in my hand, I lean forward and open my mouth, letting him place the fruit on my tongue. His eyes darken, and he strokes my jaw with his thumb as I chew.

"Georgie, what does your tattoo stand for?" I instinctively rub at the spot that's marred with ink.

"YOYOK? It stands for 'you're on your own kid'." I blush. Very few people have seen my tattoo.

"Like the Taylor Swift song?" he asks, and I shake my head.

"Funnily enough, I got this when I turned 18. It was something that my favorite, no bullshit lawyer told me when I was going through all of my crap. She wasn't exactly warm or kind, but when she said those words to me, 'you're on your own, kid,' it felt comforting. Like she saw something in me, like I could handle this life on my own. The fact that Taylor released her song is just the cherry on top."

We're quiet for a long time.

"I remember you, you know," he says, and I genuinely have no idea what he's talking about.

"Remember me?" I ask.

"Yeah. Your first day at Streamline isn't the first time I saw you."

"What do you mean?" This time he holds out a grape, and he lets out a low growl when I take it into my mouth. I make sure to swipe my tongue around his thumb as I take it.

"Last spring, at the AI symposium downtown. I spotted you coming out of one of the auditoriums with John Morello."

Morello...oh yeah. He was that guy from that company that was trying to overthrow ChatGPT. Pretty sure they've gone under since then.

"I was temping for him at the time," I say, still a bit confused.

"You were wearing that navy dress that I love so much, the one with the little bow on the front. It felt like my jaw dropped open and my tongue rolled out. I couldn't believe how stunning you were. I was frozen in place. I'd never seen anyone more beautiful in my entire life. You were holding an iPad, scrolling through it and talking as the two of you walked, so I know you didn't see me. But I saw you. Then you forgot your wallet when you were at the coffee cart."

"And you paid. I was running so late..."

No wonder I thought there was something familiar about him that first day. I was such a rude little shit, letting that kind stranger fix my mistake and running off without a passing glance. If I had taken the time to actually look at him, there's no way I would've forgotten. It's impossible to forget a face like James Adler's.

"Did you recognize me when I came into your office?" I asked softly.

"Immediately. It's part of the reason I shut down on you at first. I mean, imagine it. I walk into work, annoyed that I have a temp to train, and my mystery girl is standing in front of me, trying to shake my damn hand. I didn't know how to handle it."

"Your mystery girl?"

"Yeah, my mystery girl. I only had you for a moment, but shit, Georgie. I thought about you all the time. I was mesmerized by you. It took you all of two seconds to completely captivate me. When you offered to leave your bra as collateral for the coffee, that's when I knew I needed you. I spent every day for a year regretting not getting your name when I had the chance. Now I look at you, and I can't help but think how lucky I am. Like the universe brought you to me or something." He looks so shy and sincere as he says these beautiful things to me, it's overwhelming. I can't believe James saw me once and remembered me. Not only remembered me, but pined over me before he even knew who I was. We were there in the same city, working in the same industry- albeit very different positions- and I never saw him, never knew that this amazing man was holding a torch for me.

I stand from his lap and turn to face him. I drape my legs over either side of the chair as I straddle him.

"James Adler, you are the most incredible man I've met in my entire life." I lean in and kiss him, soft at first, but then deeper as our mouths open and our tongues dance together. He rocks underneath me, pressing his growing cock against my center, and I moan against his lips.

"Care to take this party back upstairs, sweet girl?" He nips and licks at my throat.

"No," I tell him, eliciting a surprised look. "There's something I want to do here first."

26

Georgie

I hate to admit it, but I'm not a sex goddess. Shocking, right? I can write a dirty, filthy piece of smut that would have porn stars curling their toes, but in real life? I don't have a lot of experience. One thing I do know? I've never been a fan of blow jobs. I haven't given many, and the ones I have were always out of obligation. My ex swiped me into the dining hall when I used up my meal plan for the week? He'd tell me I owe him head. He lent me his psych notes when I missed class with the flu? As soon as I could breathe through my nose again, I owed him head. I was on my period but he was hard?

Yeah, you get the gist. Not exactly what I'd describe as a fun time. But right now in this cabana, with the curtains drawn closed and James looking at me with fire in his eyes and with the knowledge that he's been pining over me for so long, I can think of nothing else but tasting him and making him come. I want him- *need him-* in my mouth, now.

I roll my hips against his hard length once more before I climb off of his lap. He goes to stand with me, but I push him back with a hand on his chest and drop to my knees in front of him.

"Georgia, what do you think you're doing?" he asks, and I shush him, pushing his thighs apart so I can fit in between them and pressing my mouth to his chest. His skin is hot on my lips, and I kiss him all over, from his pecs to his stomach. I even indulge myself and lick at a few of his abs. They're just as delicious as I imagined.

I look up and make eye contact while I run my hand over his erection through his shorts, and James groans as his head rolls back. He's rock solid hard.

"Georgie, you have to sto-unhhh- stop." He chokes around the word as I grip his cock over the fabric. "They can see our shadows." He gestures to the curtained walls of our enclosure, but the way his teeth sink into his bottom lip when I squeeze tells me he wants nothing to do with me stopping right now.

He knows as well as I do that we're the only people out here, and that Matthew won't be back unless we call for him, but I guess it's not 100% certain that we won't get caught. For a second, I'm ready to take him up on heading back to the suite, but then I have a realization. He got to see me, every inch of me completely naked and on display for him last night, and I barely got a peek at him.

Dammit. Now I'm jealous. This is happening.

"Well boss," I summon my best pornstar-y voice and yank down his trunks, "let's give them a show."

James's cock juts out, hard and heavy against his stomach. I could tell he was big when I was grinding against him last night, but seeing every inch in all of its glory is intimidating and invigorating. Its fucking beautiful. Can dicks be beautiful? Because this one is. It's long and thick, the head a shade of pink slightly darker than the skin of his shaft and already glistening with precum. Purple veins run up the length of him, just like on his bulging forearms. I drag my tongue along the thickest one from the base to tip, flicking my tongue on the underside of his head. James groans again. I look up at him and smile. He looks so sexy with his head rolled back and his mouth parted with heavy breaths.

I'm gonna take that as a good sign I think and take him into my mouth.

I honestly don't know if I'm very good at this, but I'm trying my best. I lick and suck and bob my head. I relax my throat and try to take him even further, but he's too damn big. I pump my hand around the base while I work my mouth, trying to bring him as much pleasure as I can. His breath is ragged and he hasn't asked me to stop, so that's encouraging. I swirl my tongue around his head, lapping up the salty precum that bubbles at the tip. His voice is so sexy when he moans.

"Fuck, Georgie. Look at those gorgeous red lips wrapped around me so pretty. You're perfect. So good, so fucking good."

God I love when he praises me like that. I can feel my own arousal pooling between my legs. I want to hear him make that sound again, so I repeat the motion with my tongue, and he hisses. I take him further into my mouth, my throat relaxing and allowing me to take him deeper.

"Baby, pull up. I'm getting close, you're gonna make me come."

Pfft. If he thinks that's doing to deter me, he's got another thing coming.

Instead, I moved my hand faster, pumping and twisting and looking up to catch his eyes with mine. I moan, "Yes, please."

Or I try to, at least. It comes out more like "yuun pluh". Give me a break, my mouth is full of cock.

"Fuck, sweet girl, you want that? You want me to spill down that throat? Feed you my cum right here?" He reaches down and cups my cheek as he asks. I nod, and he threads his fingers into my hair, tugging gently. He starts to move his body, helping me to take him even deeper.

I can't believe how incredibly hot it is, James pumping his hips, his cock twitching on my tongue as he fucks my mouth, the way the muscles on his stomach contract as his release builds. I'm so damn wet, I'm desperate to reach between my legs and touch myself, but I need to focus on him. I take my free hand and slide it up the inside of his thighs and cup his balls, squeezing ever so slightly.

I can feel it as every one of his muscles seizes underneath me. He calls out my name like a prayer as his hot cum starts to coat my tongue. It tastes like salt and musk and *him*, and I'm desperate to lap up every single ounce. He fills my mouth and I take it, trying to hold onto as much as I can, but rope after rope hits my throat, and I can't help but let some leak out of the corner of my mouth.

His cock is still twitching when he slowly pulls out from between my lips, cupping my jaw and stroking my bottom lip with his thumb.

"Show me," he demands, his voice still husky with arousal. I tilt my head back and meet his eyes, the proof of his orgasm filling my mouth as I open it for him. He moves his hand to my neck, wrapping his large palm around it and pressing lightly.

"Swallow." He gently works the muscles of my throat in his hand while I do as he says, savoring the taste of him as he slides down my throat. I lick at my lips, desperate for even a little more.

"Georgia," he squeezes again, harder this time as his eyes grow dark. "Sweet girl, you are in so much fucking trouble."

Why do I love the sound of that so much?

He's quiet as he stands and tucks himself away. I stay on my knees and watch as he silently begins to gather our things. Once he's gotten everything tucked into my tote bag and has thrown down a few bills as a tip for Matthew, he holds his hand out to me. I follow in step behind him back into the hotel. He doesn't say a single word to me the entire way back to the room, but the air is heady. In the elevator, he pulled me against him and gave my ass one long, slow grind with his already hardened erection.

He swipes the key to the room and follows behind me into the space. As the door shuts, he pulls at the tie around my neck. The front of my bathing suit falls, baring my breasts. He pushes the material over my hips, and I step out of it as it hits the floor.

"Don't move," he whispers. He walks towards the closet where his suits are hanging and searches for a moment. He returns with a single black necktie, one I've seen him wear a thousand times. I poke my tongue out and lick my lips.

"Do you trust me, Georgie?" My stomach flutters with anticipation. He wants to tie me up with that, doesn't he? I think that could be okay. I don't know about more though. I don't think I can handle any true BDSM kind of stuff. I open my mouth to answer, but he must sense the hesitation on my face because he continues.

"I'm not going to do anything to hurt you, Georgie. Not one single thing. I just want to play with you. I want you to hand over a little control to me. I want to see how much pleasure I can build up in this body of yours. I want to see how long you can hold on to the edge before I finally let you dip over into bliss. Does that sound like something you want to try?"

I clench my thighs together. How could I say no to that? I bite my lip and nod.

"That's my good girl. Come lay down. Put your hands over your head."

I get into the bed and lay on my back, reaching my arms up over my head like he told me to. He crawls over me, one knee resting on either side of my stomach.

"I still want you to have a safe word. If you want me to stop, just say mango. You got that?" I giggle, imagining the absurdity of someone saying such a silly word during sex. I guess that's sort of the point, though.

"Mango, got it." He gives me a nod of approval and gets to work. I stare up at him as he twists the tie in a knot around my wrist and pulls it. It's tight, but not too tight.

"Pull your wrists apart like this," he says, demonstrating a scissoring motion with his own hands. I do as he says, and the knot holding my wrists together falls apart.

"That's how easy it is to get out of this if you need to. If you hate it or change your mind at anytime, use your safe word and pull your wrists apart like that, understand?"

"I understand," I breathe. Arousal pools between my legs. I don't want to get out of it. I want to experience everything he's going to give me. He ties my wrists back into a knot before leaning down and kissing my forehead.

"Are you ready to let go, Georgia?"

27

James

⌒

"Fuck, James, please! I can't. James!" My poor girl is drenched in sweat, thrashing against her restraints, cunt leaking all over the mattress underneath her. I grip my cock, allowing myself two hard strokes while I savor the sight of her so uninhibited before me. She's almost ready.

"What do you need Georgie?" I ask her, as if I don't know the fucking answer.

"Pleeeeease!" she whines, wiggling under the weight of my palm on her stomach.

"You're so pretty when you beg for me, but only good, patient girls get whatever their greedy pussies want. So use your words and tell me what you need."

"God, James, I need to come. Please, please let me come," she cries. I lean down and croon into her ear.

"That's my good girl." I draw light circles on her inner thighs with my fingertips, high enough to tease her but nowhere close to where she needs them. She tries to clamp her thighs together, *again*, but just like every other time, I shove my hand between them and force her back open for me.

"You're all done, baby. You've done so well. Such a good little girl for me. I'm going to put my tongue back on your cunt, and when I do, you have my permission to come whenever you're ready."

She chokes out a sob, eyes snapped shut, her cheeks stained with tears and wrists bound above her head with one of my ties. Poor thing, I've been edging her for over an hour, touching and teasing her with my fingers, my mouth and the head of my cock. I brought her to the brink of orgasm countless times, pulling it away right before she tips over the edge. She needed a little punishment for the way she dropped to her knees for me by the pool.

Don't get me wrong, I fucking loved it, but that doesn't mean I didn't want to torture her a bit.

I fall back between her legs and spread her wide, pressing my tongue long and flat against her abused clit. We barely make contact before she's coming on my face with a throaty gasp. I can feel her orgasm dripping out of her and further soaking the sheets underneath us. I hold her legs to keep her as still as possible as I lick her through it, delighting in her taste – honey and salt and uniquely Georgie. Even so, she thrashes and screams above me. I hum through her violent convulsions, slowing my movements as her own body comes down.

When she finally calms, I lift myself back on top of her and kiss a tear off of her cheek while I undo my tie from her wrists.

"You did such a good job, sweet girl. How do you feel?"

Her voice is shaky, still recovering from what she just went through. "I feel like, like I still need to come."

Fuck yes, right where I want her. That first one was to take the edge off, the next one is to rock her world.

"Such a perfect girl for me."

I lower my hips, rocking my hard cock against her soft belly. "Are you on birth control, Georgia?"

"IUD." She nods, licking her sweet lips.

"Shit. I haven't been with anyone for over a year, and I've been tested." I tell her. It's the truth. I haven't wanted to look at anyone else since the moment I laid eyes on Georgia.

"I've been tested too. I'm clear." Sexy little thing is still working to catch her breath.

"Good, cause I need to feel you. Need to fuck you bare, sweet girl. I need to feel every pulse of this soaking tight cunt as it cries for me. Can I do that, Georgie? Will you please let me fuck you?"

"Yes, please, James. Fuck me. Nothing between us." She wraps her arms around my neck and I groan, pushing the tip of my cock to her entrance.

Jesus. Fuck.

Even after the orgasm, even with how wet she is from the last hour, she's still so fucking tight. I can barely work myself in, and she hisses with every movement. I go slowly, barely penetrating her blazing hot hole, trying my fucking best to be careful with her. Georgie, on the other hand, is whining, arching her back, pushing back on me, aching and needy.

"James, please, I need you."

"I don't want to hurt you," I grit out.

"You can't. Just do it."

Fuck.

"Take a deep breath," I murmur, and when her chest rises, I slam home. She yelps, then moans, and I whisper little praises to her.

"I know, sweet girl, I know. It's okay, I've got you."

I'm overcome by the sensation of her warm cunt wrapped around me. I know she's not a virgin, but her pussy is gripped so fucking tight around my cock, she might as well be. Deep inside of her, I move my hips in the smallest circle, gently rocking, trying to stretch her out and get her used to me.

If I'm being honest, I'm trying not to fucking come inside of her already.

"James," she breathes, sounding desperate. "More, please. I need more."

"Aww baby, does my filthy girl need to get fucked a little harder?" I kiss her cheek, her jaw, any place I can get my lips on.

"Please, James, hard. Oh god, please fucking pound me."

Well shit, who am I to deny my girl?

I pull almost all the way out, then slam back in, eliciting a delicious scream from her. I do it again, fucking into her over and over as she cries out. I find a perfect, punishing pace and look down at her as I slide in and out of her. Her round tits bounce beautifully with each stroke, her body shakes under my weight, and she's so fucking beautiful, I can barely stand to look. I don't deserve to. I've had plenty of sex in my life, but nothing compares to this feeling right now, the way our bodies fit together. It feels like she can anticipate my every need. Georgie was fucking made for me. I can't tear my eyes away from the spot where I'm sliding into her.

"Fuck, look at that. Look at how well you're taking me, baby. So pretty the way your pussy opens up for me. Swallowing me whole like a good fucking girl."

One of her hands leaves my neck and slides down her body to rub herself, but I swat it away. I appreciate the effort, but I need to be in control of her pleasure. I lift one of her legs over my shoulder and lean in, angling our bodies so that her clit rubs against me as I thrust into her.

"You feel that, baby? My cock deep in your cunt, fucking you so good? We were made for each other. You're mine Georgie. Your body, your pleasure, your heart, it's all fucking mine. Say it."

"I'm so close."

"Who. Do. You. Belong. To?" I force out between thrusts.

"YOU! Oh god, James, I'm yours!"

I push myself as far into her as I can, grinding my pelvis into her clit at an angle that has me pushing against her inner walls with my cock. Her mouth drops open in a silent scream, and I feel her orgasm shatter through her. Her cunt is gripping me so fucking hard, it would be painful if pleasure wasn't coursing through me. I thrust into her convulsing body once, twice, before I follow her over the edge. Every nerve in my body fires and my cock throbs with pleasure as I empty my balls into her sweet, beautiful body. She's shaking, I'm shaking, we're pulsing together. I'm still inside of her as I lay my head on her chest, basking in the sound of her beating heart as I try to catch my breath.

I hear Georgie sniffle, and my stomach drops. I slowly slide out of her and take her face in my hands. Shit. She's fucking crying.

"Hey, what happened, sweetheart? Did I hurt you?" Fuck, I hope I didn't trigger her. She was asking for more but maybe I took it too far. If I hurt her, I'll never be able to forgive myself.

She squeezes her eyes shut and shivers, shaking her head. Shit shit shit.

"No! I'm just overwhelmed. Happy. Feels too good." I let out a sigh of relief and kiss the tear running down her cheek, grateful to continue basking in this afterglow with her.

"Will you hold me?" she whines. I roll over and pull her to my chest, snuggling her into me.

"Forever, sweet girl."

28

Georgie

I floated in an out of consciousness for a long time, basking in the glow of what we had just done and the smell of James's skin. After a while, he carried me into the shower, where he gently washed my hair and body, caressing me in a way that felt sensual but not sexual before cleaning himself off.

Earlier we had discussed maybe trying an Italian restaurant near the hotel, but my body was too wrecked with exhaustion to leave the room. Instead, he put me in one of his t-shirts and ordered in sushi. I think eating in bed with James is my new favorite activity. He was telling me about Amy and Jenn and how they wanted to bring their daughter, Riley, into the office sometime soon to meet everyone.

"That sounds nice. Baby's first nine to five. Better to learn the corporate drudgery young."

"Streamline's not that boring, is it?" he asks, stealing a piece of spicy salmon roll from the container on my lap.

"It's not exactly Disneyland, dear," I tease.

"Wear that damn navy dress again and I'll bring you into my office and show you just how not boring it can be." I yelp when he bites my earlobe. "You're not wrong. I'm getting pretty tired of the corporate drudgery myself. Seriously though, I'm excited for you to meet my sisters. I know they're gonna love you."

And there it is, the invitation for me to ask the question I've been avoiding. We've been in this bubble where we kiss and hold hands and fuck for days, but I still don't know what's going on. I really don't want to be the "what are we" girl, but I think I need to know before we get home.

"Can I ask you a question?" He holds out a piece of his shrimp tempura roll between chopsticks and I take it into my mouth.

"What's up?"

I take my time chewing, trying to work up the nerve.

"Last night, after...you said something about me being your best friend. Is that...are we just friends?"

When he doesn't answer, I peel my eyes away from my lap and find his face. It's unreadable.

"Does this feel like we're just friends?" I open my mouth, but he doesn't give me the chance to answer.

"You're worried about what I said last night, but what about what I said earlier? Because both statements are true. You are my friend, Georgie, and I'm thankful for that. But you're so, so much more. I want all of the titles. I want to be your best friend, your lover, your boyfriend, your rock. I want to be the place where you feel safe, the place where you lay your head at night. You're mine," He takes my hand and presses it to his chest. "And I want to be yours. Because this right here? My heart? It belongs to you. It has for a long fucking time, Georgia. You got it?"

I nod, and he squeezes. "Need to hear you say it, sweet girl."

"I'm your girl. You're mine, I'm yours." The smile growing on his face is infectious.

"Damn right."

Is it possible to die from too many orgasms? If so, I better start counting my days. We spent the entirety of last night intertwined with each other, whether James was inside of me or just wrapped around me. Seriously, the man is the biggest snuggle bug I've ever met. He barely let me out of his reach to pee. And then just a few hours ago on the plane, he sat me in his favorite seat and spread me open, worshipping me with his tongue and his fingers. My thighs are red and sore from the burn of his beard, but I've never felt so amazing in my life.

I brought James up to my apartment for the first time earlier so that I could pack a bag to bring to his place, and even though I was nervous to let him see my space, it was endlessly entertaining to see my roommates fangirl over the CEO like he was Chris Evans and I finally figured out who's who when they introduced themselves. It was also hilarious seeing his 6 foot 6 frame trying to fit on my full sized bed as I gathered my things.

Now, we're sitting in Amir's apartment, which I didn't realize was right below James's place. He invited us and Catherine over for dinner, where he made a delicious chicken biryani. I couldn't get enough, I went back for seconds and then thirds, and now I'm fully stuffed.

I was nervous when James told me we were invited for dinner. I know that he had talked to the two of them about his feelings for me before, and that he had told them we were together, but I was still worried that things would feel different. I'd spent time with them as James's assistant, a coworker, acquaintance, but what would it be like joining the group as his girlfriend?

As it turns out, it's really freaking amazing. Besides a few "took you long enough"s thrown our way, Catherine and Amir welcomed me right into the group, as if I was supposed to be there all along. I loved hearing them laugh and tell stories about their college days and their first office space with the beetle infestation, and I told them about a certain CFO I briefly temped for last year who requested I wear a Girl Scout's vest around the office.

"So I heard from Ronan York that you two skipped his seminar on scope creep." Catherine lounged on the oversized loveseat across from us. She's in a pair of black joggers and cropped white t-shirt, so different from the sleek designer clothes I'm used to seeing her in at the office, but still so her. Amir's living room space is smaller than James's, but the minimal decor makes it feel much bigger. Am had told me once that he finds too much stuff in a room overstimulating, so I wasn't surprised to see the clean lines and simple black and white color scheme.

"We absolutely did." James topped off her scotch before cuddling back next to me on the couch. She pulled an ice cube out of her glass and tossed it at him, nailing him in the head.

"Why the hell would you do that?"

"Because he's boring as shit and I had my dream girl lying in my bed." He might as well throw her a "duh-doy" with all the attitude he packed into that sentence.

"You realize this means I'm going to have to make an appearance at his fucking executive dinner this month, right?" she whines, and James just laughs.

Amir comes in from the kitchen holding a plate of what looks like fancy donut bites.

"Ready for dessert?" I'm still completely full from dinner, but James looks ready to jump out of his skin to get his hands on whatever those things are.

"Did you make them, or did Maira?" Catherine asks, picking one of the dough balls off the plate and biting into it.

"You know I don't make gulab juman. Mama dropped them off this morning." James grabs two of the cake balls and holds one out to me.

"You have to try this. It'll ruin dessert for you for the rest of your life." I let him feed me a bite, and oh. My. God. The dough was fried with a crispy coating and soft center. It tastes like it was soaked in sugar and rose water, like an upscale glazed donut on steroids. I barely finish my first bite before I'm grabbing the other half and inhaling it.

"Holy shit," I say with a full mouth "Amir, will your mama marry me?" The room laughs, and despite my full stomach, I went back for another.

"God, I don't think I've eaten so much in my life. Amir is an amazing cook," I say later, laying in James's bed and stroking Lucifer's head. I watch as he undresses, relishing in every movement of his muscles as he pulls his shirt over his head and tosses it to his hamper.

"His mom is even better. I'll have to take you to her place next time we visit." I know from their stories that Amir's mother has been like a surrogate parent for James since their first day of college, so the idea of meeting her sends butterflies fluttering in my stomach. James turns off the lights and climbs into the bed. He shoos Lucifer off of my lap and pulls me into him.

"I hate how much my asshole cat likes you more than me, but I love having you here," he says softly before pressing his lips against mine. It's a soft, slow kiss, the stark opposite of some of the needy and frantic ones we've shared over the last few days. We melt into it, our tongues dancing and teasing against each other. I moan against his mouth, and he rolls on top of me, pulling the t-shirt that I stole from him over my head. The cool silk of his sheets add an intense tingling on my spine that has my body shaking with need. I pull at his briefs and he pushes them down as wrap my legs around his waist. His cock finds my slick entrance and he slides in, the two of us coming together as one, the way we were meant to be. He kisses me deeply as he rocks inside of me, his hands wandering from my hips to my breasts to my hair. It's slow and tender, but still so damn good. It feels crazy to think this but somehow we've already hit a point between us where we're not just fucking. We're making love.

His entire body is pressed against mine, chest to chest and a tangle of limbs. My hands float to his hair where I run the silky strands through my fingers. He groans against my mouth. The weight of him on top of me is intoxicating. The way his body covers mine completely gives me this insane feeling of being caged in, but in a way where I never want to get out. I'm so close, teetering on the edge of euphoria. I fight between wanting to hang on to the moment forever and give in to the orgasm cresting in my body. I tilt my hips just a bit to meet his so that he can hit me right where I want him to. I cry out when I come and he follows me over the edge, filling me and making me feel whole. We fall asleep wrapped up in each other, and I dream of blue eyes, sandalwood cologne, and koala bear cuddles.

It's been three glorious weeks since we've been back from LA, and I can hardly believe how happy I've felt. I've barely been back to my apartment except to grab some clothes (our matching outfits have gotten more obnoxious now that we dress together) and my external hard drive. James was kind enough to take a copy of both Ryan and Ashley's resumes as they gawked over him, but not before perving out in my room and trying to figure out which one was *the* pillow.

During the day, James and I work, eat lunch, and take as many meetings as we can from his office, where I've pretty much moved all of my work gear into. No one in the office seems to care that James and I are together, and if they do, I haven't heard any gossip about it. We keep it professional, but he's not shy about holding my hand as we enter and leave each day, not to mention the framed photostrip with our first kiss that now lives on his desk.

At night, James either takes me out to dinner or cooks for me at his place. I prefer it when we stay in because I get to take my pants off and drink wine on the counter while I watch him chop and sauté. I was shocked at how amazing he is in the kitchen, considering my signature dish is the microwavable butter chicken from Trader Joe's. I think I've gained about five pounds from all the carbonara and homemade bread. He definitely doesn't seem to mind though, because every night his hands roam my body, loving it over and over until we're nothing but two breathless, sweaty souls clinging to each other to tether ourselves to earth. I don't mind it either. My belly is still soft, but thanks to Kira and her spin classes, my legs and ass have never looked better.

"Do you own stock in lint rollers or something, Adler?" I ask him as he rolls the sticky paper over himself for the fourth time this morning. James, Amir and I are walking to their cars in the garage. James is going to pick up his sisters and niece in Sausalito, so I'm riding to work in Amir's cherry red McLaren. I'm not much of a car girl, but I gotta admit, that thing is sexy.

"Spend a few more nights rolling around on Lucifer's napping grounds and you'll see how invasive his fur is, just you wait." He leans down and kisses my cheek before helping me into the super low sports car. "Take care of my girl, man." Amir waves him off and starts the car.

"I didn't realize you two lived in the same building until the dinner you hosted. Why don't you just drive to work together?" I ask.

"James says I drive like an asshole, but really he drives like my dead grandma." He spots me looking around for an 'oh shit' handle to grab onto as he throws the car in reverse. "Don't worry, he gave me an intense lecture about keeping his precious cargo safe. I'll take it easy on you."

It turns out, 'taking it easy' doesn't really exist in a car like this. When I first felt the rev of the engine in the garage, I thought I'd be scared, but whipping up and down the steep hills of the city was actually quite thrilling, especially with the 2000's emo music playing through his speakers. It was like being on a roller coaster, but so much sexier. I can see how Amir gets so much booty driving a car like this.

I have no idea how Amir gets his long legs in and out of this contraption so gracefully. He helps me basically crawl out of the car and we head over to Espresso Yourself.

"I can do this myself, Am. I know you hate the smell. I'm fine if you wait in the car." I nudge his shoulder.

"No, I'm coming with you. I'm glad we got some alone time this morning. I actually wanted to talk to you about something." He slows his pace down, and I follow.

"Are you going to give me the 'don't hurt my friend' big brother speech?" I tease, and he laughs.

"Forget that asshole. If you two break up, I get custody of you." I lean and give him a side hug and he awkwardly pats at my back. I love this guy.

"No actually, I was talking to a friend I used to hook up with back at Stanford this week, Stacey. She's a literary agent in the city..." I stop walking, and he trails off. "Please don't be mad, but I sent her your manuscript."

I blink, once, twice.

"Why would you do that?" I ask dryly.

"Because you're fucking talented and you deserve to be a published author. She loved it, she wants to meet with you." He shrugs. I close my eyes. I don't want to be mad at him but...

"Amir, I appreciate it, but I'm not ready to put my work out there yet, and I especially don't want to get a job because I know a guy who knows a guy."

"Georgie, I'm going to be blunt with you. You're holding yourself back. I know you know that, but I don't think anyone has had the balls to tell you. You're talented. You have a solid backlog of work. You're ready for the next step, so stop fucking telling yourself that you're not." I nearly jump out of my skin when Amir takes my hand in his, the affection so out of character for him. "And one more thing. There's nothing wrong with networking, making connections, using your resources. And Stacey is a true professional. She wouldn't take a meeting with you just because I asked. She wants to meet you because she sees the raw talent that I see in you. I'm not going to tell you what to do, but she will be emailing you soon, and I think you should answer her."

I nod, and we're quiet as he opens the door to the coffee shop, trailing in after me. Rachel greets us with a big smile.

"Hey you guys! Amir, I didn't know you'd be here this morning. Want me to whip together your usual? Nonfat caramel macchiato?" she asks, and my eyes find Amir's in confusion. His are wide, and he gives me a silent plea that I take as *please don't say anything*.

"That'd be great little one, thank you."

Little one?

I catch him nervously tapping his fingertips together. We manage to make it outside before the question that's been burning inside rolls off my tongue.

"Amir, I thought you hated coffee..." I let my words trail off as he grips the cup Rachel prepared for him so tight, I'm surprised it's not exploding in his hand. His cheeks turn an adorable shade of red.

"I really fucking do," he answers, not looking at me. I don't question him further, but I do poke his arm.

"That little woman tried to guess my favorite drink the first time I came in here. She wouldn't let it go. I didn't want to get into it with her, so I just pointed to something random on the menu, a nonfat caramel macchiato. Now, when she makes them for me, she smiles the whole time." His lips curl up at the corners, an almost smile.

"Please, don't say anything to her." I can hear the pain of his unrequited crush in the crack of his voice, and my heart aches for him.

"Am, your secrets are always safe with me."

I've had this strange sensation brewing in the back of my mind for weeks, and I'm finally coming to the realization of what it is. I *thought* it was James and our magnetic pull to each other, and that's definitely part of it, but it's not just that. It's everything. So much has changed since I started this job. A few months ago, I was a loner, floating from job to job, avoiding making connections and living in my bubble of solitude.

All of a sudden, I have friends, a tribe. I have a group of people who care about me, believe in me. Shit, I have people who *like* me. I've never, ever had that before. I know it's partly my own fault. I've kept myself so fucking guarded for the last decade, and without even realizing it, I let these people under my skin.

It feels...right. And on top if it all, I have a gorgeous man that I'm falling in-

Nope. Stop. Way too soon for that.

Still, my cheeks flush and butterflies lose their shit in my stomach. Fuck.

I can keep it a secret from everyone else, but I need to admit it to myself.

I'm falling in love with James Adler.

29

James

I roar with laughter as Amy's face goes red as a tomato. I worked it out so that when we got off the elevator, Catherine would hit play on the Bluetooth speakers and Elton John's 'The Bitch Is Back' would blare through the office. Thankfully baby Riley was already awake in her stroller, because the plan went off without a hitch. Amy gives me a light smack upside the head before running into Catherine's waiting arms.

I push Riley back and forth in the stroller as my sisters ooh and ahh with their friends here in the office. I want to take her right back to Georgie, but I feel like she should meet Jenn and Amy before she meets their kid, and besides, she looks like she's really into whatever she's doing at her desk. She told me this morning that she wasn't nervous, but I caught the lie in her voice. She has no reason to be, I already know my sisters are going to adore her, but meeting the family is apparently a big deal. I wouldn't know. I've never had to do it before. Catherine takes Riley out of her stroller, and I pull my phone out of my pocket to check in.

James: Are you hiding from us, Georgia?

Georgie: Kinda. I want them to have time with their friends and stuff. They'll work their way back to me.

James: You're nervous, aren't you?

Georgie: Absolutely scared shitless.

I laugh at loud and look over to my girl, who's smiling sheepishly back at me. I give her a wink and stand back as my sisters continue their conversations and everyone fawns over the baby.

Finally, Jenn speaks up.

"Where's the girl, James?"

"*The girl's* name is Georgie, and she's back at Amy's desk. C'mon." Amy takes Riley from Catherine's arms and follows us back towards my office. Georgie stands when she sees us and reaches her hand out for a greeting, but Amy cuts her off.

"Well, well, well. If it isn't the girl that's trying to steal my job," she says with a sneer, and Georgie's face immediately falls, going white as a ghost. She's fucking lucky she's holding my niece right now.

"AMY!" both Jenn and I yell, me a little angrier.

"Geeeeez, I was kidding. Georgie knows I was kidding, don't you?" Poor Georgie just sort of shrugs, mouth slightly agape.

"No, she doesn't, because Georgie isn't a raging bitch like you."

"Children, stop it!" Jenn cuts into our argument. "Georgie, please excuse my wife. She really was kidding, she just doesn't think before she speaks. I'm Jenn, my rude wife is Amy, and this is our little girl, Riley." I watch Georgie's shoulders visibly relax, and it does a little to tamp down the anger I'm feeling towards my sister-in-law.

"It's lovely to meet you, I've heard so much about all of you." She sticks her hand back out for a shake, but Jenn grabs it and pulls her into a hug instead. Amy moves in next, offering her a one-armed, three way hug with her and Riley.

"We've heard nothing but amazing, wonderful, school-boy-with-a-crush level gushing things about you too, honey." Georgie giggles and I wipe a hand over my reddening face. "Getting under James's skin is my favorite pastime, sorry you got caught in the crosshairs."

"Oh it's fine. I think annoying him is my favorite part of this job." She pokes my side, and I can't help but love the way that tiny, intimate touch feels.

"If I had known you were all going to gang up on me-"

"You definitely knew we were all going to gang up on you," Amy interjects.

"-then I never would've let you back in the building," I continue, ignoring her. "Now come on ladies, we've got a lot to go over." Besides just visiting, Catherine, Am and I are taking today to catch up the new moms on some of the goings on while Amy's been out. As shareholders, they like to stay invested in the company's activities.

"Do you need me to take notes?" Georgie asks, picking up her iPad.

"That's ok, we're mainly going over all the notes you've taken in the past few months. Actually, if you want to take the morning off, maybe get some writing in, that would be fine." Just then, Riley starts to fuss in Amy's arms.

"Are you gonna be a little crybaby while mommies are trying to work?" she croons, then rolls her eyes. "She's gonna be a little shit all morning. She didn't sleep well last night."

"I can take her while you guys meet, if that's okay?" Georgie offers, and my sisters look to each other. "I love kids. I babysat two girls in my neighborhood so often the people in town thought I was their mother."

"Are you sure?" Jenn asks. "She really is going to be fussy."

"No problem! If I really need you, I'll knock."

Amy hands her the baby and they give her a quick rundown of the diaper bag and other things she needs to know, and we set up in my office.

Jenn asks a question about the communication platform right off the bat, but my eyes are fixated on the woman outside of my window.

Georgie is standing at her desk, rocking Riley as she fusses. I can see her mouth move as she coos at the tiny human in her arms. I can see her hips sway as she tries to soothe the fussy girl. Riley takes one of Georgie's fingers into her mouth and starts to gum on it, the same way she did to me when I pulled her out of her crib this morning, and a flutter rises in my stomach as my heart skips a beat.

Seeing Georgie with my niece, how gentle and warm and loving she is, how fucking beautiful she looks with a baby in her arms, everything I've been holding back from admitting is playing out right in front of me. I want one of those with her. I want to watch her body grow and swell with our child. I want to wake up in the middle of the night and tend to a screaming newborn while I let her sleep. I want to coach soccer with her on the weekends. I want the whole damn thing.

"Did you hear me, dude?" Amir asks, waving a hand in front of my face.

"No. Can someone shut the blinds?"

"Are you okay?" Jenn asks, and I shake my head.

"No, I'm not. Can you please shut the blinds so I can focus?" The room turns and sees what I see, sweet Georgie perched on the corner of her desk singing to Riley. Amir gets up and shuts the blinds for me, while my sisters and Catherine give me a knowing look. A look that confirms that they know what I know.

I'm so fucking in love with Georgia Hansley.

A few hours later with the boring shit behind us, I convince Catherine, Amir, Georgie and my sisters to blow off the rest of the day and walk to the Ferry Building for lunch. Jenn insisted on sitting outside on the back patio, even though no-sky July is in full bloom and fog has overtaken the bay. We settle on a seafood restaurant, where the six of us split various kinds of oysters, mussels, and a few bottles of Sauvignon Blanc.

"I can't believe I've never had an oyster before!" Georgie exclaims, slurping back a grilled Mezcal variety. I gotta say, I'm starting to see why these things are an aphrodisiac. Watching her throat work as she swallows down the little shellfish has my blood heating.

"So what's the plan for when your contract ends, Georgie?" Amy asks, topping off her wine glass. I gagged earlier when she squeezed her chest and told the group today was a pump and dump kinda day. "James says you're a writer? Do you want to do that full time or are you going to look for another temp assignment?"

It's weird. I knew Georgie was only a temp, I spent all morning going over shit with Amy about her return to office plan, but I never actually thought about her leaving. Part of my heart starts to ache at not seeing her in her cute little office clothes through my window every day, and the other part is just thankful I managed to lock down a relationship.

"Actually, Amir was kind enough to hook me up with a literary agent, and I have a meeting with her in a few days. Nothing is set in stone yet though, and since I'm not making any money writing, I'll be taking on another assignment." She sighs. "I feel like I need to look for a place outside of the city though. My shithead landlord raised my rent again and it's just not worth it."

I lower the shell in my hand. My palms start to sweat. I pull at my collar, trying to get more air into my lungs. A place outside of the city? She won't be my assistant anymore AND she's leaving San Francisco? And what's this about a literary agent? I mean, that's good, right? She wants to write? But what if she has to move- do writers have to move close to their publishers? Fuck, I'm freaking out. I wipe my palms on the top of my thighs and try to gain some composure. She could move in with me! I want her to, I need to go to bed with her every night and wake up next to her every morning. She's spent every night with me for weeks. But is it too soon? Does she feel as strongly for me as I do for her? If she's not in the city, does that technically make us long distance? Can she handle that? I know I fucking can't.

The composure never comes. I stand quickly and trip over my words.

"I have to, uhm. I gotta take a leak, I'll be right back." I feel Georgie brush her fingertips against my hand as I walk away, and the light touch fuels my panic. I enter the building and look for a bathroom but I have to stop and brace myself. I yank at my tie, loosening it and take a deep breath. I try to calm myself, but I can't.

She's leaving me...she's leaving me...

I feel a touch on my shoulder, and I turn. My older sister grabs me by the hand and leads me into a single stall restroom. Shit, we probably look like a couple of freaks trying to sneak in a quickie, but I don't care. She shuts the bathroom door and grabs a paper towel, wetting it with cool water before blotting my face. I can see her chest rise and fall as she takes deep breaths, and I work to match my own breath with hers. It's something she used to do when we were kids and I'd cry over something. I hated being coddled, but Jenn could always calm me down just by breathing with me.

"Talk, James," she says after a few minutes, after my heartbeat slowed to a normal pace.

"I love her, Jenn." I keep my eyes fixed on my shoes as I say the words out loud for the first time.

"I know, honey. Does that scare you?" she asks, squeezing the hand that's still in hers.

"I...fuck. She's gonna leave me, Jenn. She's getting a new job, she's moving, and I'm not enough for her. I'm not fucking good enough for her and she's going to see that and she's going to leave me like everyone else."

Jenn pulls me into a tight hug. In her heels, she's only a few inches shorter than me. I rest my head on top of hers and let the tears start to fall.

"James, sweetie. She's leaving the *job*, she's not leaving you. That girl loves you, too. I could see it the second she saw you walk into the room.

She lit up like a damn Christmas tree. Georgie only has eyes for you. She's not going anywhere." I swallow a sob.

"Everyone leaves me, Jenn. If I lose her...fuck. I won't be able to take it."

Jenn pushes away and pulls my gaze to hers.

"Everyone does not leave you, James. I'm here, Amir and Catherine are here, Amy is here, and Georgie will be here, too. I know it, I can feel it in my soul. She's it for you. Don't you dare let what *that woman* did to us keep you from being happy." I snap my eyes shut and will the tears to stop. "Amy found her on purpose, you know. She tracked down Morello and got the name of the temp agency he used. It was dumb luck that she was free for a new contract right when our maternity leave started, but she found her for you. She thought- we both thought that maybe if you found your mystery girl, the one woman you hadn't been able to get out of your head, maybe you'd open yourself to the possibility of more. If not with her, then with someone."

I stare down at my older sister, trying to wrap my brain around what she just said. I thought it was a fluke, Georgie showing up in my office all those weeks ago, but it wasn't. It wasn't divine intervention, it was sister intervention. Amy brought Georgie to me, delivered her to me on a silver fucking platter.

Damn. I'm gonna have to get her something really good for her birthday this year.

"Do me a favor. Take out your phone and call Dr. Patel's office right now. Get the soonest appointment you can, and after you talk to him, talk to Georgie. Don't hold this in, James. There's no reason for you to go at this alone. And Georgie deserves to know where you are. She can help you through it, I know she can." I nod and do as she says, making an appointment for 4:30 tonight. I let Jenn leave the bathroom first, splashing cold water on my face and shaking out the nerves.

I run into the adjacent bookstore and pick up a cute looking novel with a cartoon cover. I know from Amir that usually means they're smutty, and I use picking up the book as a surprise gift for Georgie as my cover for being gone so long. She kisses me on the cheek when I give it to her and I wrap my arm around her, pulling her close. Internally, I'm still freaking out, but Georgie in my arms calms me like a weighted blanket in a dark room.

I love her. I can get better for her. I can do this.

30

Georgie

Something changed this afternoon. I don't know if it was something I said, or maybe something with his sisters, but James was weird after lunch. He told me he had a therapy session that slipped his mind, but that I could hang out at his place and wait for him if I wanted to. I considered asking Kira and Rachel to meet me for a drink, but something about James's demeanor this afternoon has me yearning to stay close. As soon as he left, I slipped out of my clothes and into one of his t-shirts, not bothering with pants.

It's a quarter to six and I'm curled up on the couch with Lucifer in my lap, a glass of a fancy looking white wine in one hand and the paperback James picked out for me in the other. It was a nice gesture, made even nicer by the fact that the two women holding hands on the cover make it clear that it's a queer romance. I really love that James accepts my sexuality for what it is and has never made any gross threesome comments. There was no dramatic coming out. I just mentioned it and we moved on.

The glow of the setting sun casts the room in shades of pink and gold, and Lucifer's purrs on my lap threaten to lull me to sleep, but I can't seem to relax. Things felt so up in the air earlier, and I'm nervous about how James is going to act when he gets back.

My stomach rumbles, and I'm wondering if I should order a pizza or wait for James when I hear him open the door. The apartment is quiet, so I can hear the shrug of his jacket off of his shoulders, the click of his heels in the kitchen, and the clang of glasses as he pours what I'm sure is two or three fingers of his favorite scotch. It's a moment before he calls out my name.

"In the living room!" I call back, and I'm both relieved and worried when he joins me on the couch. He looks pale, somehow paler than he did earlier today. His tie is pulled slack and his eyes are red and swollen, like he had been crying. I put down my book and glass and turn to him.

"James, what happened?" I reach out to stroke his cheek, but he grabs my hand and pulls me into his lap instead. He nuzzles against my neck as I wrap my arms around his.

"Just a tough session. Did you eat? I could go for a pizza right now." I tell him I was thinking the same thing and he pulls his phone from his pocket, handing it to me. I pull up the UberEats app and place an order- large well-done pepperoni with extra cheese. James is still cuddled into me, and I can feel the tell tale wet slide of a tear on my skin.

"Sweetheart, do you want to talk about it?" I stroke my fingers through his hair, aching to soothe him.

"No," he sniffs. "We will, but not now. Can I please just hold you?"

"Of course," I tell him, and we stay wrapped around each other until the building concierge brings our food to the door.

We eat on the couch in silence. It's killing me not knowing what's going on in James's head, but there is no way I'm going to push him. I've had my fair share of therapy in my day, and I always needed at least a few hours of downtime after having an emotional upheaval. If that's what James needs, that's what he's going to get.

I take our plates to the kitchen and pour myself another glass of wine. I grab the blue label bottle and bring it to the living room so that I can freshen his drink as well. I hate that he's upset, but it's kind of nice to take care of him. He's usually doting all over me, I sort of like the change of dynamic.

"Thanks, baby." He smiles and I kiss his cheek.

I sit back on the couch, ready to continue giving him space, but James speaks.

"This is tough, Georgie. I never, ever want to lie to you." My stomach sinks. What the fuck could he possibly be talking about? My mind goes right to the worst case scenarios. He's married, he cheated on me, we're actually first cousins...

"I freaked out earlier. I'm sure you noticed I was...off." I nod, wondering where he's going with this. "Do you remember back when we first met, I told you about my mother?"

"Yes," I tell him, and my heart sinks lower.

"I told you a little bit about it, about feeling abandoned. Georgie, baby, I have serious mommy issues. I don't date, I don't get close to people besides my sisters and my friends because I'm terrified of not being good enough. I feel like everyone is going to leave me, just like my mom did. I got really good at keeping everyone in my life at arm's length. That is, until my mystery girl walked into my office a few weeks ago. All of a sudden, you shook up my life like a beautiful earthquake, invading my every thought, making me feel like the man I've always wanted to be. I needed you in a way I've never felt before." He sighs and runs a hand through his hair.

"It hit me today that you're not going to be my assistant forever. I knew that, but I hadn't thought about it, and then you said something about moving out of the city, and fuck. I couldn't breathe, Georgie. It felt like I let my guard down and you were going to leave me, too. I couldn't take that, not after I waited so long for you."

"James," I reach out and grab his hands. "I'm not leaving you. I might need to move but it would just be over the bridge, and-"

"I know, that, sweet girl. I know. You've done nothing to indicate that you're going anywhere, or that you're not worth these crazy feelings inside of me. That's why I had to book an emergency session with Dr. Patel today. I needed the rational part of my brain to calm down the irrational part that felt like you were slipping through my fingers." He runs his thumb over the top of my hand. "There's something more."

I hold my breath, waiting for his next statement. He was so scared of me leaving him, but now I feel like he's doing the leaving.

"Last year, when Amy and Jenn were doing IVF, I hired a private investigator to track my mother down. I told myself it was for their sake, to make sure they weren't accidentally using some cousin or long-lost sibling sperm, but really, my morbid curiosity over the years finally caught up with me. I never did anything with the information..." He trails off, and my legs shake with nerves. "Georgie, I want this with you so bad. I feel like you and me could really be something, but I have this blocker that's keeping me from giving all of myself to you. I think I need to...fuck. I think I need to confront my mother. I don't think I'm going to be able to give you every piece of my heart that you deserve while she still has part of it under her thumb."

I close my eyes and let out the air I was holding in my lungs.

"Christ, James. You scared the shit out of me, I thought you were going to end things between us. Babe, if anyone understands getting fucked up by their parents, it's me." He chuckles and I straddle him, holding a cheek in each of my palms. The brush of his scruff feels like electric shocks on my sensitive skin. "Don't ever feel like you can't share your feelings with me, or like you have to hide a part of you. I'm here for you, whatever you need." I kiss him softly, sighing at the feel of his warm lips. "When are you going?" I ask.

"Saturday," he murmurs, palming my hips and sliding them under the hem of the t-shirt I stole from his closet. "I feel like I need to rip the band-aid off."

"Do you want me to go with you?" I ask, though I don't know if it's the right thing to do.

"Desperately." He leans forward and kisses the fabric covering my chest between my breasts. "But you have that meeting. It's sometime this week, isn't it? I don't know how long it's going to take to force myself to go to her. And besides, I think I need to do this by myself. Is that okay, baby?"

"Of course," I tell him, feeling relieved. "Can I be here for you when you get back?"

"You better be. In the meantime," he pulls the hem of his t-shirt over my head and exposes my bare breasts, "I really could use a release from all this tension. Will you help me, sweet girl?" I moan as he pulls one of my pebbled nipples into his mouth and sucks. I feel him grow hard beneath me and I grind myself into him, already getting hot for him. He alternates back and forth, working my breasts with his tongue and his teeth while I rock my hips against his growing erection. My head falls back and his name rolls off my tongue in a moan. He growls and flips us, opening my legs with his knee and pulling his shirt over his head.

I lean forward and undo his belt and zipper, aching to feel his warm cock in my hands. I free him from his boxers and he hisses as I give him a few long, slow strokes. He stands and loses his own pants before yanking my panties down. His fingers slide up my thigh to my pussy, where I'm dripping with arousal.

"Always so wet for me. So fucking perfect." He circles my clit and I cry out at the sensation. I'm so goddamn sensitive, every touch feels like it could push me over the edge.

"James, please. Get inside of me, please." I reach for his cock and position him at my entrance, but he grabs himself back and teases my slit with the tip. I mewl when he presses into my clit, clawing at his shoulders.

"Desperate little thing, aren't you? So needy for my cock." He tsks and pushes at my entrance ever so slowly.

"Pleeease" I whine, because I am fucking desperate. I try to push my pelvis into his, to pull him further into my body, and he has the nerve to laugh at me.

"I think my girl needs to take over tonight, doesn't she? Do you want to get in my lap and ride my cock, Georgie? Want to wring all that pleasure out of your sweet cunt?" I don't have time to answer before he pulls me back to straddling him and I'm sliding his cock inside of me. I'm already so fucking close I can taste it. I buck and writhe with no rhyme or reason, chasing the orgasm that's building inside of me.

"Fuck yes. Look at you riding me, so goddamn sexy. I can't fucking take it, you feel too good. Where's my good girl at, huh? Tell me your close, baby," he bites out, and I moan in answer.

"I'm right-oohh- right there!" James presses the pad of his thumb to my swollen clit and I crumble. Pleasure washes over me like a baptism, renewing me from the inside out. I cry out as I come. I claw at his chest and trying to find some sort of grounding as my body spasms out of control. James takes over beneath me as soon as my body has gone limp. He pistons his hips in and out, drawing out my orgasm. It's only seconds before I hear him curse and I feel his hot cum filling me so fucking deep, it sparks another aftershock of pleasure. I love the feeling of his release inside of me. It's so dirty and perfect to hold a part of him inside of my body even after he pulls out. He keeps me in his lap as he slides out of me. He cups my cheek and peppers soft kisses against my lips.

"Fuck, Georgie. You're so amazing. I lo-" He stops and swallows the syllable, but I know what he was going to say. I press my forehead against his and nod. A mutual understanding washes over us. We might not be ready to say the words out loud yet, but we both know it's true. The feeling is palpable between us. Whether we're talking or making love or simply being together, it's there.

James and I are in love.

He goes to the bathroom and returns with a warm washcloth to clean me up, and we spend the night cuddled on the couch watching The Office and making out like we have all the time in the world, trying to ignore the gravity of what tomorrow might bring for him- and us.

31

Georgie

I woke up Saturday morning to soft lips brushing against my own. The only light in the room came from the cracked bathroom door, and all I could see was the shadow of James hovering over me.

"Don't get up," he whispered as I moved to throw the blanket off of me. "I'll call you when I land." He kissed my forehead as he tucked me back in, and I drifted back to sleep.

Sure enough, I got a call around 7 hours later that James had landed and was on his way to his hotel room. He hasn't gone to see his mother yet. I don't know exactly when he's planning on doing that. He didn't even tell me where he was going- only that it was on the east coast- and I didn't think I should ask. What he's doing- confronting his mother, facing his past in an attempt to open up his future- it's huge, and I'm not going to push him any further out of his comfort zone than he already is. I'll be here to support him, and whatever he is willing to share with me, I will happily accept.

We ended the call with a promise to FaceTime later tonight, and I invited Keeks and Rachel over for an in-home spa day. Right now, the three of us plus Lucifer are lying in the guest room bed in matching white, fluffy robes with Olaplex in our hair and avocado masks on our faces. 13 Going On 30 is playing on the TV, and I've got a giant bowl of caramel popcorn on my lap that we're all picking from.

"Seriously, G. This place is amazing. Why would you leave the city when you could move in here?" Rachel asks me around a mouthful of popcorn.

Not for a lack of thinking about it. I've spent every single night here for weeks. I have my own drawer in his dresser and contact solution in the bathroom. I'm paying overpriced rent for a shit hole apartment that I haven't seen the inside of in days. Why the hell wouldn't I move in with my sexy as hell boyfriend instead of leaving the city I love and all my new friends?

"Because he hasn't asked me to, Rach." James and I haven't spoken at all about my living situation since yesterday. We've been distracted by other things. I know he doesn't want me to leave San Francisco, I certainly don't want to leave San Francisco, but everything feels so delicate right now. I'm not going to add more to his plate.

"Don't wait for him to ask, just don't renew your lease. By the time he notices, you'll already be getting your Christmas cards mailed here," Kira says, swiping another coat of red polish onto her toes. I laugh.

"That's brilliant, Keeks. Then when he realizes I moved in against his will and kicks me out-"

"You'll come stay with me and we'll plot his demise." She wiggles her eyebrows and all three of us fall into a fit of hysterics. Lucifer stands at the end of the bed and stretches before pouncing to the floor and sauntering off. He's clearly not a fan of our antics.

"It sucks he's away this weekend. My TikTok engagement is going to drop way down without your goofy hunk in the front row of my class this morning." It's true. James has been coming to Spin Sync with me every week since that first class, and every week, a clip of him goes absolutely viral. The first week it was him watching me. The next week it was him whipping his towel like a fan to "Levels" by Avicii. The third week, it was a compilation of zoom in shots of his behind in the mirror captioned "An Ode to the Blessed Butt of Spin". I couldn't even be mad about it. He has a fantastic ass.

"He made sure the hotel he was staying at had stationary bikes in the gym. There's no way he'd miss a Saturday Kira class." Like me, James fell in love with indoor cycling after his first taste. He actually bought two home Spin Sync bikes for his home gym so that we could ride on demand classes together. He says he loves feeling moved by the music, and it's invigorating after years of running being his sole form of cardio. "Besides, Brian should have come and taken his place. It could have been like the rotating hunks of Spin Sync."

"Oh my god, G! James should totally audition to be an instructor!" Rachel practically jumps out of her skin next to me, completely ignoring any mention of her boyfriend. It's weird how little she talks about him. I haven't even met him yet, though Kira doesn't seem to be his biggest fan. "He's hating his job right now anyway, and he'd be so freaking perfect, don't you think?"

Before you go judging me, no, I did not tell Rachel that James hates his job. He told her himself a few mornings ago when requesting a fourth shot of espresso in his latte. He notably left out the tidbit that he'd been up making love to me until three in the morning the night before.

Kira squeals next to me. "I mean, he'd have to get certified, but he does have amazing energy and stage presence. I mean his peachy butt cheeks aren't the only thing that stands out about him. You should mention it to him!"

Maybe I will. Maybe he's in a season of change- hell, maybe we both are. It looks like we have a lot to discuss when he's back in California.

Speak of the devil, my phone vibrates with an incoming call. I totally forgot about the time difference when he said he'd call at 9, and I also forgot about the green mush on my face before I hit 'answer'.

"Hey, it's Elphaba!" He flashes a wicked, toothy smile at me, and I groan.

"Shut up, I messed up the time difference and we're doing face masks."

"Who's we?" he asks, and both Kira and Rachel lean in and wave.

"James, guess what? You're gonna get certified and come work with me as a spin instructor at the studio!" Kira bounces and steals my phone from my hand.

"Oh, is that so?"

"Yup, I make your decisions now, buddy. Get used to it."

"In that case, is there anything else I should know?"

"Yeah, Georgie's not renewing her lease. She lives with you now."

"Jesus, Keeks, give me my phone back!" I manage to snatch it back from her and walk out of the room, while she and Rachel cackle behind me.

"Ignore her, she drinks too much." I roll my eyes and cross into the closest bathroom, propping my phone on the sink and wiping the gunk off of my face.

"I don't know, babe. Both of those ideas are intriguing, particularly the one where you live with me now." I feel my face heat and I know it's not a reaction to the mask.

"That's not really a conversation we should have over FaceTime 3000 miles away from each other," I say, wiping at my hairline.

"You're right. We can discuss it when I get home, but I'll tell you right now sweet girl, I know what the outcome is going to be." He winks at me, and I blush. I want to tell him so badly, I want to scream the words "I'M IN LOVE WITH YOU," but that's another thing I don't want to do over FaceTime.

"Anyway, I'll let you get back to the girls. I just wanted to see your beautiful face before I went to bed." I cringe.

"Sorry that face was just caked with goop."

"It's okay, Georgie. You're still gorgeous. And since your friends are there and I'm doing the gentlemanly thing by not asking you for a FaceTime quickie anyway, you can make it up to me by sending me something naughty to get through the night." His face melts into a lazy smile and I swoon. He's so freaking beautiful. I take a few steps backwards and tug at the ties on my robe.

"Get ready to take a screenshot." I let the robe fall to the floor, revealing my bare chest and red lace thong. My nipples are rock hard and poking towards him, begging to be touched. James runs a hand over his jaw, and I see him work the phone in a way that lets me know he's capturing this moment.

"Fuck, baby. So beautiful. Turn around and bend over." I do as he says, spreading my thighs ever so slightly in hopes that he can see the damp spot of my arousal between my legs. God, I get so turned on just knowing how much *I* turn *him* on.

"Such a filthy girl for me, aren't you, Georgie?" I grab the robe and slowly roll myself up standing, slightly swaying my hips as I go. I drape the fabric over my shoulders as I turn back to face my phone.

"Think that'll get you through the next few days?" I ask innocently, biting my lip. He chuckles.

"For a few hours at least. Georgie..." he says, followed by a pregnant pause. The air is thick with tension, and I know he's fighting to keep the words in, too. Both of us are bursting at the seams, but neither is willing to waste the moment like this. I simply nod and say, "Me too."

I can see in his eyes that he knows what I mean, and he visibly relaxes as we blow each other kisses and say goodnight.

32

James

∽

I briefly considered staying in Manhattan when my plane landed this afternoon, checking into the Four Seasons and calling Georgie for some phone sex, but I know myself too well. If I stay too far away, I'll never get the nerve to face my demons. Instead, I picked up my rental car and drove the hour and half from JFK into the suburbs. The irony of the woman who gave birth to me currently residing in the same town where Georgie grew up is not fucking lost on me. I didn't tell Georgie exactly where I was flying today. I worried that the information might be triggering for her and I knew I wouldn't be able to leave her alone if that happened. I'll tell her when I get back, though. I don't plan on keeping secrets from my girl.

The Westchester Little Inn isn't the most luxurious hotel I've ever stayed in, but the room is air conditioned and the bar has a decent selection of scotch, so I have no complaints. After my call with Georgie, I hopped into a hot shower and relieved some of the tension that's been building all day, thinking about her sweet tits and the way she gets so wet for me, even when I'm miles away. Now, I'm picking at another slice of the pizza I ordered earlier. Georgie is right by the way, this pizza is way better than anything I've had in San Francisco. I stare down at the address I wrote down on a Post-It note.

Technically, the address was emailed to me over a year ago, but once I decided to make this trip, I scribbled it down on piece of paper, tucked it into my wallet and deleted the email. I don't know why. Maybe it feels like if the address lives on a silly little Post-It, I can easily crumple it up, toss it, set it on fire, and it will no longer exist. If it no longer exists, I don't have to do this. It's giving me the illusion of choice, and I'm leaning hard into that illusion right now.

I turn off the light and TV and crawl into bed. I send Georgie a goodnight text with a kissy face emoji, and she sends me back a picture of her, Kira, and Rachel on my couch making kissy faces back at me.

Scratch that- it's not my couch they're sitting on, it's our couch. I've been trying to think of ways to broach the subject, and Kira just went ahead and did it for me. This is probably the only time I'm going to say this- I'm thankful for her big ass mouth. Georgie can think her moving in is going to be a discussion all she wants, but I know it's happening. As soon as I get home, I'm taking her in my arms, telling her I love her, and then packing up the rest of her shit at the apartment and bringing it to ours.

Actually, I think I'll eat her pussy first. Maybe twice.

My mind wanders to the other life decision Kira made for me today. I don't even know where it came from, working with her at Spin Sync? As an instructor? I mean, a consultant, maybe. Maybe join the board of directors, but instructor? I've only taken like, five spin classes in my whole life, and don't you need to have a degree in...body...physics? Something? I'll look it up.

It does sound...intriguing. Besides being with Georgie, I've had the most fun of my life in those five classes. The dark room, the music, the energy of the people around you, it's magnetic. Every time I listen to a song now, I think of the beat of the music and where it would work into a playlist for a good workout. And really, how different can leading a spin class be from leading a shareholders meeting, anyway?

Probably very different. And probably a lot more fun. I'll just tuck that idea in the back of my mind for now. I'm going to see my mother for the first time in thirty years tomorrow. I need to get some rest.

I did not see my mother for the first time in thirty years yesterday. I chickened out. I never even put the address into the rental car's GPS. Instead, I drove to McDonald's and ate two sausage egg and cheese biscuits and three hashbrowns. I folded a ring out my straw wrapper and put it in my pocket for safe keeping, so I can slide it onto Georgie's hand when I get home. Then, I walked over to a nearby park where I literally tossed those biscuits up in a trash can. I tried swinging, but my legs are too long, they kept dragging on the ground with each pass. As soon as a mom turned up with her two little kids, I felt like a total creep and left.

So much for healing my inner child.

After that, I drove around with no plan for a few hours- terrible for the environment, but cathartic for the mind. For someone like me who has lived in a city his whole life, White Plains definitely gives off small town vibes, but it's not actually that small. For example, I passed four different elementary schools, two libraries, and a handful of chain restaurants, all of which could be somewhere Georgie once spent time. Under normal circumstances, she and I would visit her hometown together. I'd hold her hand as she walked me around her childhood neighborhood. I'd listen while she pointed out the monkeybars she fell off when she was 6, I'd press my lips against hers on the park bench where she fumbled through her first kiss to remind her that all the rest of her kisses belong to me.

But Georgie and I didn't grow up under normal circumstances. She might have lived here, but this is not her home. I don't feel her here. I don't want to. I don't want to think of what she suffered through here. I don't want to picture her walking to school in pain, hiding a canvas of bruises under her clothes. I don't want to think about her living alone at 17, struggling to feed herself. I wish I could take away every ounce of anguish she has ever felt. I know I can't, I know her experiences helped shape her into the strong, fiercely independent and loyal woman she is today, but it doesn't stop me from resenting every square mile of this godforsaken suburb.

Last night, I called Georgie when I got back to the hotel room and told her about how I skipped out on my mission that day. I was feeling like such shit, all I wanted was to be curled up with her in my arms, but she calmed me down. She told me not to force it and reassured me that

I didn't have to rush into anything I wasn't ready for for her benefit, that she'd be by my side while I try to heal, no matter how long it takes.

I rewarded her amazing kindness and understanding with multiple orgasms via a vibrator that I can control with an app on my phone.

Best. Purchase. Ever.

I promised myself I'd go today. I'd get it over with. There's no way I could spend another night away from Georgie, and she has her meeting with the literary agent. I need to get back to her. I checked out of the hotel, knowing it was now or never. I got in the car, I entered the address into the car's GPS, and I followed the directions all the way to a mobile home park on the edge of town. I parked a few trailers down and sat.

And sat.

And sat.

I was frozen. I watched the front porch of the dilapidated trailer for what felt like hours. I'm surprised no neighbors called the cops on the freak stalking out on their street. There was nothing going on upstairs, no thoughts in my head. I was utterly and completely blank.

That is, until just now, when a woman in an oversized sweatshirt throws open the screen door at the address I was avoiding.

I can't see her face, its masked by the large hood, but I can see the flick of a lighter and the angry red tip of a cigarette burning between her lips, and I know in my gut that the woman is Amber Adler. I watch her inhale a puff of nicotine, and I'm instantly transported back to being 6 years old and berated for getting sick in the car, the stench of Marlboro Reds causing me to lose the contents of my stomach because she refused to roll the windows down while she smoked.

Her bare legs are long and bony, riddled with red spots and varicose veins. The hand that holds her cigarette is wrinkled and dotted with dark marks. The years have not been kind to her. I stare like the world's worst private detective as she smokes with one hand and scrolls through an iPhone that's at least a few years old and cracked across the back with another. I don't know how she hasn't noticed me yet. The Toyota Camry I rented is unassuming, but it still stands out amongst the other rusted and old cars parked around here.

I watch as Amber pulls her hood down, revealing the face I haven't seen since I was a boy. It's changed, of course. Her cheeks are hollowed out, lines creased around her lips and eyes, and her skin has a slight yellow tint to it, likely from decades of nicotine use. Underneath all of that, I can see the woman who held my hand on the way home from my first day of preschool, the one who did Jenn's hair for her class's holiday pageant, the one who left us on Aunt Janine's doorstep and never looked back.

It's not lost on me that the woman is living around the poverty line, and the thought of it makes me sick. Not because I feel pity for her, but because my success hasn't exactly been a secret. I mean, I'm technically a self-made billionaire. Streamline has made national news time and time again. I've spoken all over the country, I've lobbied in Congress, I gave a fucking TED talk for god's sake. I've been impossible to ignore for the last 15 years. Part of me knows that Amber knows about my money, not to mention Jenn and Amy's. It's fucking sick, but the fact that she never cared enough to come after us for money pisses me off. She well and truly does not fucking care. She never has.

She chose this life. She chose New York, she chose the trailer, and judging by the track marks on her arm, she no doubt chose the drugs. She chose all of that over me, over her own children.

I want to call Georgie, I want to hear her voice and tell her I'll be home to hold her tonight but one look at the clock tells me she's probably still in her meeting. Instead, I turn on some music, hitting shuffle on a playlist she put together for me last week.

Mean (Taylor's Version) starts to play, and I sing along with the radio. I've really gotten into Miss Swift in the last few weeks. I like her pop music, but personally I lean more towards her country albums.

As I sing the lyrics, I feel myself start to get pissed. I am living in a big city. I am big enough so she can't hit me. She is mean. I'm running away in fear, and that leaves the power in her hands. She owes me a fucking explanation, and I'm going to get it.

I pull a U-Turn and head back to the mobile home park.

33

Georgie

Walking into the lobby of Stacey's building, I'm weirdly not nervous at all. I don't know if it's a false sense of confidence, or its the fact that Stacey has already read my work, the most vulnerable part is over. Either way, my hand is steady and I haven't broken into any cold sweats, so I'm calling that a win. I'm wearing the same white silk blouse I wore in LA, but this time I paired it with a pair of super dark straight leg jeans and a pair of black heels. I curled my hair and tied it into a high ponytail. I feel like the look gives big "professional but still artsy" energy. My heels click across the floor as I make my way to the receptionist.

"Can I help you?" the young woman asks from behind her iMac.

"Yes, Georgia Hansley for Stacey Marple?" Even my voice sounds grown up and confident. I am nailing this.

"Oh yes, she's expecting you. Down that hall, third door on your left."

An hour later, I'm walking out on cloud freaking nine. Stacey and I bonded immediately over our love for what she calls "drugstore romance"- the kind of books you buy for $8 from the end of the candy aisle at CVS. We talked about my finished manuscript that Amir had sent her, as well as my little universe outlines for the four other standalone books in the series. I thought I was there to prove myself, but Stacey was really pitching herself to me. She told me all about the success she's had getting other romance authors in with The Big 5. She even represents one of my favorite authors who she found through her AO3 work. Even though she's in traditional publishing, she really has a soft spot for the little guys. Despite all of that, I didn't sign the contract. Not because I was afraid, but because this meeting solidified something I already knew. I want to pursue self-publishing. I don't want to be locked into a contract or any harsh deadlines. I want to publish what I want, when I want, and I finally have the confidence to do it.

I check my watch as I walk down the street. It's about 5pm on the east coast. I could call James, I haven't heard from him since this morning, but I'm hoping that means he's actually going to go to his mother's house today. I've been trying to be as supportive as possible the last few days, but the longer this goes on, the more I worry that it's not good for him. I know he feels like he needs to face his demons to clear his future, but what if it's doing him more harm than good?

Of course, I wouldn't say that to him. I think I feel this way because there is no way I'd be brave enough to face my own.

Instead of bothering him, I shoot a text to Rachel and Kira to see if they want to meet up for a late lunch slash early glass of wine. I'm met with resounding "fuck yeah" from Kira and a thumbs up emoji from Rachel (truly a perfect representation of their respective personalities). I tell them to meet me at the Peruvian place down the street from here, and I head over to grab us a table.

While I wait, I draft an email to my landlord, CC'ing my roommates to let them know that I will not be renewing my lease. I don't care what I said on the phone the other night. Kira's right, I want to live with James, and based on what he said, he wants me to move in. I think I'll head over to my (old!!) place and pick up some more of my stuff to bring over to make my decision obvious when he gets back.

Nothing says "I live here now" like a desktop computer and a box of tampons.

"Are we celebrating or crying and manifesting a plague on that bitch?" Kira asks, sliding into the booth next to me and sipping from my glass of water. Rachel sits down across from us and smiles.

"Are you kidding, look at the way she's beaming. We're celebrating, right G?"

"We are most definitely celebrating!" I clap my hands together and my friends woo. Kira utilized her superior food ordering skills to secure us a bottle of Rosé, ceviche, and anticucho de carne and I tell them all about the meeting and my decision to take it all into my own hands.

"And what did James say when you told him?" Rachel asks, topping off her glass of wine. We burned through the first bottle before the food came and just started on the second.

"I bet he squealed like a girl. That man has such cinnamon roll vibes for you, G," Kira says, picking a fingerling potato off of my plate and popping it in her mouth.

"I actually haven't told him yet. We haven't talked since this morning." I'm surprised at the tear that pricks the corner of my eye.

"You ok?" Rachel asks, placing her hand on top of mine. I grab the napkin Kira holds out to me and use it to dot at my eyes.

"I'm fine. I just feel emotional. James is so raw and vulnerable right now and I feel like everything I say and do is the wrong thing. He cried to me on the phone last night and I just wanted to crawl through the screen and hold him. I've only seen him cry once before when I-" I cut myself off. I never told my friends about the incident down on the wharf. I was so embarrassed that I lost my shit so publicly like that.

"When you what?" Kira presses, nudging her shoulder with mine.

I sigh. "It was a while back, before we were technically together. We were down by the water, and there was an incident with some jerk and a guy trying to sleep on the sidewalk. James got involved and when the asshole hit him, he hit him back. I had an...episode. I got sick and passed out in the street. That night I told James about my parents. That's the only time I've seen him cry."

"God that man loves you so much," Rachel practically whispers. Tears well in my eyes once again, and this time I'm completely unsuccessful in holding them back. I drop my face into my hands to try to muffle my sobs. It feels like everything that's happened in the last few days, even the last few weeks is suddenly sitting heavy in my stomach. I feel Kira rub her hand across my back and shiver at the touch.

"I just feel like I'm not enough. I've put him through so much with my own stupid fucking drama and now he's putting his heart out on a limb for me, and I can't handle it. I'm not worth all the trouble I've been putting him through. He's putting it all out on the line and I don't fucking deserve it." I sniffle. I've never been a cute crier, I've got a full on snot bubble happening right now.

"Georgie, you have to stop that. You're worth all of it. You're brilliant and kind and loving. You bring so much light to all of us." Kira's voice is as calm and smooth as I've ever heard it. I look up and Rachel is nodding, wiping a lone tear from her own cheek. "You could have turned out so different, given your circumstances. You had every right to grow up angry and reclusive, to be a fighter instead of a lover. But you didn't. You took your crappy childhood and created a beautiful life for yourself, and you share that beauty with every person you meet. You're an amazing woman, G. And James knows it too. That's why he looks at you like the damn sun shines out your ass. To him, it does." Leave it to Kira to make me want to laugh and cry at the same time.

Rachel squeezes my hand and I squeeze back.

"It's ok to feel your feelings," she says, "especially with us. But we're not going to sit back and let you talk shit on yourself like that anymore. I don't let people treat my friends the way you're treating yourself."

I feel overwhelmed by the existence of these women. I can't believe how incredibly lucky I am to have them in my life.

"The feelings mutual, babe." Kira pulls me close into a side hug. I didn't realize I had said those words out loud.

After we down the second bottle of wine, we decide to share a pezcado a lo macho and another bottle of rosé. I'm thoroughly stuffed and quite tipsy when I notice my phone screen is black.

"Shit, phone's dead. Can I use one of yours to call an Uber?" Kira shoves her iPhone into my hand, and I send a quick text before opening the app.

Hey, it's Georgie. Phone died while I was out with the girls. Going to my apartment to pick something up. TTYL

I'm giddy with excitement the whole ride back to my apartment. Maybe I'm just drunk, but I want to tell James that I'm moving in with him tonight. I can barely wait to charge my phone and call him. I'm hoping he flies home tonight, but if not, I think I'll put on some lingerie and give him a striptease show over FaceTime.

My Uber driver Dimitry pulls up to the curb and I give him a bit-too-loud 'thank you' as I stumble out of his Prius.

I float upstairs and give myself a main character moment. I slowly open the door, lean against the doorway, put my hand on my chest and sigh dramatically. This isn't my apartment anymore. I'm moving on.

I'm going home.

34

James

This time when I pull up in front of the mobile home, I don't hesitate. I barely think. I'm fueled by anger and burning hot spite. I get out of the car and slam the door so hard I can feel the reverberation on the pavement beneath my feet. I stomp up the rickety steps and pound on the splintered wood with the full force of my fist. The door swings open, and I'm met with the stench of stale cigarette smoke and day old beer. Amber is tall, but I still have a few inches on her. She's clearly annoyed by the intrusion, but still I search her face for any sort of recognition that the man banging down her door was once the chubby cheeked boy she left behind. I get my answer quickly.

"You're wasting your fucking time, James." She tries to shut the door in my face, but I stop it with one strong grip on the side. She stumbles back a step, but I don't give a shit.

"I think you owe me this, Amber." I push my way past her and into the small space. I look around at the yellow tinted furniture, the surfaces layered with dust, the burn marks in the carpet. I peer into the kitchen, where the counter is littered with pizza boxes and dirty dishes. I have to fight the urge to find a lint roller and clean myself up.

"Nice place," I sneer, and she scoffs back at me.

"What do you want, James? Do you want an apology? Want to kiss and makeup? Want me to be your mommy again? It's not going to happen." She places a cigarette between her lips and flicks her lighter. I watch her crepey skin hollow out as she inhales, and I fight the urge to gag when she exhales up towards my face.

I've thought about this moment a thousand times. I let go of any notion that she'd welcome me with open arms years ago, so her passive attitude doesn't get to me. I meet her bored stare with one of my own. She and Jenn have the same green eyes, but the whites of Amber's are a dull orange and bloodshot. Her ratty locks are a similar brown to my own, if not duller and streaked with gray. She's pieces of us taped together haphazardly to form a shell of a person.

"Why'd you do it?" I ask plainly, and she laughs- a throaty noise that turns into a fit of mucus-laden coughs. I can't help but roll my eyes at the pathetic scene unfurling in front of me as she finds a plastic red cup to spit into.

"Shit," she draws out sarcastically "I've done so many things in my day. You'll have to enlighten me- why did I do what?" Her spitefulness rolls right off of my back.

"Amber, do not fuck with me. Answer the question." I watch as she takes another deep drag, the cherry glowing red and angry between us. She runs her eyes over me, taking in my form with an air of disgust. She turns and walks to the refrigerator, opening the dingy door and pulling out two silver cans.

"Beer?" she asks, and I take one from her. I don't really want it, the last thing I want to do is share a drink with this woman, let alone a cheap, piss flavored brew. Not taking it feels more unnatural somehow, so I crack the tab and raise it to her in a sarcastic "cheers". She motions for me to have a seat, but if my jeans touch her furniture I'll have to burn them, and that would be a big waste of a thousand dollars. I shake my head no and she shrugs, lounging back onto the couch while I stay standing in the middle of the room.

"There's no sob story," she sighs.

"I didn't think there was," I answer.

"This isn't going to redeem me."

"I assumed."

"I never wanted you. Your sister, I wanted. I thought I did, anyway. When I found out I was pregnant with her, I was so happy. Your shithole father couldn't have cared less, but I was ecstatic. I wrote name ideas in a journal. I crocheted a little blanket. I used to sing to my belly at night. So fucking stupid. She was a mess as soon as she was born. She tried to come out backwards so they had to cut her out of me. I was in so much pain for days. I resented her immediately. I was always alone with her while baby daddy drank his life away at the bar down the street. She never fucking stopped crying. All day, all night. She screamed constantly. One time, I put her outside in her carseat and left her there to scream just so I could get some fucking sleep.

"It got better when she got a little older, but the damage was done. I hated her. She ruined my life, ruined my body, my independence. I couldn't wait to put her in school so I could get a break from her once in a while. I used to fantasize about running away. Packing my shit in the middle of the night and just leaving. Imagine my disappointment when I missed my fucking period. My girlfriend gave me a cocktail she swore would take care of it, and I threw myself down the steps for good measure. I was bleeding like crazy, I thought it worked. I didn't figure it out till I was six months along. By then, your dad had already overdosed. Good fucking riddance. Man, all that drinking I did, I'm surprised you didn't turn out more fucked up." She laughs like it's a fond memory, and my stomach churns.

"You were a better baby, at least. Quiet. Even as a kid. You kept to yourself, left me alone. You were more interested in playing with Jenn, and thankfully she didn't mind. That's how I survived it. You two kept each other busy so I could ignore you. I hated being a mother so much. I resented every stupid question you'd ask, every scraped knee you wanted me to tend to, all of it. I kept it bottled up for as long as I could. The dam finally broke. I was watching you two play in the living room, and I was fantasizing about putting you in the car and turning on the engine, letting you rot in the garage." She's fully emotionless, a true psychopath as she tells me that she once wanted to kill me.

"I didn't want to end up in jail. A bad TV movie about a murderous mom. I packed your shit up and told you you were having a sleepover at Aunt Janine's house. You two went inside, and I drove east. I never looked back."

I stare at her, the condensation on the can I'm holding mixing with the sweat of my palms. I take a deep breath before I speak.

"Thank you for your honesty."

"I don't regret it. Not one fucking bit."

"I know," I say, and I do. For the first time, I don't care. It's not that I wasn't good enough for her, she wasn't good enough for us. She didn't deserve us. She chose her path and Jenn and I are better off for it.

"Will you please leave now?" she asks, and for a second I actually do feel sorry for her. She sounds...not sad. Drained maybe?

"He's not going anywhere, Amber. The man is fucking loaded, he owes us for breaking and entering! We should call the cops on this guy unless he writes you a check." A small man, probably a full foot shorter than me appears from somewhere in the back of the trailer. His skin is red, like a permanent sunburn. What's left of his hair is buzzed close to this skull. His track marks are almost identical to my mothers. His eyes...

Fuck. I'd know those eyes anywhere.

I think this guy has Georgie's eyes.

I take in the shape of his nose, the bow on his chapped upper lip, and the dark freckle on the crook of his neck.

I really think this could be Georgie's father.

I push down the panic unfurling in my chest. This is not the time to lose my shit. I adjust my sleeve to hide the tremor in my hand.

"You think I owe you money? Go ahead, call the police. I'm sure they'll be happy to arrest me and ignore the clear smell of chemicals wafting from back there. They might take an interest in the empty boxes of Sudafed under the kitchen table. Fancy yourself the new Heisenberg, buddy? I really should get out of this place before it explodes." I turn, and the ham fisted little shit has the nerve to grab my arm.

"I don't think so, pretty boy. You can't just come here and fuck up my woman's life without a little compensation. We wouldn't want anyseedy skeletons crawling out of your perfect closet, huh? Might not be good for business if your people know about your shady past." He spits as he talks, and the urge to physically recoil is strong.

"Funny, you of all people being concerned about fucking up a woman's life. Although I suppose you're more interested in fucking up the lives of children." He thinks his grip on me is strong, but I pick his fingers off one by one like specks of lint.

"What the fuck are you talking about?" he sneers.

"Ever put your hands on a kid? Ever kick someone smaller than you because you could? Did it make you feel like a big man? Did it make you feel tough every time you watched her hit the ground? Did you like the way it felt when the bones of her nose crushed under those pathetic fists of yours? Did you enjoy it, making Georgia cry?"

He's fucking pissed. His chest is puffed, his fists are curled into tight balls at his sides, and he looks at me with fire in his eyes.

"That fucking girl is such a liar. She disobeyed me, and I spanked her. I'm her damn father, it was my right to discipline her."

"You wanna know something, Craig? It is Craig, isn't it?" He nods, almost involuntarily. "I'm glad you're a piece of shit. Truly, I am. I mean, don't get me wrong, I could kill you for hurting her. Seriously, I could wrap my hands around your neck right now and I wouldn't think twice about it. But I'm glad you're so fucking horrible that she was able to get away from you. She's so fucking smart and beautiful. She's the strongest person I've ever met in my entire life, and she did that herself. You would have sucked the life out of her, so thank you for being so supremely, unfathomably horrible that she got to leave."

I roll my eyes when his fist flies out at me. You'd think the dude would at least aim for my stomach, but he goes high towards my face. Maybe he's too high to realize that he's not tall enough to land a blow there, or maybe he's just that fucking stupid. I step back and let him follow through, punching the air.

"Hmph. Too bad I'm not as small as your usual targets." I'm already turning on my heel to leave this hellscape.

"Get back here and fight me like a man, you little bitch," he spits. I'm pushing open the screen door and on my way out as I answer.

"I'm the only man in this room, Craig. I think you already know that."

I only make it a few blocks before my body seizes and I have to pull over to the side of the road, vomiting in the grass.

35

James

I make it to the airport on pure adrenaline. I have no memory of calling my plane service and driving up to the tarmac, nor do I remember pouring a drink and sitting in the chair that Georgie and I defiled just a few weeks ago, but here I am. I think I just took my first full breath in hours. I want to call Georgie and let her know I'm coming home, but I got a text from Kira's number saying that her phone is dead just a couple minutes ago. It's probably for the best because I don't know what the fuck I'm going to tell her. I swear I don't want to lie to her, but I don't know if she'll want to know that I met her father. I couldn't even tell her where I was going for fear of triggering her. What am

I supposed to do? Waltz in to her apartment and lay it out like it's nothing?

Oh hey Georgie. Just found out my mother fantasized about murdering me when I was a kid. Oh and she's sleeping with your dad, you know that guy that used to beat you? I'm thinking Chinese for dinner.

Yeah, no.

"Annie," I call out, and she's by my side in a moment. "Do you mind setting up the room for me? I could really use a nap."

"Of course, James."

"Annie, if you were estranged from an abusive parent and found out your boyfriend met him and he's shacked up with your mother, would you want to know?" She looks at me quizzically, then gestures towards my nearly empty glass.

"Can I freshen that for you?" My head slumps and I hand the glass over to her.

"Yeah, that's what I thought," I lament under my breath. I take my drink into the shower and finish it as I rinse off. I climb into the made bed, happy to be rid of the smell of stale cigarettes. I pull out my phone and send an email to Dr. Patel. Simple. Three words.

I did it.

Moments later, my inbox pings.

Do you have time for a session now?

I run my hand over my jaw. I'm fucking exhausted, but I know I need to get this over with. I log into Zoom and start a call.

"James." My name from Dr. P's mouth in *that voice* causes my stomach to drop. We've been working together for years, I know when he's had enough of my shit, and I really pushed it this time.

The thing is, when I came up with this hare-brained attempt at self healing, I sort of implied that Dr. Patel was in on it and that we had made the decision together.

We did not. In fact, in our last session he explicitly told me why confronting my mother was a horrible idea. He drilled into me how opening that wound would do nothing but leave me bleeding. He told me how easily all the progress I've made over the years (and more specifically, over the last few months) could come undone. He warned me that picking at this scab could revert me back to the dry, unfeeling asshole I once was when it came to the thought of relationships.

I fucking hate that he was right.

"It felt like the right thing to do, Dr. P. In my heart, I thought I needed it."

"Tell me everything." And I do. I tell him every part, from puking in the park to puking on the tarmac. I told him every vile, hateful world she spit at me. I told him about Georgie's father and how badly I wanted to indulge him in a fight. How I ached to feel his bones break under the weight of my fists.

If there's only one good thing about this disaster, it's that I kept my damn hands to myself.

"And how do you feel now?" he asks. I've heard him say those exact words so many times, they don't even sound like real words.

"Numb," I answer. He studies me through the camera on my phone. I watch him jot something in his notebook. He's such a cliche with his sweaters, thick glasses, and his insistence on continuing to use a physical notebook when the rest of the world has moved on to iPads.

Usually, I find these qualities comforting. Right now it's just pissing me off, especially because he's refusing to speak.

"Just fucking say it, Dr. P," I spit, growing uncharacteristically impatient.

"You're not usually angry when we speak, James." His calm tone is grating on my last nerve.

"You don't usually beat around the bush so much. Just tell me I fucked up and we can get this over with."

"Do you think you fucked up?"

I scoff and roll my eyes. He's seriously fucking annoying today.

"James, you don't seem numb to me. You seem angry."

"Of course I'm fucking angry! How could I not be angry?" I yell, startling myself with the growl in my voice. I just got a weird image of Annie and the pilots at the door of this bedroom with glasses to their ears. A front row seat to my complete and utter breakdown.

"Why don't you tell me?"

"Jesus fucking..." I mumble.

"James. Take a breath." I do. "Now another. Good. Tell me why you're so angry."

I feel tears prick at the corners of my eyes.

"I fucked it all up," I start, quietly. "I don't know why I thought having some big closure moment would make me feel better, feel less scared. It felt like if I never faced it all head on, then it would never really be over. I was so fucking stupid. I didn't listen to you, and now I just feel...fucking broken. All that hurt I thought I had gotten past, it's burning inside of me. And I feel like a goddamn fool. I did this to myself. I thought I knew better and I didn't. It's so embarrassing."

"Why do you think you feel embarrassed?" His questioning is slightly less annoying this time. I blink, and I feel the tears run down my face.

"She's just...she's too good for me," I say, barely above a whisper.

"Who? Your mother?"

I snort/sob at that.

"Georgie. She's too good for me. She's perfect. She's been through so much in her life, so much worse than what I have, and somehow she's just perfectly well adjusted. And even since I met her, she's grown so much. Every single day she gets smarter, funnier, more clever, more fucking beautiful. And I'm just a goddamn mess. She deserves better than me."

Dr. P sighs and pulls his glasses off of his face, rubbing the lenses between his sweater in his pinched fingers. That's his tell. He's about to tell me like it is.

"James. You made a mistake, but it's done. You did not undo a decade's worth of work in one day. You and I, we'll get through this. I know that you know that it's not always going to feel like this. As far as Georgie goes, I've never met her so I can't speak to her mental state, but if what you've told me about her past is true, I can almost guarantee that as well adjusted as she seems to you, she has her days where she feels like you do right now. Put yourself in her shoes. Don't you think she's ever looked at you and all that you have to offer her and thought that she was the one who wasn't good enough?"

Doubtful. I spent weeks as a thorn in her side before I wormed my way into her life like a parasite attaching themselves to their host. I've made so many mistakes with her, I don't know why she gives me the time of day.

"Do you remember your mantra? We haven't had to use it in a while."

I nod. He's referring to the mantra we came up with a few years ago. I'd repeat it in each of our sessions, and whenever I found myself spiraling I was supposed to come back to it.

"Can I hear you say it, James?"

"I am not broken. I am a person who is worthy of love."

"Again."

"I am not broken. I am a person who is worthy of love."

I repeat the phrase three more times before Dr. P starts to ask questions to unravel my feelings of anger. To be honest, I was only half present for the rest of our conversation. I had only one thing on my mind.

Georgie.

Georgie is the one who isn't broken. She's the one who is worthy of love. She deserves better than what I can give her.

When Dr. P ends our session, I pull up my text thread with Georgie. The selfie she sent me this morning before her big meeting stares back at me. I send a message with just a heart emoji. It turns green instead of blue. Her phone is still dead. Thank god.

If I'm gonna take the coward's way out, I might as well go all the way.

I read and reread the message four times before I hit send, and then I lay down and cry myself to sleep.

36

Georgie

I'm practically buzzing with excitement as I open the door to James's penthouse. I stopped downstairs first to see Amir and tell him all about my meeting today. I brought him flowers as a thank you for giving me the push I needed, and he blushed so sweetly as he put them in a vase with water.

Sometimes men deserve flowers too.

My phone is still dead, and I'm dying to see if James has called yet. I really hope he's coming home tonight. I miss him so much. I plug my phone into the charger by the couch and then go to find Lucifer and make sure he has enough food and water.

When I come back, my phone has enough juice to turn on. Butterflies flutter in my stomach when I see two messages from James.

They quickly die when I read the words under the heart emoji.

James: Georgia, I made a mistake. I should have never pursued a relationship with you. It was completely unprofessional. It was wrong of me to put your reputation on the line like that. Furthermore, I don't think I'm in a headspace to be in a relationship right now. I have too much going on, it wouldn't be fair to you. I think it's best that we finish out the last few weeks as my assistant in a strictly professional manner and when it ends, we can politely part ways. Thank you for the memories.

Excuse me, what?

I stare at the words until they blur together into one white and blue blob, willing them to make some kind of sense.

I made a mistake.

I don't think I'm in a headspace to be in a relationship right now.

Thank you for the memories.

What kind of out of left field bullshit is this? He's breaking up with me, just like that? We've been holding back on admitting that we're in love for days and now he just wants to kick me to the curb?

I wait for the sadness to overwhelm me, but it never does. I just feel confused. Confused and pissed off. This obviously has something to do with this trip he's on. I haven't talked to him since this morning but he must've spoken to his mother today. It can't have gone well if this is how he's acting out.

How did he expect me to react to this?

"Thanks for the opportunity, Mr. Adler. I'll always remember your magic dick."

Part of me wants to cry, to scream, to break his things and set his clothes on fire. I don't want to dignify this ridiculous break up text with a response. I want to run out of here and never look back.

I'm not going to give him that satisfaction, though. This isn't a romance novel where I freak out over a third act miscommunication and storm off, leaving the door wide open for him to come through and win me back with a grand gesture that knocks me off of my feet.

No way. James Adler is going to sit down and talk to me like an adult. If he wants to breakup with me, he's going to have to do it to my face.

I sit on the couch in silence. I have no idea when he's coming home, but I want to be here when he does.

I don't have to wait long. A little less than an hour later, I hear the front door open. A bag drops to the floor. Feet stomp across the kitchen. Ice clinks in a glass. Lucifer lifts his head from my lap to inspect the source of the noise for a moment before dropping back to sleep.

I think I'll have to claim custody of him in the divorce.

James enters the living room, pausing when he sees me sitting there. He looks disheveled. His clothes are wrinkled, like they'd been slept in. His hair is standing up. It's clear he's been tugging at it. His eyes are stained red with purple bags hanging below them. He's been crying.

I say nothing. Neither does he.

Finally, he gestures to the phone sitting on the table in front of me.

"Is it still dead?" he asks. His voice is hoarse and low.

I shake my head. "No."

"Then what are you still doing here?" He sets his glass down and crosses his arms. That felt like a punch to the gut. I have to fight the

311

urge to cry. Just like our first fight all those weeks ago in the office kitchen, I refuse to show weakness in front of him.

"James, don't do that. Talk to me. Tell me what's really going on."

"I told you." He sounds so monotone. "I made a mistake. I need to correct it." I roll my eyes.

"You're a terrible liar, you know that? I know you didn't just have a sudden realization that our relationship was unprofessional or that you don't have the time for me or whatever other bullshit you're trying to spin. I can tell that something set you off. Just sit down and talk to me."

"I'm so fucking done with talking. Why doesn't anyone get that I don't want to fucking talk anymore?" He says it like it's a rhetorical question posed to someone else, not me. I'm a patient person, but there's only so much I can take.

"Well, that's too fucking bad, James," I spit out as I stand and stalk towards him. "If you're really ending things between us, I deserve to know the real reason why." I poke his chest, hard.

"That's exactly the point," He mutters so low I could barely hear it.

"What was that?"

"I said that's exactly the point! Fuck, Georgie! You deserve better, why do you not fucking get that? I'm not good enough for you. I'm so fucked up in the head. I have nothing to give. Even my own fucking mother hated me enough that she wanted me dead rather than to love me. I don't know how to do this. I don't know how to love you. Jesus Christ, Georgie. Can you just fucking leave and let me live my pointless, piece of shit existence on my own so I can stop dragging you down with me?" I've never heard James raise his voice like this. I wince at his harsh words. I close my eyes for a moment to catch my breath. The self-loathing makes me feel sick. This man in front of me is everything. He's kind and caring and so ridiculously beautiful, inside and out. He's everything I never knew I needed and everything I never allowed myself to want. I move to hug him. I want to pull him close and tell him all of that, to finally tell him how much I love him.

When I open my eyes, the sight of him shakes me to my core. His chest is heaving and flushed red. Sweat gathers at his hairline and trickles down his skin. He clutches the collar of his shirt, pulling it away from his body like that will help him get air into his lungs. Now I'm the one freaking out. I know a panic attack when I see one. I wrestle his shaking hands away from his collar and interlace his fingers with mine.

"James, sweetheart, are you okay?" He says nothing. The pace of his breath starts to slow, if only slightly.

"Baby, I'm gonna ask you some questions and I want you to try your best to answer them, okay?" Still no response, but I press on.

"What do you see? Right now, tell me what you see." He doesn't answer right away, but when he does, the sound of his voice is quiet and hoarse.

"Your lips. I see your red lipstick." I melt into a smile.

"What can you smell?"

"Vanilla. Your lotion."

"Good. What do you hear?" He doesn't answer right away, so I ask again. "What can you hear, James?"

"Your voice. I hear your voice, Georgie." I pull him into a close hug, squeezing my arms around his middle as tightly as I possibly can. I know he's somewhat back to earth when I feel him hug me back.

"I'm sorry, Georgie. I'm so fucking sorry," he whispers, before he leans his head on top of mine and starts to cry.

37

James

I feel like my body isn't my own. Every limb feels foreign and wrong. I want to crawl out of this damn skin.

When I broke down, Georgie gently pulled me to the floor where I laid across her lap and sobbed like a baby. When my sobs slowed, she led me upstairs and into the bathroom. I felt like a ghost floating behind her. She helped me out of my clothes and into the shower, where she slowly and gently washed my body. I watched as the dirt and grime of the day, physical and metaphorical, washed off of my skin and down the drain. It was all I could do to bend over so she could reach my hair to shampoo it.

Now we're both wrapped in towels, me sat on the edge of the bed and Georgie standing in the closet, braiding her hair in the mirror on the door. I can see her sneaking peeks at me, and I'm dying to know what's going on in that head of hers, but I can't be the first one to speak. I know she can sense my hesitation, because she turns and says "You don't need to talk about it if you don't want to."

I don't want to. I don't want to talk about how badly I fucked up. I don't want to apologize and grovel for breaking my promise to her. I don't want to tell her that I saw her reaction to my raised voice. I don't want to admit that I'm not the man she thought I was, that I'm just like the fucking others who've hurt her. I don't want to give her the opening to tell me that it's over, that I've thoroughly and completely ruined the love that we share. I want to go back in time and stop myself from ever getting on that plane to New York. I stare at my hands in my lap.

"I don't even know where to start. I'm just so sorry. I'm so fucking sorry, Georgie. I can't believe how badly I screwed up. I can't believe I broke my promise to you. I just, fuck. Everything that happened in New York with those two piece of shit humans...I just wanted to see you, hold you." Tears start to prick at my eyes again.

"What happened in New York, James?" she asks, barely above a whisper.

I might as well tell her. I have nothing left to lose.

"My mother...she lives there. White Plains, New York." I don't look up, but I feel her stiffen beside me. "I talked to her, and it was awful. And then this man came out and I couldn't fucking believe it." I pause and take a deep breath, trying to steady the shake in my chest.

"It was your father, Georgie."

The seconds drag out as I wait for her response. She never looks away from me.

"How did you-"

"His eyes, baby. They're your eyes."

"His parting gift," she snorts, her words dripping with sarcasm. I push forward. Now that I've started, I need to get this out.

"I went in. I got my answers. Amber truly never fucking wanted me, she said so herself. That's not what was bothering me, though. The whole time I was in that shitty little house, I was seething with rage, but it wasn't because of her. I couldn't figure it out. Then there he was. The piece of shit who hurt you, who left you all alone when you were just a fucking kid when he was supposed to be the one person who loved you unconditionally. He came out and had the fucking nerve to demand money from me, and I saw red."

Her lips tremble, but she doesn't let the tears fall.

"Did you give it to him?"

"No. I told him I knew who he was and that he could get fucked. He tried to hit me but he missed. I wanted to swing at him. I wanted to hit him so bad. I wanted to break his fucking face in for what he did to you, Georgie. I didn't do it, but I really fucking wanted to. It fucked me up in the head so bad. I was confused and angry and all I could think about was you. I don't want to drag you into my shit, baby. I'm so messed up and it's ridiculous because you've been through so much more and you're fine. I feel stupid and embarrassed and weak. I really don't feel like the man you deserve."

One lone tear rolls down her cheek. I want to reach out and wipe it away with my thumb, but if she recoils from my touch I'll never be able to take it. I keep my hands to myself. She just looks at me for a long minute. My pulse is racing, I'm so scared that the next words out of her mouth are going to be "How fast can you get the fuck out of my life?"

"What happened out there James? What triggered you?" she asks.

"I...I yelled. I yelled and you winced. I scared you, and I hate myself for that."

"That's not why I winced."

My eyebrows draw together in confusion. I just shake my head. I don't know what to say.

"You didn't scare me, James. I didn't wince because you were yelling. I winced because I hated the way you were talking about yourself. Did I freak out? Did I have an episode? Did I try to run away from you?"

"No," I whisper.

"What did I do?" she asks.

"You...hugged me."

"I hugged you."

"Then you took care of me."

"And then I took care of you, that's right. Do you know why? Because I'm in love with you. You needed me, and I refuse to let you push me away. You say you're not a good man? That's fucking bullshit, James. You were triggered. You don't act out for no reason. You don't set out to hurt people. I think...I think you just love me so much that you would do anything to keep me safe, even if you're the thing you think I'm afraid of. I told you that first night I ever came to your house, I'm not scared of you. I never could be."

I don't know when I started crying again.

"I also need you to stop making comparisons between us and how we've dealt with our trauma. I am not perfect. I'm not well-adjusted. I'm just trying my best every day, just like you. We're both flawed, imperfect people and we're always going to have shit to deal with, but we need to do that together."

I don't know how she always knows exactly what I need to hear.

"I have never in my life hated someone as much as I hate your father, not even Amber. I wanted to kill him, Georgie. I wanted to kill him for what he did to you. I wanted to wrap my hands around his neck and not let go."

She ponders that for a moment. Her little tongue peeks out, wetting her bottom lip.

"Well, it's a good thing I wasn't there, because I would have let you do it."

God, she's so fucking strong. This little pint-sized woman has more courage in her thumb than I do in my entire body. I want to be her when I grow up.

"You're not gonna leave me." It's not a question this time. I know it. Georgie isn't going anywhere. She shakes her head and smiles.

"Georgie, please can I please touch you? Feel your skin? Fuck, sweet girl, I need it, need to feel you." I know I must look pathetic right now, crying like a child and from an anxiety attack that would make Milton from Office Space seem neurotypical.

She doesn't make me beg. She stands and turns, her back facing my front. Slowly, she unwraps the towel covering her and lets it slide down her body. My cock starts to harden instantly. She bends at the waist, sliding down the panties I didn't notice her slip on and giving me a delicious view of her plump ass cheeks. I reach out and trace my fingertip over one of the beautiful pale stretch marks that decorate her perfect ass, so light I doubt she can even feel it.

"Can I make you come?" I rasp, and she looks at me from over her shoulder, mouthing 'yes'.

She turns to face me, and I stand, ready to flip her onto the bed and eat her pussy until she passes out, desperate to sear the taste of her on my tongue, but she pushes me back, palming me through the towel.

"Fuck me," she says, standing between my spread legs. My stomach flips and I shake my head, even though I'm hard as a fucking rock- so aroused at the sight of her that a slight breeze might push me over the edge.

"Baby, I just wanted to make you feel good. I don't deserve-"

She straddles me, gripping my chin between her thumb and forefinger, forcing my eyes to meet hers. It's a dominant move I'd never expect from my sweet girl, nor did I expect my cock to jump at this shift in control.

"James, shut up. You deserve the fucking world, and I'm not going to sit here and listen to you talk down about yourself anymore today. I'm not going to make you do anything you don't want to do, but listen to me. We come together- you inside of me, filling me the way only you can- or I don't come at all. Do you understand?"

She holds onto my chin, keeping her gaze locked to mine. I've seen her eyes dark with lust before, but I've never seen the devious glint behind them until now. She rocks her soaked sex against my lap, the hitch in her breath telling me she likes the strange new sensation of friction the towel provides. Slowly, I nod, reaching down and pulling the towel away. I line myself up with her slick entrance, and she moans as I inch in.

She seats herself fully, taking me to the hilt. Letting go of my chin, she runs that same hand through my hair. She tugs at the roots, pulling my head back and dropping her mouth to my neck, peppering light kisses on my flesh.

"That's my good boy," she whispers against my ear, so soft and sexy, I nearly blow my load right then and there. I've never been praised like that during sex. With Georgie, I'm the one in control. I tell her what to do, I whisper dirty things that make her go wild. She's my good little girl. That's what she needs, and it's what I like- I like being in charge of her, in charge of us. But fuck, those sweet words coming from my Georgie's lips unlock something that I didn't know I needed, but she did. She knew how to flip the script on me, knew how to remind me that I'm hers as much as she's mine.

This woman fucking owns me. There will never be anyone else, I belong to her.

My cock slides in and out of her tight hole as she rocks above me and my balls tighten up to my stomach, my orgasm boiling under my skin.

"If you want us to come together, you'd better be quick, filthy girl." I hiss out, and she leans back, planting her palms on my knees as she rides me, exposing the apex of her pleasure to me. I wet my thumb with my tongue before I press it against her swollen clit, rubbing tight circles that I know will drive her insane. She gasps, her entire body shudders, and at the first clamp of her blazing hot cunt, my own release rips through me. We're animals-her moaning and writhing with abandon and me roaring as I pump her full, her pussy spasming and squeezing every last bit of cum out of me.

Tears spring from my eyes as we both come down from the high. I feel Georgie's soft lips on my skin as she kisses the salty liquid off of my cheeks. She takes my face in her hands and when I look up at her, I see that she's crying, too.

"I love you, James. I need you to try harder not to hate yourself, but I also want you to know that I love you enough for both of us."

"I love you too, Georgie. I love you so fucking much, sweet girl." Finally saying those words out loud to her and hearing them back from her lips is like a thousand pound weight being lifted from my chest. I want to hold her here forever and never let her go.

She stirs, sliding off of my lap. She reaches into a bag I didn't notice on the floor and pulls out a ratty blue t-shirt that I recognize instantly. It's the InstaHam shirt she wore in the very first picture I ever got of her on my phone. I run my finger over a small hole in the belly when she pulls it over her head.

"Let me get you cleaned up." Another action I usually handle post sex, but I know Georgie wants to take care of me right now as much I want to be taken care of by her. She comes back with a warm washcloth wipes at my skin with featherlight strokes. She kisses the inside of my thigh before returning to the bathroom. I lay back horizontally on the bed, thrilled to be back on my silk bed after long nights on hotel sheets. I hear that gorgeous Georgie laugh coming from the other room, and my smile unravels on my face like The Grinch Who Stole Christmas.

"What's so funny in there?" I call out. I prop myself up on my elbows when she gets to the doorway, holding two shirts in her hand. In one, a silk white blouse and in the other, my wrinkled button up.

"We matched!" she giggles, causing me to laugh too, because of course we did. We were made for each other. I hold my hand out and she takes the hint, grabbing it and letting me pull her down to snuggle into my chest.

"Georgie, please move in here with me."

She looks up at me and bites her lip.

"I sort of already did..." She trails off.

"You mean it?" She nods.

"I told my landlord I wasn't renewing my lease. I only have two months left here and then I'm out. I brought some more of my stuff over while you were gone. There's only a few more things I need to grab." I take her by the chin and pull her lips to mine. The kiss is slow and languid. Neither of us is in a hurry to get anywhere, and I take my time enjoying the taste of her.

"Georgie, you're home?" I whisper against her lips.

Pressing herself even closer to my body, she murmurs back to me.

"I'm home."

38

Georgie

Twelve Weeks Later

James absolutely insisted that we throw a housewarming party for our friends, which is not only ridiculous because he's lived here for years, but because all of our friends have already been here. Several times, in fact. Many of those times were over the course of the last few months!

But he's excited, so we're humoring him.

To be honest, a gathering with our friends feels like exactly what we need right now. After everything that happened the day James returned from New York, we knew we had a lot to work on individually and as a couple. We had a few joint sessions with Dr. Patel, who referred me to a colleague for my own purposes. I've been seeing her for three weeks and we've started working through some of the aspects of my past. It's been difficult but I know I need this. It's going to be good for me. I spent so many years isolating myself and convincing myself that I wasn't worthy of love or positive attention, and I am so done with that.

It hasn't been all smooth sailing. Healing is never a linear journey, and we still have days where James fears losing me, or I freak out over the dependency I've built around my new family. We're both doing our best, and we made a pact to never let that line of open communication fail again. It's James and I against the problem, always.

It only took us a few hours to pack up my stuff and move it here. Ryan and Ashley even helped bring boxes down to the car, and they both hugged me before I left. James had encouraged me to make any changes to decor or bedding that I wanted, insisting that this be *our* place where *we* make the calls, not just him. I haven't done much. I always thought the place was pretty perfect to begin with, but there are some new additions. I switched out some of the kitchen appliances with pops of pink. A stand mixer, the toaster, even the coffee maker are all shades of cotton candy now. The vinyl shelf is now full of Taylor Swift albums in addition to James's original collection, and there's a couple fluffy blankets on the bed that Lucifer adores. If you're wondering if *that pillow* made the trip across town with me, the answer is no. I have something much better to ride now.

The biggest change is in the home office. It used to be one desk, one computer, one chair. Now we have two large desks that face each other, his always kept neat and tidy and mine littered with post-it notes and candy wrappers. Behind me, I have a bookshelf wall that I've started to fill in with my book collection. James said I needed to keep the middle, biggest shelf clear for my own books so that they sit behind me like a crown while I write. It's empty now, but it won't be soon. I've had so much fun working with alpha and beta readers and designing my cover art. I can't wait to hold the final product in my hands. The whole room is set up so that James and I can look at each other while we work when he's here, just like we used to at Streamline. Writing romance heroes is much easier now that I have my very own muse in my face- and sometimes, between my legs- while I work.

Speaking of Streamline, my temp job ended a few weeks ago and Amy is back to work. She says she misses Riley dearly, but she missed Espresso Yourself coffee more.

I think she was kidding...

Personally, I don't miss the job. I liked working there, but I like sleeping in more. I do have my fond memories of Streamline, not only because it brought me to James. On my last day, he decided it was the perfect time to act out the boss/sexy assistant fantasy he'd had since my first day. It started out clumsy. Neither of us could stop laughing when he swept the contents off his desk, consequently breaking both of our company laptop screens. Once the fits of giggles stopped, he laid me out on that desk and fucked me until my voice grew hoarse from screaming his name. A wonderful send off, if I do say so myself.

I obviously did not take on another assignment and I've been spending my days writing full time. I'm not the only one job-jumping, though. James is officially stepping down as CEO in a few weeks. So far, only Amir, his sisters and I know. He'll be recommending to the board that Catherine take his place. He said he's known for months that his heart just wasn't in it anymore, and he felt like he was doing the company that he loves a disservice by not having the best person he can at the helm of the ship. He'll be keeping his ownership shares, of course, and retain a seat on the board of directors, but pretty soon he'll be the artist formerly known as Streamline CEO, and I've never seen him more excited. He says he hasn't decided what he wants to do next, career-wise, but I did see information about the City College of San Francisco's Personal Training Program left up when I borrowed his iPad the other day, so who knows?

It's warm tonight, the early October air bringing in the little bit of true summer weather us San Franciscans get. We have the windows and balcony doors open to cool the penthouse down. We don't have to worry about Lucifer getting out because he hates all of these people. He won't come out from under the bed until they're all long gone. Most of our guests are outside, where James set up a makeshift bar and is currently shaking a cocktail for Catherine.

It's a small party, just Kira, Amir, Catherine, Jenn and Amy, Rachel and Brian, Ryan and Ashley- who I became weirdly close with only after I moved out and who, to my surprise, have actually been dating this whole time- a few other Streamline execs and Warren Yates. I don't know him well, but I remembered him from a meeting that he was once apart of. He's nursing a glass of warm amber colored liquid and watching Kira intently as she tells the story of James's first time in her class. Dottie wanted to fly in, but she had an influencer event she couldn't get out of, so the girls and I FaceTimed her earlier instead.

I see Amir take the last sip of his IPA, so I grab another out of the cooler and bring it over to him.

"Cheers!" I say, lifting my glass of white to clink his new bottle.

"Thanks, Peaches." he says, his voice sounding like it's a million miles away.

"Are you having fun?" I ask, and he doesn't answer. He gets like this sometimes, like he disappears in on himself and needs to be coaxed back out. Usually it happens when we're eating together, and I can usually tell right away that he has left the chat. I don't think that's what's happening right now, though. He doesn't look like he's lost in thought. He looks focused, intense. Maybe even a little angry? I wouldn't know, I don't think I've ever seen Amir angry before.

"What are you looking at?" I ask, following his line of sight. When I catch it, it clicks into place.

Across the balcony, Rachel is standing next to her boyfriend, Brian. She looks beautiful in her cotton white dress that hits right above her knee with little bows tied at her shoulder. She's a stunning woman, she'd look gorgeous in a potato sac. Tonight in the light of the low evening sun, the light breeze lifting her blonde lock away from her face, she's fucking luminous. Brian is telling some kind of story to Jenn, who quite honestly looks like she's trying to find a polite way to leave the conversation. He has a glass of red wine in one hand, the other sits on top of the high tables we rented for the night. I watch as Rachel reaches for that hand, wanting to hold it in hers. He gives it a light squeeze and a pat before he drops it, never stopping whatever he's saying to look at her. Rachel's face falls for a "blink or you'll miss it" moment before she plasters a smile back on and sips from her champagne glass. I know Amir catches it too, because he audibly winces beside me.

"Oh, Am." I sigh and he shakes his head. I won't push him if he doesn't want to talk about it, but I know he has feelings for Rachel. That had to hurt him. He doesn't move away when I lie my head on his shoulder and when I lace my fingers with his, he squeezes twice.

We stay cuddled like that for a few minutes, watching the sinking sun over the bay until he excuses himself to the restroom.

By now, James is away from the bar, leaning over the balcony and sipping from his glass. His black t-shirt has ridden up just a bit, enough that I can see a hint of skin peeking out of his low slung jeans. I watch the cords of muscle in his forearm flex as he lifts the glass to his lips. When his throat works to swallow the scotch down, I want to press my mouth against it and feel the action on my lips. I walk over to him and when he sees me out of the corner of his eye, he turns and smiles like a little kid on Christmas morning.

"There's my girl! I missed you."

"I've been here the whole time, you goof."

"Yeah but I haven't talked to you in-" he checks the watch on his wrist, dramatically "23 minutes and 52 seconds."

"Wow. It's been that long?" I tease.

"Yes, and I won't have it happen again. Get in here." He leaves his glass on the ledge and pulls me into his arms. When I tilt my head up, he kisses me soft and slow. His lips are warm against mine. The taste of scotch lingering on his mouth mixed with the scent of leather and sandalwood and *him* dizzies me. He nips at my bottom lip and then kisses it again, just a quick peck this time. The kind of kiss that reminds me that all of my kisses belong to him, that we have all the time in the world.

When we pull apart, he stares at me with the look only he can give me. The same look he's been giving me since we first met, before I even knew what it meant. The look that makes me feel safe, warm, loved, cherished. The look that says "you're mine".

"What's on your mind, Adler?" I ask him, and he kisses my forehead before reaching into his pocket. He pulls out a paper ring made out of a straw wrapper and holds it up to me. I love these. I've saved every single one he's ever given me in that same jar from my old bedroom. I must have thirty or more now.

He kisses me again before he answers.

"You, Georgia. You're on my mind, always."

I blush, taking in his sweet words and holding them close to my heart. I gesture towards the straw wrapper he's still holding. I stick out my left hand dramatically and ask "Aren't you going to give that to me?" I pout my disappointment when he shakes his head.

"No, not this time. Actually, I was thinking..."

I swear to God, the whole world shifts to slow motion when James reaches into his pocket and drops to one knee. My vision blurs, and when I blink, I realize my eyes are filled with tears. Even on his knees, James's enormous height means he's face to face with my breasts, a fact I know he enjoys because I catch him sneaking a peak at my cleavage before looking back up at me. He holds up a small velvet box. In it sits a single, large oval cut diamond set on a simple gold band.

"I know it's not paper," his voice shakes, and I stifle a giggle through my tears, "but what do you think, sweet girl? Will you marry me anyway?"

I barely let him finish his question before I yell out an enthusiastic "YES!" and rush to kiss him, accidentally knocking us both to the ground in the process. The happy tears continue to fall, the salty liquid mixing into our mouths as we kiss each other in a tangle of limbs on the ground.

"What the hell are you two doing?" someone asks. I think maybe it was Amir? James pulls himself from my lips long enough to exclaim "She said yes!" before he presses his mouth back against mine.

Our friends are a glorious chorus of "oh my god"s and happy clapping. Kira stands over us as we continue to make out on the ground. I know she kicked James in the shin because he pulls away and winces.

"Put your tongues away. Let's see the ring!"

Oh yeah, the ring. I kind of forgot about that. James reaches over to the black box, discarded the moment I said yes and attacked his mouth, and slips the band on my finger the same way he's done a hundred other times with straw wrappers.

We stand, and James wraps his arms around me from behind as the women come over to ogle my new jewelry, and the men give him pats on the back. It was the perfect proposal. All of our friends are here to celebrate our love with us, but the moment was just ours. I know it's fast, but I don't care. My soul has been tied to James Adler's for my whole life. I just needed to find him.

Here on this balcony, held tight in James's arms and surrounded by family that I chose for myself, I'm deliriously happy.

I'm safe. I'm loved. I'm home.

Epilogue

Georgie

Nine Months Later

"I can't do this. I want to go home."

"You can do it. We're not going home, Georgie."

"What if I get stage fright and forget how to talk?"

"You won't. And if you do, I'll talk for you."

"What if no one shows up and I sit here all alone like a loser?"

"People are going to show up, and you're not alone. I'm going to be here with you the whole time, sweet girl."

James takes my shaking hand and kisses the back of it. I close my eyes and take a deep breath. I'm so fucking nervous, I've never done anything like this before.

It's the first day of Spicy Lit Con, a convention for romance authors and readers to meet, talk, get their books signed and have fun. I was here once before a few years ago, as a reader.

Today, I'm here as an author.

I think I might crap my pants.

My booth is decorated in shades of pink. I have a couple boxes filled with paperbacks, a candy jar, bowls of stickers with things like 'smut slut' and 'sweet girl' printed on them, and a full supply of pink Sharpies for signing. It looks really good and inviting, if I do say so myself.

My first book, *Whispers And Wisteria* was officially released three months ago. I built a pretty solid social media following prior to its release (being outed as the woman who took James Adler off the market caused an uptick in some people's interest in me), which helped me find an audience of readers quickly. It also helped that all of my friends have showered me with love and support, particularly Kira and Dottie, who are always pimping W&W out to their combined millions of followers.

I can't believe how much has changed in the last year. This past summer, I was broke, single, had no friends, a string of crappy jobs that I hated and a hard drive full of smut I wouldn't dream of letting anyone read. Today I'm a published author, I have a solid group of friends who have my back no matter what, and I no longer have to fight the urge to lose my lunch when an unexpected action sequence pops up in a movie.

Kira started giving me private boxing lessons last fall when my therapist suggested that finding my own power might help me deal with anxiety of feeling overpowered by others. It was tough at first. I would get nauseous at the thought of throwing a punch, but Kira was patient with me. Now I love nothing more than getting my knuckles bloody while beating up the bag. We train together a few times a week, and Rachel has even joined in.

Oh, and one other thing. I'm freaking married.

That's right. James could not wait to tie the knot. The second he slid that beautiful ring onto my finger he was ready to put me over his shoulder and drag me to city hall.

I made him wait it out until February. I found a gorgeous lacy white dress that pushed up my boobs and flared at my waist, and James donned a stunning black tux that would have put James Bond to shame. We invited just our close friends, Am's Mama and James's sisters to The Presidio, where Amir acted as our officiant and married us on the sprawling green grass, the sun setting over the Golden Gate Bridge in the background. It was intimate and beautiful.

I'll never forget the look on James's face a week later when the author proof of W&W came in- the one whose cover had been designed weeks before- featured the name *Georgie Adler* instead of Hansley on the bottom. He didn't know that I had always planned on branding my baby that way, whether we were married yet or not. His presence in my life has changed me for the better. It's his love that makes me feel brave and keeps me warm. It's his name-our name- that deserves to be my legacy, not my father's.

But back to today. I might have been brave enough to publish my work, but I'm still chicken shit when it comes to meeting my readers. I mean seriously, what if no one comes by my booth? What if I leave today with a stack of unsigned books and my tail between my legs? Ugh, I know it's only 9am but I need a drink.

Like a mind reader, James pulls two nips of something brown out of his pocket and hands one to me.

"Just one, to calm your nerves." He winks and untwists both caps.

"To Georgia Marie Adler, accomplished author, loving wife, and my very own good girl." We clink our tiny bottles and toss back the shots, the alcohol burning my throat but soothing my anxiety.

"You promise you're not gonna leave my side?" I ask as the doors open and the overhead announcement tells the room that the convention has begun. He kisses me, soft and quick.

"Never, sweet girl. Never."

Dottie, Rachel, Amir and Kira are my first visitors. They each demanded a signed and personalized copy of Whispers and Wisteria, even though they've all already read it.

To my surprise, a line forms behind them.

A line of people...for me. Wanting to meet me. Talk to me. Read my book.

I feel like I'm dreaming.

The day went by in a blur. I had so much fun meeting readers, discussing W&W, and teasing my next release. When I had downtime, I got to meet and talk to some of my favorite authors. I swear I was like a star struck lunatic when my favorite regency romance writer stopped by my booth and told me how much she adored *Whispers & Wysteria*.

James took us all out to dinner to celebrate the success of my first author event. He had made reservations for somewhere fancy but cancelled them when I said I could go for a pizza. We downed slices of pepperoni and cheap beers with our friends, and then he took me back to our hotel room where he made love to me soft and slow. He kissed me everywhere, whispering beautiful praises and telling me how proud he is of me while bringing me wave after wave of pleasure.

He's asleep now, my back plastered against his front, his arms squeezing my middle tight, the same koala bear position we sleep in every night, just a naked tangle of limbs. I'm still awake, basking in the afterglow of the day. I think about the people I met. The woman who told me W&W got her out of a months long reading slump, and especially the one who teared up when she thanked me for the way I handled the darker undertones of the characters lives. I think about Amir bouncing around like a kid in a candy store and the stacks of paperbacks he left with. I think about Rachel and Dottie, and the way they had no idea that Kira was sticking NSFW stickers to their backs all day.

And more than anything, I think of James and the way he beamed at me with pride all day, only ever taking his hands off of me to grab a reader's phone and take a picture for us. (He even posed for a few pictures for some of the *cough* thirstier readers. I didn't mind, my husband is hot as hell).

My mind drifts to the tattoo on my ribs. It still holds meaning to me, as it's a reminder of my past and the strength I needed to have to get to where I am today. But it's not true anymore. I'm surrounded by so much love that sometimes it's overwhelming. It's amazing.

I'm not on my own anymore.

James

Seven Months Later

I walk through the door of the penthouse, completely and thoroughly wrecked. This was the longest day I've had since I became an instructor at Spin Sync a little over a year ago. Not only did I teach two live hour-long classes with students in the studio with me, I spent the rest of the afternoon filming on demand classes that will be released periodically during my upcoming time off. I took it easy, sticking to the low end of my own call outs all day, but 7 hours of cardio is gonna be killer no matter what. All of that followed a two hour meeting this morning concerning expanding our equipment's ability to access other streaming platforms so that users can watch TV while they ride. (Yeah, I couldn't stay out of tech long. Warren Yates brought me in as Lead Technical Consultant right after he bought the company). I love my job, but right now all I want to do is have a drink and cuddle up in bed with my wife.

My. Wife.

It's been more than a year, and I'm still not used to it. Georgia Marie Adler is *my wife*.

I'm the luckiest son of a bitch in the world.

I walk out to the balcony, expecting to find her laying out and reading like she usually is at this time of day, but she's not out there. That's weird.

"Georgie?" I call out, and then I hear a faint sob coming from the bedroom. I run to her, afraid she's upset or hurt. What the hell could have happened? I know I was gone all day, but we texted during all of my breaks. She seemed perfectly fine.

I fling open the door to our bedroom and panic laces my voice. "Georgie, what's wrong?"

"Nothings working!" she sobs, and I have to stifle a laugh when I see her. Laid out on the bed, naked and flushed pink, Georgie is desperately rubbing her thighs together and plucking at her nipples while tears stream down her face. Just like that, my energy level is off the charts. I whip off my shirt and crawl into bed next to her, kissing a stray tear from her skin.

"Sweet girl, I'm so sorry. I thought I took care of you. You came three times before I left this morning." It's true. I woke up to her straddling me, rubbing her dripping wet center on my cock, her tits bouncing in my face, just begging to be sucked on.

Fucking glorious.

"You did," she cries "But I was writing-"

"And you turned yourself on. Baby, we talked about this. You're not supposed to write when I'm not around, especially the spicy stuff." Georgie has been insatiably horny since the start of her second trimester. It was a welcome relief from how sick she was during the first. I was out of my mind trying to do anything to help her. We've had more sex in the last few months than I think I've had in my entire life, not that I'm complaining. My hot as sin wife wants me to act like her personal dildo? Sign me up. It only became a problem a few weeks ago when she realized that her belly had grown so big that she was struggling to touch herself. I've been more than willing to tend to her needs whenever she asks. If the mood strikes her while I'm at work, however, she has trouble scratching that itch. Hence the 'no writing while I'm away' rule.

I've been trying to convince her to slow down a bit anyway. She's released five books in the last two years, and because they're brilliant and sexy, she's gone mega viral. She's done a ton of author events and signings, even up until a few weeks ago when it was no longer easy for her to travel. She even has her sixth book set to release around 12 weeks after she gives birth (I'm still working to get her to push that back).

I will miss her book touring. She always gets real touchy feely after a signing. We're pretty sure we conceived the night of Spicy Lit Con.

"I can't help it when inspiration strikes! I'm an artist, James, an artist!" she sobs again and punches her cute little fists into the mattress. "Please just touch me. I'm aching."

My cock throbs in my shorts. I've been hard ever since I saw her lying here with no clothes on. Georgie has always been drop dead gorgeous, but the pregnancy adds another layer to her sexiness. Her tits are fuller and much more sensitive, the curve of her hips wider to accommodate the swell of her belly. Her skin is pink and glowing, and her pussy is always- and I mean always- wet and ready to take me in.

"What do you want baby? My hands, my tongue, or my cock?" I ask her between soft kisses and nips at her jaw. My fingers alternate between her breasts, rubbing light circles around her pebbled nipples.

"Anything. Everything. Please," she whispers. I pull a pillow from behind my head and help her prop her hips up, laying her on top of it to try to relieve some of the pressure of the pregnancy on her pelvis. I kiss my way down her body, stopping to play only at her most sensitive parts. I'd normally like to take my time, teasing and nipping at her all the way down, licking and massaging her inner thighs, but my poor girl needs release quickly.

She's already so fucking wet, two fingers slide right into her warmth with ease. I stroke her inner walls a few times before my tongue joins the dance, lapping and flicking at her aching clit. I know she wants to hold onto my hair and crush my face to her cunt, but she can't reach, so she squeezes her thighs against the side of my head instead. It only takes a few moments before she cries out, clenching around my hand and soaking my face.

That's another fun thing we learned around the second trimester. Pregnant Georgie is a squirter. Not every time, but when I hit that sweet spot inside of her just right, she gushes like a fountain. It's incredible.

I drink her up as she grinds out the waves of her orgasm on my tongue. When she settles, I stand and quickly yank my shorts down and give my cock a few strokes while Georgie rolls over onto all fours-our favorite position in her current state. I climb up behind her and rub my hands over her ass cheeks.

"Fuck, sweet girl. Look at this perfect cunt, dripping and begging to be filled. Such a filthy little girl you are. Growing our love in your belly but still so desperate for my cum." I drop one hand between her legs and run a finger up her slit, circling her tight hold but not penetrating.

"Isn't that right, Georgia," I continue. "You're aching for me to pump you full, aren't you?"

"Yesss" she whines, pushing herself back in an attempt to get my finger inside of her. "Please give it to me. I need you. I feel so empty."

I move my hand and line my cock up to her entrance.

"That's my good girl, so fucking pretty when you beg for me." She moans and I slam into her on a whimper.

"Baby," I whine, unable to keep my alpha shit up when her tight cunt is choking me so perfectly. I start fucking relentlessly.

"Jesus, fuck baby. So tight and warm. So good, every fucking time. How are you always so good?" She groans and throws her head back. I grab a fistful of her hair and tug.

"Need you to come for me, Georgie. Need to feel you milking my cock. Can you do that? Can you be a good girl and come for me right fucking now?" Her response is an incoherent symphony of hitched breaths and garbled moans as she clenches around me. I reach around her to roll one sensitive as fuck nipple between my fingers and she shatters, her pussy drenching me as she falls apart. Three deep strokes and I'm following her over the edge. Stars explode behind my eyes as I come, stuffing my pregnant wife full.

I lean forward and kiss the skin on her spine as I pull out. I want to pull her into my arms and cuddle her, but if I do that, we'll both fall asleep in this wet mess and wake up feeling icky. Instead I help her out of the bed and hold her hand as she waddles to the bathroom. I start the shower and when it's warm enough, I pull her in with me. Her eyes drift lazily as I soap her up, rinsing her skin and running my hands over every inch of her.

"I'm sorry," she says, barely above a whisper and I pause. I cup her cheek in my hand.

"What could you possibly be sorry for?"

"For being so needy. I know you must be so sick of this pregnancy by now, and we still have two months to go." I can't help but chuckle as I lean down and kiss her.

"You've got it all wrong, sweet girl. I'm the needy one. I'm obsessed with you, with your body. I can't get enough. You're so sexy like this, Georgie. When these two come out, I'm gonna fuck another set into you as soon as I can."

That's right, two babies, IUD be damned. We weren't expecting that at all. Neither of us has twins in our family- that we know of anyway. I'm not saying I have hyper viral sperm, but I'm not *not* saying that either. We thought we wanted to be surprised, but a few weeks ago we decided we couldn't wait and had the doctor tell us the genders.

We're having a little girl, who will be named Taylor James, and a little boy, Ethan George.

She leans her head back and groans. I take the opportunity to kiss her throat, then I turn her so I can wrap my arms around her and massage her belly.

"God, I hope it's just one next time. The twins are in a battle of 'who can kick mommy's bladder the most' and they're both winning."

"Don't worry, sweet girl. I'll fight them for you as soon as they pop out. Nobody kicks my wife and gets away with it, not even my babies."

She laughs and tells me I'm stupid.

I smile and tell her she's beautiful.

We towel off and i help her into a pair of my sweats and a hoodie, pulling on just some underwear to my own body. We move to the couch, where I cuddle her into me and wrap us up in a blanket. Lucifer snuggles onto Georgie's belly, purring like a mad man. He's incredibly protective of his mother and unborn siblings. Whenever we have guests over, they can't even think of touching her stomach without Lucifer breaking out his claws at them. Georgie leans her head against my shoulder and falls asleep almost instantly. I don't know when I became so emotional, but I have to fight to hold back a tear as I marvel at the wonder of my life. My entire world is here in my arms. Mine to love, mine to protect, mine to cherish.

Mine.

Kira's 90's Pop Ride Playlist

Summer Girls - LFO
Barbie Girl - Aqua
Livin La Vida Loca - Ricky Martin
...Baby One More Time - Britney Spears
Spice Up Your Life - Spice Girls
Genie In A Bottle - Christina Aguilera
MMMBop - Hanson
C'est La Vie - B*Witched
Pony - Ginuwine
Believe - Cher

EMILY SHACKLETTE

Wonderwall - Oasis

Kira's "Drive Him Wild" Ride Playlist

♡

Buttons – The Pussycat Dolls
Lean Back – Terror Squad ft. Fat Joe & Remy Ma
Hot In Herre – Nelly
My Humps – The Black Eyed Peas
Candy Shop – 50 cent ft. Olivia
Fergalicious – Fergie ft. will.i.am

Get Low – Lil Jon And The Eastside Boyz ft. Ying Yang Twins

I Wanna Be Bad – Willa Forde

There It Go (The Whistle Song) – Juelz Santana

Thong Song – Sisqo

Salt Shaker – Ying Yang Twins ft. Lil Jon And The Eastside Boyz

Goodies – Ciara

Milkshake – Kelis

Get Ur Freak On – Missy Elliot

Fantasy – Ludacris ft. Shawanna

Eat Your Way Through

⁌

SPOILERS AHEAD

Food is a love language to me. You might have noticed a light theme of food insecurity running through this book. I was adamant that I feature Georgie eating well as often as I possibly could, and I combined that with one of my favorite things about San Francisco- the incredible restaurants. So for you, dear reader, I've compiled a list of everywhere our characters eat in the book so that if you're ever in the City By The Bay, you can eat like James, Georgie and their gang.

Le Marais Bakery – the real life inspiration for Espresso Yourself

Posh Bagels – Amir orders breakfast for the office

Atwater Tavern – the bar on the bay where James and Amir have dinner

Boudin Bakery – where Catherine orders lunch from

Il Casaro Pizzeria & Mozzarella bar – the pizza James and Georgie share in his office

Zazie – the girl's brunch spot

Wine Down – the girl's happy hour spot

Gott's Roadside – the 'diner' where James takes everyone for lunch

Izzy's – where James and Amir have their date night

Alioto's – James and Georgie's first date

Senor Sisig – Amir orders from here at work, and then James and Georgie order it at his house

Canela Bistro & Wine Bar – where the girls eat before shopping

House of Nanking – the Chinese food James has delivered to Georgie

Spire 73 – the rooftop bar in LA

Hog Island Oyster Co. – where James takes everyone when his sisters visit

Bocado – where the girls eat while James is gone

The Spicy Stuff

For you, dear reader, a list of all the spicy scenes in this novel, whether for closed door modifications or ~reasons~, I don't judge. Happy reading <3

EMILY SHACKLETTE

Reading is our safe space, our happy place, and I want this book to be an enjoyable experience for each of you. With that in mind, I've done my best to compile a full list of potential triggers and content warnings within the pages of this book. If you need any additional information in order to safely read Georgia On My Mind, please do not hesitate to reach out to me.

Georgia On My Mind is an adult romance novel and is not intended for younger readers or anyone under the age of 18.

In this book there is

- Explicit language

- Childhood abandonment

- Childhood trauma

- Anxiety

- Characters on the Autism spectrum

- Obsessive tendencies

- Possessiveness (consensual)

- Violence against a person (witnessed and experienced)

- Panic attacks

- Death of a parent (DWI)

- Mentions of abortion (in the past, thought about and attempted)

- Vomiting

- PTSD

- Domestic violence (witnessed as a child)

- Child abuse (MC) (happens o/ page in the past but is described by the MC)

- Alcoholism (not MC)

- Alcohol consumption

- Explicit, on page sex acts (masturbation, sexual fantasy, nipple play, oral sex, vaginal penetration, edging, bondage, soft sub/dom play, MF sexual intercourse, dirty talk, public sex)

Acknowledgements

Gosh, where to even begin? Much like Georgie, I found my love for writing as a kid, scribbling in a notebook, and then as a teenager writing Haylor fanfiction and posting it anonymously on the internet. It's a part of me I've held close to my heart for over a decade, and I've finally found the strength to share my words with you.

Thank you to all of the early readers of Georgia On My Mind for believing in this project and helping me to polish the mess that was the first (and second...and third) draft.

All my love and thanks to my girl Taylor for accepting the fact that I will never stop sending you unhinged, horny dialogue in the middle of your work day and for generally being my one woman hype squad. Your love and support (and the endless pictures of your adorable baby) keeps me going.

Thank you to my other girl- Taylor Swift- for writing the soundtrack of my life and coincidentally, the soundtrack to this story. (If I had a nickel for every time I devoted my life and love to a tall blonde bombshell named Taylor, I'd have two nickels. Which isn't a lot but it's weird that it happened twice).

To Naria, who co-wrote our very first story with me when we were only 12 years old and has forever been a fellow lover of words.

To Kristen, queen of positive energy and white heart emojis.

To Alaina, the best long distance bestie a girl could ask for. Thank you for dealing with my unhinged fan girl behavior and keeping me endlessly entertained with Barbie memes and hare-brained Taylor Swift conspiracies.

Elizabeth, my sweet baby sister. Thank you for keeping me up to date with the gen z lingo and trends (and making me reconsider how many times I wrote the word 'cock' in this book).

Mommom, my lifeline. Thank you for supporting every dream I've had. I wouldn't be the woman I am today without you. (Please don't read this book, I will never be able to look you in the eyes again).

My therapist- thanks for talking me through the imposter syndrome week after week. I have a feeling I'm going to continue to keep you very busy with my messy mind for a long time.

To John, thank you for being my rock, my supporter, and my number one fan. Thank you for believing in all of my wildest dreams and helping me to make them a reality. Even though I know you'll never read any of my books, you and your lint rollers are an integral part of them. I love you, honey. You make me brave.

To the booktok/bookstagram community, you all changed my life. Thank you for the endless support and love. I feel so honored to be a part of a group of such loving and supportive women.

Finally, thank you to every single person who takes a chance on me and reads this book. I hope you love James and Georgie as much as I do.

About the Author

Emily Shacklette is an avid reader, Swiftie and cat lady. She loves romantic tension and spice that lasts for pages. She currently resides in the heart of beautiful San Francisco with her husband and Olive, Punky, and Chicken (her cat children). When she's not reading or writing, you can find her watching Community, riding her Peloton, or listening to Taylor Swift as loudly as the volume will go. Find her on Instagram (@authoremilyshack / @emilyshaack) YouTube (Emily Shack) and TikTok (@authoremilyshaack). authoremilyshack.com

Milton Keynes UK
Ingram Content Group UK Ltd.
UKHW020647041223
433752UK00018B/1145

9 781088 237878